An Unv

Candida felt strange in her white riding habit, fitted carefully to enhance her young figure. But Major Hooper assured her that there was nothing like a handsome rider to show off a handsome horse—and nothing was too good for her black stallion, Pegasus.

As they neared the crowd of people in Hyde Park, Candida was aware of a sudden hush, of many eyes turned toward her.

"Just ride on," Major Hooper said behind her. Then, after they'd passed through the crowd, another man on horseback joined them. What happened next chilled her to the bone.

"That's a fine stallion," the man told Hooper breathlessly. "How much do you want for him?"

"This horse is not for sale," Hooper said. "Unless of course you can meet my special conditions."

THE PRETTY
HORSE-BREAKERS

Barbara Cartland

PYRAMID BOOKS • NEW YORK

THE PRETTY HORSE-BREAKERS

A PYRAMID BOOK

Pyramid edition published April 1972
Fifth printing, June 1975

© Barbara Cartland 1971

All Rights Reserved

ISBN 0-515-03789-3

Printed in the United States of America

Pyramid Books are published by Pyramid Communications, Inc.
Its trademarks, consisting of the word "Pyramid" and the portrayal
of a pyramid, are registered in the United States Patent Office.

Pyramid Communications, Inc.,
919 Third Avenue, New York, N.Y. 10022

AUTHOR'S NOTE

"The Pretty Horse-breakers" are a historical fact, although little has been written about them. In the nineteenth century, breaking a horse to the side-saddle was carried out by professional lady riders, and every livery stable employed them. Then in two or three of the more fashionable riding schools in the West End of London it became the practice to invite a select audience to the gallery to watch their performance, and wealthy young bloods soon persuaded the more attractive of the horse-breakers to become their mistresses.

There was never any question of professional prostitutes learning to break horses, but there was an alliance between the well-known "procureur" and the fashionable livery stables. The "procureur" would invest money in the flashy riding-habits of the "Pretty Horse-breakers," and the consequent sales of horses ridden by them became a lucrative business. In the absence of "film stars" the "Pretty Horse-breakers," who met at the Achilles Statue, became the rage with the public in Hyde Park.

The severity of the "Pretty Horse-breakers" is again a historical fact, most side-saddle riders with only one heel available could only hope to control their horses with the use of a spur. The modern dummy spur was not invented until the early twentieth century.

It was the predilection of the "Pretty Horse-breakers" to use their sharp and vicious spurs severely on all occasions. G. J. Whyte-Melville in his book *Riding Recollections,* published in 1878, deplores the lack of mercy shown by ladies in the use of the spur:

"Perhaps because they have but one, they use this

stimulant liberally, and without compunction. From their seat, and shortness of stirrup, these vigorous applications are unsuspected by lookers-on; and the unwary wonder why, in the streets of London or the Park, a lady's horse always appears to go in a lighter and livelier form than that of her male companion.

"It's a woman's hand," says the admiring pedestrian.

"Not a bit of it,' answers the cynic who knows, 'it's a woman's heel.' "

1

"Steady, boy, there is no hurry," Candida said pulling at the reins, yet knowing even as she spoke that there was the need for haste and she was but putting off what lay ahead.

She kept saying to herself:

"This is the last time—the last time I shall ride Pegasus, the last time perhaps I shall ever be mounted on a horse like him."

As the words repeated themselves over and over again in her head, it seemed to her that the horse's hooves on the road endlessly reiterated:

"The last time!"

"The last time!"

"The last time!"

She looked about her at the countryside through which she was passing: the hedges sprouting with the first green buds of spring; the meadows new-born with a lush freshness; the primroses peeping through banks of moss at the roadside and the anemones making a carpet, white and virginal, in the woods.

"The last time! The last time!"

"Oh, Pegasus," Candida whispered, bending forward to pat the horse's neck, "how can I bear to let you go? How could it have come to this?"

She felt the tears gather in her eyes and bit her lip to stop them falling. What was the use of crying? It was all so hopeless. There was nothing she could do to save Pegasus, or indeed herself.

She must have known that this would happen after her Mother had died a year before. "A wasting disease" the doctors had called it for want of a better name. Only

Candida had known how hard her Mother had fought to keep her husband from knowing what agonies she suffered, or to disguise from him her weakness, which grew greater day by day.

Candida thought now that she might have known her Father would never survive without her—her gay, affectionate but weak Father, whose whole world collapsed when he no longer had the wife he loved to support him.

He had taken to drinking at "The King's Head" night after night, and Candida had realised it was not for the convivial company, in which he had no interest, but merely because he dreaded the emptiness of the house, and most of all the bedroom where he must sleep without his wife. She tried to help him, but he was like a man suddenly blinded, who could see nothing but his own darkness.

"How can she have left me?" he used to ask furiously when he was drunk.

"Where has she gone to?" he would demand, and often, as Candida helped him up the stairs to bed, he would shout "Emmeline, Emmeline!" his voice reverberating round the house, the echo of it seeming to come back to him, "Emmeline, Emmeline!"

She should have known, Candida thought, that when he went out that last night she would never see him again. It had been cold and damp all day, and at dusk it had started to deluge with rain.

"Do not leave home tonight, Papa," Candida had begged, as she heard him order old Ned to saddle Juno, his chestnut mare.

"I have an appointment," he answered, but he avoided her eyes as he spoke and she knew only too well that the appointment was at "The King's Head" with a bottle of their raw brandy.

"See, Papa, I have built a fire in the Library," she coaxed. "I believe there is a bottle of your favourite claret downstairs. Let me fetch it from the cellar and you can drink it here by the fireside."

"Alone?" he asked sharply, and she heard the pain in his voice.

"I will sit with you," she said a little shyly.

8

For a moment she seemed to break through the misery which enveloped him.

"I believe you would," he said, "and carry me up to bed afterwards. You are a good child, Candida."

He bent to kiss her and she had a short-lived hope that she had persuaded him into staying. Then almost roughly he pushed her aside.

"I must keep my appointment," he said, and there was an agony in his tone that she knew only too well.

It was when his utter despair at his loss swept over him that he could not stay in the house. He could not look at familiar objects which reminded him all too poignantly of his wife—her favourite chair with the ridiculous little cushion she had embroidered with beads; the tables on which she had arranged vases of fragrant flowers; the inlaid sewing-box which had always stood beside her so that she could busy herself while they talked or when he read aloud the poems which he had written and which she tried so hard to appreciate for his sake.

It was these poems, Candida had learnt, which had turned her Mother's family against the marriage. When she was a child she had often wondered why she had so few relations while other girls of her age had grandparents, aunts, uncles and cousins. She must have been very young when she first sensed there was something strange about the isolation in which they lived.

They were poor, but she accepted that without question. Sometimes unexpected money would arrive from the publishers and then there would be special celebrations—food, which seemed to Candida like ambrosia; wine, a luxury seldom enjoyed; and her Mother would go to the piano and play songs, which her Father would sing. The whole house seemed as golden as the money which had been earned by her Father's writings.

"Gladys's grandfather has given her a pony for Christmas," she remembered saying once to her Mother. "Why haven't I a grandfather?"

Her Mother had looked apprehensively over her shoulder.

"Hush, darling, do not speak of it now," she begged, "you will upset your Father."

"Why?" Candida enquired.

9

For many years she always received the same evasive answer. Finally from some chance remark she learnt that her parents had eloped.

"Oh, Mama, how exciting! How could you do anything so brave, so daring!" Candida exclaimed. "Tell me about it, please tell me about it."

Her Mother shook her head.

"I cannot, darling. I promised your Father that I would never speak to anyone of my life before I knew him."

"You must tell me, Mama," Candida had insisted. "When the other children whom I meet in the village talk about their relations, I feel so foolish, and indeed so strange having none of my own."

"You have Papa and me," her Mother had said. "Isn't that enough, darling?"

"Of course it is," Candida replied, impulsively throwing her arms round her Mother's neck. "I love you, I could not have a more wonderful Mother and Father if I searched the whole wide world for them. I love you both so very much, but . . ."

She paused, and her Mother, with a little smile, finished the sentence.

". . . you are curious."

"Yes, of course," Candida answered. "Can you not understand?"

She had been twelve years old at the time and she could remember now how often she had felt embarrassed, sensing that other people thought there was something strange in the fact that her Mother never spoke of her parents or where she had lived before they came to Little Berkhamstead.

Little Berkhamstead was a tiny village in Hertfordshire of less than a hundred inhabitants, with a few cottages nestling round a grey Norman-built church. Candida's parents lived in a small Elizabethan manor.

It had low oak-beam ceilings, small rooms and a garden which was her Mother's delight and which, unlike other ladies in the neighbourhood, she tended herself—growing not only a profusion of flowers, but many herbs, with which she made remedies for those who were sick and could not afford a physician.

She was deeply loved in the village, and when she

was buried in the little churchyard there were no large or expensive wreaths, but the grave was covered with blossoms, most of them only in small bunches, but each given with love and gratitude.

"Please tell me, Mama," twelve-year-old Candida had pleaded, and finally her Mother had risen and walked to the lattice-paned window to look out on the flower-filled garden.

"I am so happy," she said softly, almost as though she spoke to herself. "I hoped the past would be forgotten."

Candida had not spoken, and after a moment her Mother had gone on:

"Still, I suppose you have a right to know. But you must promise me you will never speak of what I tell you to your Father. Any mention of it upsets him, and you know I would never do anything that would cause him distress."

"No indeed, Mama, and I promise you faithfully that if you confide in me I will never relate your secrets."

"It all seems a very long time ago," her Mother began. "I was young and I had many of the things that you, my darling, will never be able to have, and, of course, the gowns to wear which to any woman are the most important part of a social scene."

"Oh Mama, I would have loved to see you," Candida exclaimed. "You must have looked beautiful. Did you wear a crinoline?"

"No, but our gowns were very full," her Mother replied, "because we wore innumerable petticoats. They were perhaps more becoming and certainly more comfortable than being encumbered with an enormous hoop which the *Ladies Journal* tells me in 1860 is still the vogue."

She spoke a little wistfully, and just for a moment Candida sensed that she missed the fashionable silks and satins, the jewels, the furs and all the elegance which must have made her look even lovelier than she was in her plain, home-made dresses.

"It was all very gay," she went on, "and I suppose I should be foolish if I did not confess that I was a success. I had many suitors, Candida, and my parents

11

favoured a gentleman—who shall be nameless—but who, I can tell you, was of noble birth and truly distinguished."

"Was he handsome?" Candida asked.

"Very handsome," her Mother replied, "and I was deeply envied because I had attracted his attention . . . But then I met your Father . . ."

There was a long pause and Candida felt as though her Mother had somehow forgotten her.

"Pray continue, Mama, this cannot be the end of the story."

It was almost with a start that her Mother seemed to come back to reality.

"No indeed," she answered, "it was only the beginning."

"Did you fall in love with him, Mama?" Candida asked.

"Deeply and irrevocably," her Mother declared. "I cannot explain why—he was certainly good-looking, but he had not the presence or distinction of my other suitor, but—what was more detrimental in my parents' eyes—he had no money."

"No money at all?" Candida enquired.

"A mere pittance," her Mother replied, "a small legacy from an uncle. But we thought it was enough."

"Enough for what?"

"Enough to live on, enough for us to be married, because we needed each other so desperately."

"But why did you have to run away?" Candida asked.

"What a lot of questions!" her Mother exclaimed. "But, as I have said, you have a right to know. Life might have been very different for you had you been the child of the marriage that my parents desired for me."

"But I would not have been the same if my Papa had not been Papa, would I?" Candida enquired.

Her Mother had suddenly put her arms round her and drawn her close.

"No, darling," she said, "and that, of course, is exactly the right thing to say. You would not have been the same, and I would not have had these wonderful, golden, marvellous years with a man I love and who loves me with all his heart."

"But why did you have to elope?" Candida asked, determined that she should hear the end of the tale.

"My Father—your grandfather—was enraged," her Mother replied. "He was a very overbearing, autocratic man who was not used to having his wishes crossed. He had chosen, as he thought, a suitable son-in-law, and he was not going to be circumvented by a penniless and unimportant poet. My Father abhorred poetry! He man-handled your Father from the house!"

"Oh, poor Papa! Did he mind?"

"He minded terribly," Candida's Mother replied. "It was done in a most humiliating and brutal manner. Your grandfather also threatened to horsewhip him if he ever spoke to me again."

"How cruel!" Candida exclaimed.

"It was indeed, and it was something your Father was the least fitted of anyone I have ever known to bear. He was too sensitive, too decent in himself, not to be wounded by such a sadistic assault."

"And so you could not see him," Candida suggested.

"I saw him," her Mother replied, and now there was a note of triumph in her voice. "I went to him. I crept out at night and went to his lodgings. It was an out-rageous thing to do, but your Father had been treated outrageously. We knew then there was only one thing we could do—that was to go away together."

"How brave, how very brave of you!" Candida cried.

"I was frightened that your grandfather would pre-vent us actually getting married," her Mother said, "but I need not have been troubled. The moment I crossed his wishes I was dead as far as he was concerned."

"How do you know?" Candida asked. "Did you go back and speak to him?"

"No, I could not do that," her Mother replied, "but a year later, when you were born, I wrote to my Moth-er. Of course I did not tell your Papa I had done so, but I knew she loved me and I knew that, even if my Father was unforgiving, I was still her daughter and close to her heart."

"Did she reply?" Candida enquired.

Her Mother shook her head.

"No, dearest. Your grandfather must have found the letter before it reached her, and recognising my writing returned it unopened."

"How cruel of him," Candida exclaimed.

"It was what I might have expected," her Mother said. "I knew then there was no going back—the past must be forgotten, wiped out of my mind, even as your Father had asked me to do."

"Do you ever regret having run away with Papa?" Candida asked in a low voice.

Once again her Mother swept her into her arms.

"No, darling, never, never, never!" she replied. "I am so happy and your Papa is so wonderful to me. No woman could have a more unselfish, considerate, adoring husband. It is only that we are so poor, and I mind for your sake. I would like you to have the social life, the balls, the gowns that I enjoyed. But there is no use wishing for the moon, and I only pray, my darling, that you will be as content as I have been."

"I am happy, and you know that I love you and Papa," Candida cried.

"Then if you truly love your Papa you must never speak of this again," her Mother admonished her. "It distresses him so deeply to remember how badly he was treated. He is also always afraid that I will compare my present circumstances with the life which I lived when he first met me. It is stupid of him—no money in the world could buy what I have now.

She smiled.

But any reference to the past makes him long so desperately to give me all the things I had then."

"I understand, Mama," Candida assured her, "but you have not told me what was your name before you married."

To her surprise her Mother's lips tightened and for the first time there was a hard note in her voice.

"My name is Emmeline Walcott, I have no other name. There is nothing else for you to know, Candida."

It was only when she was alone, thinking over this strange and exciting story which her Mother had told her, that Candida had wondered, not once but many times, who her Mother had been. It was obvious that

14

her grandfather had been rich, and he must too have been a man of importance.

It was tantalising that her Mother would tell her no more, but there had been a firmness about Mrs. Walcott's refusal which had warned Candida against further indulging her curiosity—nonetheless she could not help wondering.

Sometimes she told herself stories that her grandfather was a Prince or a Duke, and that he suddenly decided to forgive her Mother and came to see them bearing luxuries which they had never been able to afford.

This story alternated with one in which her Father suddenly achieved fame. His poems sold not in the few hundreds which were achieved year after year, but in thousands, so that overnight he became famous like Lord Byron, admired and acclaimed, and once again her Mother could have beautiful clothes and jewels.

Candida wanted nothing for herself. As long as she had Pegasus, which her Father had given her when he was only a foal, she was happy.

The foal had been a birthday present, bought from a travelling horse-coper. He had grown from an adorable, rather gawky, long-legged animal into a coal-black stallion of unbelievable beauty and elegance. Candida knew whenever she rode him that she was admired and envied by everyone who came their way. Yet now Pegasus had to go.

There was nothing else left to sell. When her Father had taken that five-barred gate in the rain on his way home from "The King's Head" he had broken his neck and Juno, with two broken legs, had to be destroyed.

It was then that Candida found the house was mortgaged. Furniture had to be sold to pay the creditors, fetching a pitiful sum. Many of the pieces which her Mother had cherished and loved had been bought by the villagers more out of kindness than because they attached any value to the well polished wood or the carvings on which the gilt had been chipped away by age.

Some of the things had belonged once to her Father's parents, who had died when he was still very young, and Candida had always believed them valuable. But caring for one's possessions was a very different thing,

15

she discovered, from obtaining money for them. When everything was disposed of and the debts paid off, there was nothing left save a few personal belongings of her Mother's and Pegasus.

At first she fought in a wild panic against the thought of disposing of him, but she realised that she had to make some provision for old Ned. He had been with her Father and Mother since they were first married— groom, handyman, nursemaid, and cook.

He was too old at nearly seventy to get another job. He must have some source of income in his retirement, and the only way she could provide that for him was by selling Pegasus.

It was Ned who told her there was to be a Horse-Fair at Potters Bar. In her misery at her Father's death she had no time to think of anything but coping with the mortgage, settling the tradesmen's accounts and deciding which of the few clothes and books her Mother had left behind she would keep for herself.

"A Horse-Fair at Potters Bar?" she had repeated almost stupidly.

"Ay, Miss Candida. 'Tis the annual one, and the dealers and some of the gentry from London comes to it. Ye often get a better price there, they say, than anywhere else in the country."

She felt as though Ned's words stabbed at her heart, so that she almost cried out with pain. Then she knew, looking into his kind old eyes, that he was thinking of her, that she must have money on which to live, or at least to keep herself until she could find employment of some sort.

"I suppose I could be a governess," Candida murmured beneath her breath, wondering at the same time how she could get a position without a reference.

But whatever she decided to do, she had first to sell Pegasus. It was not possible for her to travel round the country with her horse, and besides she must ensure that Ned did not starve. It was, she thought, almost a sacred trust imposed upon her by her Mother.

"He is such a dear little man," she had often said. "What would we do without him, Candida? He can turn his hand to anything."

It was indeed Ned who made certain that there were

always fires in the house, lit from the wood he managed to collect without cost from adjacent estates. It was Ned who brought in a snared rabbit when there was nothing else in the house to eat.

"You have not poached it?" Mrs. Walcott would ask sometimes in horror, knowing the heavy penalties for anyone who poached game.

"Oi 'ave done no trespassing, if that is what ye mean, Ma'am," Ned would reply. "If the poor creature strayed onto our land, that be his own foolishness."

There had been an occasional pheasant that "strayed", and more than once rook pie had helped them over a particularly lean period. Always it was Ned who provided what was necessary: he could not now be allowed to go to the workhouse because he was too old to find other employment.

"I am young," Candida told herself, "I will manage somehow."

When she reached Potters Bar and saw the horses travelling towards the Fair, when she heard the bustle and noise of the Fair itself, she felt as if she was taking the horse she loved to the slaughter-house.

A number of hay-carts had been drawn up to make a rough circle in which some horses were being paraded, while others were being walked round on the outside. Some were rough animals led by a dark-eyed Gypsy or a vacant-looking farm-yokel with a straw in his mouth.

Others, with their coats brushed until they shone, their manes and tails combed and trimmed, were ridden by grooms in the livery of a local squire or mounted by a tradesman's son dressed in polished boots and smart pantaloons.

There was a babel of innumerable voices punctuated by loud guffaws from those who had already visited the local inn and the shrieks of children rushing about, stimulated by the excitement of their elders, and getting under the horses' hooves and in everybody else's way.

For a moment Candida felt at a loss. The only thing she really wanted was to turn round and ride for home, and then she remembered home was no longer hers—already it had passed into alien hands and tomorrow she must remove herself and her few meagre belongings.

17

It was with a sense of relief she saw Ned waiting for her by the entrance to the ground.

"Ah there ye be, Miss Candida," he said, coming up to take Pegasus' bridle. "Oi'm awondering what could have happened to ye."

"I could not hurry, Ned," Candida answered honestly.

"Oi knows that, Miss," he answered. "Here, ye jump down. I've seen a gentleman who might be interested, he has bought two or three of the top-notchers already."

"Yes, you take Pegasus," Candida said as she slipped to the ground.

She put out her hand to touch the horse, and instantly he turned his nose to nuzzle it against her neck with a gesture she knew so well. At his touch she felt she could bear it no longer.

"Take him away, Ned," she said, and her voice broke on the words. "I cannot bear to watch him go."

She walked into the crowd, her eyes blinded with tears. She did not want to see or hear what happened, she only knew that everything she really loved had gone from her. First her Mother, then her Father, and now Pegasus. They had been her whole world; now there was nothing left, nothing, except emptiness and a sense of despair which made her only want to die and put an end to her suffering.

How long she stood there, with the crowd milling round her, seeing and hearing nothing but her own misery, she had no idea, until suddenly Ned was at her side.

"He wants to buy him, Miss Candida, ye'd best come and talk to him. Oi've got him up to seventy-five guineas, but Oi thinks he would go a mite higher if he saw ye."

"Seventy-five guineas!" Candida repeated.

"It ain't enough for Pegasus," Ned said, "a hundred is what Oi hoped for. Come and talk to the gentleman, Miss Candida."

"Yes, I will talk to him," Candida said.

She suddenly felt that if she had to sell Pegasus she would sell him only at his proper worth. She would not allow him to be insulted by being knocked down for the paltry sum of seventy-five guineas. Ned was speaking the truth when he said there was not a horse to touch him at the whole Fair—there would not be, there could not be, there was no animal in the world like Pegasus.

Without saying anything further she followed Ned through the crowds to where in a corner of the field she saw Pegasus held by a groom. Beside him was the gentleman whom she knew must be the person interested in purchasing her horse.

At first glance Candida recognised his type all too well. That he was a man accustomed to being with horses was obvious. He almost looked like a horse with his long, lined face and weather-beaten skin.

The fit of his coat and breeches, and the neatness of his legs with their polished boots, told her that he had always ridden, and ridden well; a man who would be a hard rider to hounds; a man who undoubtedly knew a good horse when he saw one and would never make a mistake.

"This be the owner of Pegasus, Sir," she heard Ned say, and she looked up to see an expression of astonishment on the man's face.

"My name is Major Hooper, Ma'am. I am interested in your horse."

"Are you buying him to ride yourself?" Candida asked in her soft voice.

She saw it was not a question he had expected her to ask.

"I keep a livery stable, Ma'am," he replied. "I cater for the nobility and the smartest ladies in town. Your horse will be well looked after, my grooms know their job."

"And Pegasus will stay with you?" Candida enquired.

"Unless I am offered an exceedingly large sum for him," Major Hooper said, "then he will go to some Ducal stables. He is a fine animal. I promise you, Ma'am, that he will not be degraded into pulling the mail or sent to some posting-house."

Pegasus had turned to nuzzle his nose against Candida's cheek and she patted him gently. Then, looking at Major Hooper in what he described to himself as a scrutinising manner, she said:

19

"I believe what you tell me, but this is a very exceptional horse, unusual in many ways."

She saw a faint smile twitch his thin lips as if this was something he had heard often enough before. Impulsively she said:

"Wait, I will show you."

She made a gesture to Ned, who understood. He helped her into the saddle, then, taking the reins, Candida guided Pegasus into the next field away from the crowds. There were few people there, only a number of farmers' carts with their horses tied to a fence awaiting the return of their owners.

Candida put Pegasus through his paces. She made him trot, first in an ordinary manner, and then throwing out a foreleg at each step. Then at her command he knelt, rose, turned round and round, first one way and then another, until with a touch of her whip he stood up on his hind legs and walked, pawing the air in front of him.

She trotted him round once again, and then back to Major Hooper.

"Those are only some of the things he can do," she said, "and you should see him jump. He takes any fence, however high, as if he had wings."

She had concentrated so hard at showing off Pegasus that she had no idea that Major Hooper was watching not only the horse, but her. Now, as she looked down at him from the back of the big black stallion, he took in every detail of her appearance—the small, oval face crowned, beneath a weather-beaten riding-hat, with hair such as he had never seen before on any woman.

It should have been pale gold, the colour of ripening wheat, and yet in it there was a hint of fire, a touch of red which made it appear to have captured the rays of the sun.

It was perhaps the red in Candida's hair which was responsible for the whiteness of her skin, which was like the petal of a Madonna Lily. Smooth, soft and utterly flawless, it was not the skin of a girl who had lived all her life in the country, and had it not been for her shabby habit and battered, broken boots, Major Hooper would not have believed it possible for a woman to have such a skin without resorting to artifice.

But if her hair and skin were sensational, her eyes were even more so. Dark-lashed, they seemed unnaturally large in the thinness of her face, and though he tried he could not determine what their colour might be.

When he had first seen her he thought her eyes were flecked with green, but now, because she was anxious concerning his decision, he thought they were almost purple.

"My God, she is lovely!" he said to himself, and then as Candida dismounted he said abruptly:

"Why are you selling him?"

He saw the elation which had been in her face at Pegasus' performance vanish as though a dark blind had been drawn over a lighted window.

"I have to," she answered briefly.

"I am sure you could persuade your Father to keep him: you match each other so well."

"My father is dead," Candida replied in a low voice. "You do not suppose I would part with Pegasus unless I were compelled to do so."

"No, I can understand what he means to you," Major Hooper agreed. "I have worked with horses all my life. They become a part of one, especially if one is fortunate enough to own a horse like this!"

"You understand then," she whispered.

His sympathy had brought the tears back into her eyes, and Major Hooper, watching, wondered if any woman's eyes could look more expressive or more in need of a man's comfort.

"It is a pity you cannot show off Pegasus yourself," he said suddenly. "You would get a proper price for him in London—far better than I can offer you—if you were riding him."

"I would do that willingly," Candida said, "but how? I have no knowledge of London."

"What would your family say if I offered to take you there?" Major Hooper enquired.

"I have no family," Candida replied. "Walk Pegasus round the field, Ned, I would like Major Hooper to see him once again at a distance."

Ned took the bridle and did as he was told. As soon as he was out of earshot Candida said:

"I will be frank with you, Sir. I have to provide for

21

Ned. He has been groom to my Father and Mother for twenty-one years, I cannot leave him penniless. Anything you give me for Pegasus will provide for his old age. I can only beg you to be generous."

"And what will happen to you?" Major Hooper enquired.

She looked away from him across the field to where Pegasus, in high spirits, was pretending to shy at a piece of paper blowing in the wind.

"I will find employment of some sort," she said vaguely. "Perhaps I could be a governess or a companion."

Major Hooper suddenly slapped his whip against his riding-boots, and the sound made her start.

"I will give you £100 for Pegasus," he said, "if you will come to London with me and show him off in my school."

"School?" Candida queried.

"I have a Riding School attached to my livery stable." Major Hooper explained. "Many horses that I purchase need further breaking before they are competent to carry ladies in a side-saddle for their rides in London and the Row."

"I can help you do that?" Candida asked.

"Yes—and you can show Pegasus off to those who are interested," Major Hooper said.

"I would love to do that, it sounds too wonderful. Are you sure I shall not be any trouble?"

"You will be no trouble," he assured her.

"B-but . . . my . . . clothes," Candida stammered.

"Everything will be seen to," he promised. "You can trust me not to let you down on that score."

"Oh, thank you, thank you!" Candida cried. "I can stay with Pegasus! I cannot tell you what it means to me."

"I can understand that," Major Hooper said unsurely, "and now I should be getting back to town. If you come with me it will make things easier."

"At once? Do you mean now, just as I am?" Candida asked.

"I'll see that you are not wanting for anything when you reach London," Major Hooper said. "If you have any luggage of any sort, then perhaps your groom can bring it up to you tomorrow. I'll pay his expenses and give him now a note of hand for £100, which he can change at a bank. It would not be wise for him to carry such a large sum about with him."

"No indeed not," Candida replied, "it is kind of you to be so thoughtful."

"I'm used to such dealings," Major Hooper said. "May I be frank, Ma'am, in saying that never before have I been fortunate in finding at a country Fair of this sort such a magnificent animal or such a very attractive owner."

He saw Candida blush at the compliment. Just for a moment the lily whiteness of her skin took on the soft pink of a rose-bud. Then she smiled at him and he could only think once again that he had never seen such fantastic eyes.

"My God, I've got a bargain!" he said to himself as he watched her run across the field towards Ned to tell him the news.

Not even the dowdy, threadworn habit could disguise her grace, and Major Hooper, a man little given to sentiment, found himself muttering beneath his breath:

"She's lovely, and she'll pay for it! Poor little devil!"

2

As Candida drove into London beside Major Hooper in his fast yellow and black phaeton, she felt that a new world was opening before her.

It was not long before the green fields of Potters Bar gave way to suburban houses with flower-filled gardens, and then the increasing traffic told her that they were nearing the great city, which she had visited only twice in her whole life.

It was the horses which interested her more than anything else. She stared at a pair of well-matched roans drawing a ponderous family carriage gleaming with brass, the cocked-hatted coachman wearing many-tiered driving-capes. On another such vehicle the horses' heads were held high by bearing-reins and there were a brace of powdered flunkeys on the dicky seat.

Sometimes, as they flashed by, she would have a glimpse of an attractive face at a window or the rosy-hued nose of a rich owner.

Then her eyes would be attracted to the chestnuts drawing a fashionable Victoria open to the afternoon sunshine and conveying a vision of fashion holding a ridiculously small lace-trimmed sun-shade.

She found it hard to take her eyes also from the riders on horseback. Their sleek, well-groomed mounts made her wonder how Pegasus would compare with them; but it was a question with an easy answer—he was undoubtedly incomparable.

"We do not pass any shops," Major Hooper said, thinking that, as Candida turned her head eagerly from side to side, she was, like so many women, window-gazing.

"Are the shops only in the centre of London?" Candida asked.

"The ones that will interest you are," he replied. "I live the park side of St. John's Wood—a very fashionable quarter at the moment."

He glanced at her sharply as he spoke, as if he expected her either to challenge the statement or to show that she was aware of something that he implied. The lovely little face turned up to him showed no emotion other than the ordinary interest that any young girl might have shown in his conversation.

"It is a good position then for your livery-stable?" she asked innocently.

Major Hooper's lips twitched as he replied:

"My customers are all around me."

"That must be very convenient," Candida remarked, no longer attending but watching a young gallant, his top hat at a saucy angle, coping with his stallion that had shied at a coster's barrel.

Pegasus was being ridden to London by one of Major Hooper's grooms. He had bought three other horses at the Fair, but Candida had known without being told that the chief groom would be in charge of Pegasus.

It had been a poignant moment when she had said good-bye to Ned, but he had been so overwhelmed and grateful at the vast sum of money she had bestowed on him that he was almost incoherent.

"You will be able to rent that cottage you like in the village," Candida told him. "And I am sure there will be lots of small jobs you can do which will bring you in other money from time to time."

"Do not worry yer head about me, Miss Candida," Ned replied, "'tis ye Oi be athinking of."

"I shall be all right," Candida replied with a bravery which, though cleverly assumed, did not deceive Ned.

"Are ye sure ye be doing the right thing, Miss?" he asked, pulling her a little to one side so that Major Hooper could not overhear what he said.

"It is an opportunity to be with Pegasus," Candida replied, "and Major Hooper seems a nice man."

It was not exactly the word she would have chosen to describe Major Hooper; she did not really know quite what she did feel about him. At the same time he seemed frank and open. Besides, if she did not go with him, what was the alternative?

She had no knowledge of Domestic Bureaux from which fashionable ladies engaged their servants, nor did she think that her appearance in London, ill-dressed and without references, was likely to find her anything but employment of the most inferior sort.

Besides this she was certain that her youth and her looks would be against her. She was not conceited, but she was well aware that society ladies did not usually fill their houses with attractive young women who were not by birth intended to be domestic servants.

No, there was nothing else she could have done but accept Major Hooper's offer, and indeed she was deeply grateful to him for the chance to remain with Pegasus and to know that for a short time at least she would be able to ride her horse.

It was not long after six o'clock when finally they reached the wide, well cared for streets of St. John's Wood. Major Hooper tooled his phaeton skilfully into a narrow mews, with stables on either side of the cobbled roadway. Finally they came to a large door surmounted by an arch on which was inscribed "Hooper's Livery Stables."

"Here we are!" Major Hooper exclaimed.

They drove through the gateway and Candida found herself in a square stable-yard surrounded on all sides by horse-boxes. Their occupants were looking out over the half-open doors, and she had a quick impression of dozens of attractive and elegant horses, more than she had ever seen in one place in her life before.

It seemed to her as though all the horses watched her descent from the phaeton. She had a feeling that they welcomed her with more enthusiasm than human beings could possibly have shown.

Without waiting for Major Hooper she walked towards the nearest horse-box and stroked its occupant—a young bay. He was quiet and gentle to her touch, and she knew he was the type of horse that any woman, even an inexperienced one, would be happy to ride.

She looked to the right and left. There were long vistas of bays and chestnuts, greys, blacks—some with

26

a distinguishing white blaze upon their forehead. There was a flush on Candida's cheeks and a sudden light in her eyes as she turned towards Major Hooper.

"Fancy you having all these fine horses!" she cried "They are indeed magnificent! No wonder you have a lot of important customers. Yours must be the best stable in the whole of London."

"It is perhaps the best known," Major Hooper said, and again there was a faint under-current in his voice which however escaped Candida's attention.

"How long will it be before Pegasus gets here?" she asked. "And where are you going to put him?"

"There are two or three empty boxes at the far end," Major Hooper replied, making a gesture with his hand. "In the meantime I must find somewhere for you to live."

"Oh yes, of course," Candida said, "but I have no luggage."

"I've remembered that too," Major Hooper assured her, "it need not trouble you. I'm going now to see a lady who I know will be delighted to accommodate you and to provide you with all that is necessary. But first I would like to speak with her alone."

"Yes, of course," Candida agreed.

"So I am going to leave you in the Riding School," Major Hooper said, walking across the stable-yard.

Candida followed him. There was another arched doorway that she had not noticed at the far end of the yard. It was not as large and impressive as the doorway from the mews, but when Major Hooper opened the door and she followed him in, she gave a cry of delight.

She found herself in a large Riding School lighted by a glass roof. It had been modelled—though she was not aware of it then—on the Imperial Riding School in Vienna.

The school had been built, she was to learn very much later, by an elderly Peer who had been besotted by the beauty and the equestrian prowess of his mistress. He liked to see her put his horses through their paces, but as he preferred to watch her ride, as Lady Godiva had ridden, in the nude, it had been essential that they should have a private place in which she could perform.

27

When the Peer had died Major Hooper had been able to buy the Riding School at considerably less than it had cost to erect. The panelled walls were still painted pale blue, and in the gallery in which the Peer had sat to watch his naked Venus, the seats were covered in blue brocade. There were mirrors on the walls to reflect the horses and their riders from every angle.

"What an unexpected place to find in London!" Candida exclaimed.

"It is useful," Major Hooper answered, "and you will be able to exercise Pegasus here. As you see, I have erected some high jumps. I have at the moment two or three horses that may be sold for quite considerable sums if I can satisfy their prospective owners that they can stretch out over a high fence."

"Pegasus can do that," Candida said proudly, and then she almost bit back the words, realising that Pegasus might be sold if he took the fancy of some rich nobleman who wanted an unusual mount.

As if he read her thoughts by her sudden silence and the look of anxiety on her face, Major Hooper said reassuringly:

"Do not worry, I'm not considering selling Pegasus as yet."

"Oh, thank you!" Candida cried. "Thank you! Thank you! He is the only thing I have left. I can never tell you what I felt today as I rode towards the Fair knowing I must lose him."

"I can understand," the Major said kindly. "Now go up to the gallery. If anyone comes here, which is very unlikely since the school is closed, I want you to keep out of sight. You are not to speak to anyone, man or woman. Do you understand?"

"Yes, of course," Candida said in some astonishment.

He watched her climb the staircase which led to the gallery, before he walked out of the Riding School. Hearing him close the door firmly behind him, she walked to the end of the Gallery and sat down in a corner on one of the brocaded blue seats. There was still a glint of sunshine coming through the glass roof and she appraised the jumps one by one, calculating how she would ride Pegasus up to them.

She was so intent on her thoughts that she gave a start when suddenly she realized there was someone in the school. She had not heard the door open, but now she saw a lady mounted on a rather frisky chestnut and holding him in check as she bent to speak to the gentleman standing beside her.

"I will put him over the jumps," Candida heard the lady say, "and you can judge for yourself."

"I am prepared to believe you, Lais, you know that, the gentleman answered. "It's just the price which bothers me."

Remembering Major Hooper's instructions not to be seen or to speak to anyone, Candida drew back further into the corner and sank a little lower in the chair she occupied. She realised it was very unlikely that the people down below would see her. She could look down at them, but it was far more difficult for them to look up and see her, small as she was, crouching in the corner.

She watched them both with interest and curiosity. The lady riding the chestnut was lovely. Candida thought she had never seen anyone so attractive before.

Not only was her face with its high cheek-bones and long dark slanting eyes so arresting, but also the shining dark chignon on which was perched a high hat swathed with an emerald green veil which floated out behind as she rode.

Her riding-habit was green too, and Candida thought she had never seen one cut with such close-fitting shoulders or such a tiny pulled-in waist. The emerald velvet skirt of the habit moved when she jumped to display a narrow coquettish boot with a high heel, to which there was strapped a twinkling spur with a sharp point.

As the chestnut approached the fences the rider used her silver-handled whip sharply, and Candida knew as she watched that here was one of those women who enjoyed supremacy over a horse and would exert it even to the point of cruelty.

At the same time here was no doubt that the lady in the emerald green habit could ride—and ride magnificently. Round and round the riding-school she went, increasing her pace until finally she was almost galloping between fences, and yet somehow lifting her horse

29

over them with such skill that Candida found it difficult not to clap as she drew the animal to a halt with almost unnecessary severity.

"Bravo! Bravo!" the man watching her cried. "That was well done, Lais. If anyone genuinely deserves the title of being a Pretty Horse-breaker, it is you."

"I am gratified by your approval, M'Lord" Lais replied mockingly. "Well, are you going to buy Kingfisher for me?"

"You know damn well I am," the gentleman answered, "although Hooper is asking a hell of a price."

"Not really," Lais replied. "You can lift me down."

A groom appeared from the shadows and took the horse's bridle. Lais put down the reins and held out her arms to the young man, who lifted her from the saddle. As he did so Candida gave an audible gasp. The horse's flank was red with blood and she knew that his rider must have driven in her pointed spur at every jump.

"How could she be so merciless?" Candida asked herself, and thought if anyone treated Pegasus in such a fashion she could not endure it.

Below, the gentleman, having taken Lais in his arms, did not put her down. The horse was led away, and now his arm tightened round the slim, elegant body and his lips came down hard on the laughing red mouth.

"You little witch," he said. "You inveigle me as usual into spending more money than I intended."

"Am I not worth it?" Lais asked.

"You know you are," he answered hoarsely.

"Well, if you are not satisfied there are others who will be," she told him coolly, and extricating herself from his arms she turned towards the door.

"Damn you! You know as well as I do," the gentleman exclaimed, "that I can refuse you nothing, although the Devil knows what my Father will say if I land up in Dun Street."

"That is your business," Lais said, but her inviting smile somehow softened the harshness of the words. "Now I must go and get dressed for dinner."

"You are dining with me?" he said eagerly.

"I suppose so," she replied with a provocative glance, "that is if I do not find a better invitation when I get home."

30

"Curse it, Lais, you cannot treat me like that," the gentleman expostulated, but now the door of the Riding School shut behind them and Candida could hear no more.

She sat looking down wide-eyed at where they had been. Never had she heard a gentleman speak to a lady with so many swear words in his conversation, and now Lais was no longer there to bemuse her with her elegant clothes and fashionable appearance, Candida realised that her voice had not been very cultured.

"Perhaps she is an actress," she thought, "that would account for her good looks and for her sensational habit."

She had hardly noticed the gentleman, but remembering now that he had spoken of his father she thought he appeared very young. He too had been dressed in the height of fashion: top hat on the side of his head, gold-mounted cane in his hand, pale elegant pantaloons surmounted by a wide skirted coat and a dazzlingly fancy waistcoat.

It was what Candida knew gentlemen of the nobility would be wearing in London, but she had not realised how graceful they could look.

The conversation between the pair who had now left the School was very puzzling, and yet there was no doubt how well Lais, whoever she might be, could ride . . .

Only a short distance away from the livery-stable Major Hooper was raising the polished knocker on the door of a porticoed house in one of the quiet streets off Regent's Park. The door was opened almost immediately by a powdered footman wearing a discreet livery with silver buttons.

"Evening, James," Major Hooper said. "Will Mrs. Clinton receive me?"

"She is alone, Sir," the footman replied.

"That is what I wanted to know," the Major replied. "I will show myself up."

He went up the stairway two at a time, and opened the door of the L-shaped Drawing Room. The room was lit by gas, but the light was soft and seductive and

31

made the woman rising from the fireplace to greet him seem younger and more attractive than her years.

Cheryl Clinton had been on the stage when she was taken under the protection of a rich and successful businessman. She had progressed from him to a distinguished nobleman, who in turn had passed her on to several other gentlemen well-known in the Clubland of St. James's Street.

It was only when her charms were fading a little that Cheryl Clinton made the decision to go into business for herself. Her first protector had taught her a great deal about money and how to handle it. Subsequent gentlemen on whom she had bestowed her favours had given her an inside knowledge of masculine taste in the frail female. She had also learnt of the extreme laziness of the wealthy and the aristocracy when it came to exerting themselves in pursuit of their desires.

Cheryl Clinton set herself up to introduce gentlemen who could afford it to the type of young woman that they wished to know and whom it was far too much trouble to find for themselves.

Cheryl Clinton had in her youth met Mrs. Porter, whose boast it was that she had introduced Harriet Wilson—then the head of her profession—to the Duke of Wellington.

She had been shocked later on to hear that Mrs. Porter had fallen on bad times. This was something she had no intention of doing herself. If she made money she intended to keep it.

Mrs. Clinton was convinced it would be easy to make money if one was expensive enough. She had discovered during the course of her life that men would always pay for the best, and if she provided the best, then she would ensure that she obtained the best price.

Every evening Cheryl Clinton could be found in her charming Drawing Room in her quiet, well-ordered house in St. John's Wood. Gentlemen would arrive to call on her. They would sit gossiping on general topics, imbibing a glass or two of champagne. Then, the formalities over, they would come to the point.

"I know exactly what you want, My Lord," Mrs. Clinton would smile, "and I have the very girl to suit you. As a matter of fact she is a young married woman and her husband is away from home. You will find her very accommodating."

As she spoke she would touch a little silver bell by her side. James would open the door and a note would be despatched to the house of a pretty young grass-widow who seldom lived far away.

There would be more champagne and more conversation until the lady in question arrived, when His Lordship would escort her to dinner in one of those restaurants which had discreet supper rooms upstairs.

Mrs. Cheryl Clinton contrived it all very cleverly. In fact she was by now so well-known in the West End of London that practically every introduction of importance was handled by her.

"Well, Major," she said as Major Hooper entered the room, "this is a surprise! I was not expecting you this evening."

"You must forgive my calling on you just as I am," Major Hooper said, "but I have been at the Horse-Fair at Potters Bar all day and have had no time to change."

"I am convinced that what you have to tell me is important," Mrs. Clinton said with a smile. "Please sit down. Will you have some champagne?"

Major Hooper shook his head.

"No thank you, I must hurry or your attention will be occupied elsewhere. Mrs. Clinton, I have found something unusual and I might almost say unique—a girl who is lovely, unspoilt and inexperienced. She is a really beautiful creature, far more beautiful than any of those who have patronised my stable in the last ten years."

"I do not believe it," Mrs. Clinton teased him. "Who is this paragon?"

"She is a lady of breeding," Major Hooper said bluntly, "with a horse such as every riding man dreams of possessing—an animal that occurs once in a life-time."

"I am not interested in the horse," Mrs. Clinton said gently.

"That I know," Major Hooper said, "but they go together. I promise you this is a couple such as you have never seen in your life."

"Who is she?" Mrs. Clinton asked.

"She told me all about herself. She is an orphan of gentle blood, whose father broke his neck ten days ago. She hasn't a penny-piece to bless herself with."

"That is not always a disadvantage," Mrs. Clinton replied softly.

"She is also as innocent as a new-born babe," Major Hooper continued.

Mrs. Clinton raised her eyebrows.

"It is true," he said, seeing the disbelief in her eyes. "She has lived in the country all her life—her father was a recluse, a writer of some sort. She knows nothing of the world. I'm convinced she has not only never heard of the expression a "Pretty Horse-breaker" or the like, but that if she did she would have no idea what it meant."

"It is not necessarily a part of a young lady's education," Mrs. Clinton said with a smile.

"No, but you know what I am trying to say," Major Hooper said. "You will have to handle her with kid gloves or she will take fright. I swear to you, valuable though that horse may be, its value is increased a hundredfold when she is on its back."

"What do you want me to do?" Mrs. Clinton asked.

"You must have her to stay here in the first place," Major Hooper said.

"That is impossible!" Mrs. Clinton exclaimed. "You know I never have women in my house."

"This girl is different," Major Hooper retorted. "As I have told you, she is a lady—and I mean that. You cannot put her into lodgings or in some dingy hotel. For one thing, she is far too pretty. Let anyone see her and they will be round her like flies round a comb of honey. The only thing that astounds me is that no one has discovered her before."

"She must indeed be outstanding to affect you in this manner," Mrs. Clinton said in surprise. "I thought, Major, you were past being excited by the fair sex, knowing how much you have to do with them. At least, that is what you have always told me."

"I would rather deal with a horse than a woman any day," Major Hooper said. "But this is business, Mrs. Clinton, as well you know. I can get a thousand guineas for that horse if the girl goes with it. I might even try

34

for two thousand. Our arrangement is as usual—fifty-fifty."

"What does she look like at the moment?" Mrs. Clinton asked.

"Like someone from the alleys round Drury Lane," Major Hooper replied. "I have never seen such a habit as she is wearing, it must have come out of the Ark. I did not stop to let her pick up her other things, they wouldn't have been any better. You will have to start from scratch, Mrs. Clinton."

"You really intrigue me, Major Hooper," Mrs. Clinton said. "It is not often I am interested in such propositions these days. I have my hands full, and as things are there are more doves about waiting to be soiled than there are men looking for them. Of course the quality is not as good as it was when the Crimea War was on: the names on my list then had to be seen to be believed! But I am not complaining!"

"I should think not indeed," Major Hooper said. "Since it has become the fashion for the "Pretty Horse-breakers" to meet at the Achilles Statue my business has doubled, there was never a better shop-window."

"And yet we have our failures," Mrs. Clinton said gently. "Do you realise, Major, that the Marquis of Hartington has given Skittles an annuity of two thousand pounds—but he did not meet her through my introduction."

"I thought he did!" Major Hooper exclaimed.

"Unfortunately not," Mrs. Clinton said crossly. "Skittles was under the protection of someone to whom I had introduced her, but she had set her cap at Hartington. She contrived to collide with him and fall at his feet in Hyde Park—of all old tricks! She caught him right enough! She fancies herself as the future Duchess of Devonshire."

"You have to hand it to her," Major Hooper ejaculated with a grin. "She's never yet funked a fence, however high!"

"And the same thing has happened with Agnes Willoughby," Mrs. Clinton continued. "She has recently married young Windham, who is mad but very rich. She has had the grace to send me £50 for all I did for her. It was a gesture, at least, but Windham did not proffer me a farthing. Said he met her with Kate Cooke, who, if I am not mistaken, will become the Countess of Euston."

"Oh well, I suppose there is an element of luck in your business as there is in mine," Major Hooper said.

"You may take it philosophically," Mrs. Clinton said, "but I do not. And I will tell you someone whom I would like to make pay and pay and pay!"

"Need I guess?" Major Hooper said with a grin.

"You know to whom I am referring!" Mrs. Clinton said grimly. "Three of my best girls my Lord Manville has taken from me one after another. Mary he set up in a most elegant villa, buying her three horses."

"Which he did not purchase from me!" Major Hooper ejaculated.

"And she was so puffed up at his patronage," Mrs. Clinton continued, "that when I saw her in the Park driving in the pony-carriage he had bought her, she looked right through me."

"I never did like that girl!" Major Hooper remarked.

"And then there was Clarissa," Mrs. Clinton said. "I spent no less than £150 on that chit, and His Lordship carries her off as brazenly as if he were a highwayman. Her sapphires were the talk of the town, and not a penny-piece have I had from that investment."

"Well, if you want to put His Lordship in his place, here is your chance," Major Hooper said. "There's no better judge of horseflesh in the length and breadth of Britain. So listen, Mrs. Clinton, for we have not much time. I have an idea which should benefit us both."

There was a knock at the door.

"Excuse me, Ma'am," James said. "His Grace the Duke of Wessex is downstairs and craves a word with you."

"Show His Grace into the Morning Room and ask his indulgence. I shall be with him in a few moments."

"Very good, Ma'am," James said respectfully as he shut the door.

"Now, tell me," Mrs. Clinton said. . . .

Waiting in the Riding School Candida grew a little afraid. It was growing dark, the school seemed full of shadows. She was suddenly conscious of how utterly

36

alone she was; she was also, womanlike, aware of the contrast in appearance between herself and Lais.

She was accustomed to think very little about her clothes for the simple reason that she had so few, but now she knew her habit was a disgrace and her boots beyond repair. She thought of her hair pulled back into an untidy bun, while Lais' had been plaited in a smooth, elegant chignon.

It was hopeless! How could she possibly manage in London? How could she even expect to ride Pegasus where there would be anyone to see them? She would be the laughing-stock of any fashionable throng, and, looking as she did, she would certainly not enhance the value of her horse.

She felt a sudden surge of homesickness, not only for her Father—who, even when he drank, had been kind and considerate to her—but for everything that had been familiar—the shabby little house; Ned shuffling round it, Pegasus in the broken-down stable; the quiet; the sense of belonging to herself and being free. For, despite the lack of money, friends and clothes, she had been free—free to ride her horse, free to do as she wished. But now what lay ahead?

She had a sudden moment of panic. Perhaps she should not have come, perhaps she should go away. Would her Mother have wanted her to do this? And then she asked herself to do what? What did Major Hooper envisage for her? And what did she know about him?

Impulsively she jumped to her feet. She moved along the gallery, down the staircase and onto the floor of the Riding School. Her hand had actually gone out to open the door which led into the world outside when Major Hooper appeared. It was too dark for him to see her face, but he must have sensed her agitation because he said soothingly:

"It's all right, I'm sorry to have been so long. Come along, there is a lady who is going to look after you. You can stay with her in her house."

He turned to go but Candida did not move.

"What is it?" he asked.

"I shall not fit in here," Candida said in a low frightened voice. "I think I had best go back to where I came from. I will find something in the country."

"Frightened are you?" Major Hooper asked. "Well, you need not be. It is all right—you're going to have a good life and a comfortable one. Listen, Candida, you are a very attractive girl. You will be admired, fêted, made a fuss of—that is what all women want."

"I do not think I want that," Candida replied.

"Well, what do you want?" he asked.

"I think I want to be safe," she answered. "I want a home."

"That will all come in time," he said quickly. "Now, we can't hang about. I've done my best for you and one day you will be grateful to me."

He put out his hand and laid it on her shoulder. She was shivering, and he thought to himself she was like a young foal finding its legs in a strange meadow, uncertain and nervous.

"Come along, girl," he said kindly. "The first fence is always the worst, you know that; and you've got the courage to take them all."

"Have I?" Candida asked.

"I'm prepared to bet on it," he answered.

She smiled up at him.

"You must think me very stupid," she said in a low voice, "but I am grateful for your kindness, I am really."

"There was really nothing else I could do, was there?" he asked, and she wondered at the question in his words and did not understand the sudden doubt in his tone.

They walked through the stable-yard. The horse-boxes were all closed and she could hear the grooms singing and talking in a lighted room at the far end.

"How far is it to the place where I am staying?" Candida asked.

"Only a few streets away," Major Hooper replied. "Do you mind walking?"

"No, I like it," she told him.

They moved side by side up the cobbled mews. In the street outside the broughams, with their lamps lighted, were clop-clopping past. There seemed so many of them. They all looked prosperous—the horses sleek and well fed, the coachmen on the hammer-cloth flashily dressed.

They walked in silence until Major Hooper stopped before a porticoed door. Candida was just about to climb the steps when the door opened. To her surprise Major Hooper took her tightly by the arm and drew her quickly away.

"What is it?" she gasped, as she saw coming through the door in a shaft of light two tall top-hatted figures.

"Do not look round," Major Hooper said.

"Why not?" Candida asked.

"I do not want them to see you," he answered.

They were still walking down the street. Major Hooper looked back. The two gentlemen leaving Mrs. Clinton's had stepped into their carriage. There was a crest on the door, a footman on the box, and the coachman whipped up the horses.

"They have gone now," Major Hooper said with relief. "Come on girl, we don't want to dawdle about in case someone else arrives."

"The lady you are taking me to is not giving a party, is she?" Candida asked nervously.

"No, no, just seeing—friends," Major Hooper answered.

Candida noticed the little pause between the last two words, but already they were at the door and the footman opened it at Major Hooper's knock.

"Madam said it would be best if you went into the Dining Room, Sir," she heard the footman say to Major Hooper.

"Yes, a good idea," he replied.

He led the way to a room at the back of the house; small, square, tastefully set out with polished mahogany furniture, and two large silver candelabra on the sideboard. The gas-globes on either side of the fireplace were lit.

"I will inform Madam of your arrival," the footman said.

Candida looked round her apprehensively. There was nothing to frighten her, the room was in good taste, and yet she felt afraid. It seemed to her that Major Hooper was also nervous. He kept looking at her and she could not understand the expression in his eyes.

"Why don't you take off that vastly unbecoming hat," he suggested.

"Of course, if you would like me to," Candida smiled. "It is ugly, is it not?"

"No self-respecting horse would be seen dead in it," Major Hooper replied, and they were both laughing as Mrs. Clinton came into the room.

She stood for a moment in the doorway, taking in the picture of the girl who stood beside the Major. She was small and fragile, with an amazingly white skin and two huge eyes sparkling now with amusement.

It was her hair that made Mrs. Clinton draw in her breath a strange mixture of pale gold, and in the gaslight touched with little flames of red.

She stood there staring, and then met Major Hooper's eyes across the Dining Room table. There was a look of triumph in them, the look of an owner who has won first prize at a show. Mrs. Clinton gave him a faint smile and glided forward with both hands outstretched.

"My dear child," she said to Candida, "I am so very, very glad to meet you."

3

"It is not fair!" The words seemed to burst from the lips of the young man standing tense and pale in the elegant Morning Room of Manville House which overlooked Berkeley Square.

"Naturally you think so," His Lordship replied suavely, "but in the years to come, Adrian, I promise you that you will thank me."

"I cannot understand why you should dictate to me in this matter," Adrian retorted. "You may be my Guardian and have control of my money until I am twenty-five, but that does not entitle you to interfere in my life and prevent me from marrying whom I wish to marry."

Lord Manville raised his eyebrows.

"It does not?" he questioned. "I should have thought that was exactly what guardians were for. But it is no use arguing with me, Adrian. I have made up my mind, and the answer is no. You cannot get married when you are still only twenty and at Oxford."

"If Lucy was not a lady I could understand your opposition," Adrian said, "but even you cannot say that morally she is not a suitable person for me."

"I was not suggesting that morals were concerned," Lord Manville replied. "Moreover I accept your statement that the lady on whom you have set your affections is of gentle blood, and that her father, being a parson, gives an air of sanctity to the whole affair. Nevertheless, Adrian, you still remain too young."

"I suppose," Adrian said in a bitter voice, "you would make no objection if I set up some sordid little dancer in a villa in St. John's Wood. That would come

41

within your peculiar beliefs of what is correct for me at my age."

"While I am prepared, my dear boy, to ignore your somewhat offensive tone of voice," Lord Manville said, rising from the breakfast table and walking towards the fireplace, "let me tell you that such a liaison at your age would not only have my consent but my blessing."

"I was sure of it," Adrian retorted furiously. "Your own reputation stinks. People talk about you, and do you know what they call you?"

"I assure you I am not interested," Lord Manville answered blandly.

"They call you 'The Heart-Breaker'," Adrian stormed, "a shaming way to have one's Guardian described! Oh, I'm not saying that a lot of my friends do not envy you your wealth and your fine horses, but they snigger about your conquests—snigger! Do you hear me?"

"It would be difficult not to," Lord Manville replied, "considering that you are shouting. Do try, my dear boy, to have more self-control. It is exceedingly unbecoming for a gentleman of fashion to lose his temper simply because he cannot obtain exactly what he desires."

The quietness in Lord Manville's tone seemed to check his young cousin's fury. Adrian choked and, walking across the room to look out into Berkeley Square, said after a minute in a very different tone:

"I apologise."

"I accept your apology," Lord Manville said, "and let me assure you, Adrian, that, although you do not believe it at the moment, I have your best interests at heart. You have seen very little of life. When you leave Oxford you will go to London and meet a great number of people, including many of the female sex. Then if you are of the same mind about this young woman who has captured your heart, I shall be prepared to listen."

Adrian swung round, his eyes alight.

"In the meantime, may I be engaged to her?"

"Certainly not," Lord Manville replied promptly. "There is to be no attachment, no public recognition, nothing to proclaim that you mean anything more to each other than can be summed up in the all-embracing word of 'friendship'. Even an 'understanding', my young Don Juan, would put you in chains. I want you to be free to see life for what it is before you shackle yourself to any woman, however attractive, however alluring she may appear at the moment."

"So you want me to become like you," Adrian muttered in a dull voice, "nearly thirty-five and unmarried."

"And with the reputation of being a heart-breaker!" Lord Manville finished for him. "Well, Adrian, each to our own choice. May I assure you that whatever you and your contemporaries say about me, I am a contented man."

"You are out of date," Adrian declared. "Can you not understand that all this raffish woman-chasing is something which belonged to the beginning of the century? Men are more serious today, they look at life from quite a different angle to what you do."

Lord Manville threw back his head and laughed as if he could not help it.

"Oh my God, Adrian, you will be the death of me!" he exclaimed. "Students are all the same: they always think that they are going to reform the world; that they are different from their fathers' generation; that they are made in a different mould from their elders; that their ideas are something entirely new."

"We do think differently, I assure you," Adrian said hotly.

"Spare me the details, I beg of you," Lord Manville pleaded. "Go back to Oxford and get your degree. Then we can talk about what you are going to do with your life."

"There is only one thing I want to do," Adrian replied.

"I know," Lord Manville said, "but despite all your arguments you have not convinced me. I am sorry, the answer is still—no."

"What would you do," Adrian asked slowly, "if Lucy and I eloped? It might not be hard to persuade her."

"If you were so foolish," Lord Manville said, and now his voice was like ice, "as to do anything so unconventional and so detrimental to the good name of the young woman you pretend to love, then I should indeed be ashamed of you. But I think that even a parson's daughter, accustomed as the young lady must be to living in straitened circumstances, would find it hard to exist on an income of precisely nothing a year. That, Adrian, is what you would both have."

"You would stop my allowance?" Adrian asked incredulously.

"Immediately," Lord Manville replied. "And let me say that is not an idle threat. The day you did anything so unconventional, and indeed so despicable, as to persuade a lady of gentle birth to accompany you to Gretna Green, you would no longer be worthy of my consideration. In fact, I should not think of you again until I handed over your estates—doubtless more enriched because there would be less spent—on the day you are twenty-five."

"There is nothing I can do, is there, in those circumstances?" Adrian said sullenly.

"Nothing," Lord Manville agreed.

For a moment the young man stood staring at his guardian as though he would plead with him. Then, with an inarticulate sound that was half an explosion of anger and half a hastily smothered sob, he strode from the Morning Room, slamming the door behind him.

Lord Manville sighed, and picking up *The Times* newspaper scanned the headlines. The morning sun coming in through the window enveloped him, and it was hard to imagine a finer or more handsome looking man as he stood there in a dressing-gown of oriental brocade, an azure-blue satin scarf round his neck and his legs encased in tight-fitting yellow pantaloons.

Lord Manville had dark hair growing back from a square forehead. His features were almost classical in their perfection, and while he wore fashionable muttonchop side whiskers elegantly trimmed, the rest of his face was clean shaven.

He had eyebrows which, when he was angry, nearly met across the bridge of his aristocratic nose. His eyes were sharp and penetrating, but when he was amused they could sparkle with a hint of mischief.

It was a handsome face; at the same time, despite his assertion that he was a contented man, there was an air of cynicism in his lips, which could set themselves in a hard line and smile disdainfully as if he stood back from life and defied it to dominate him.

Lord Manville was just in the process of putting down *The Times* and picking up *The Morning Post* when the butler entered.

"Pardon me, M'Lord, but the Dowager Duchess of Thorne has called on Your Lordship. I have shown Her Grace into the Salon."

"My grandmother at this hour of the morning?" Lord Manville glanced at the clock over the mantelpiece. "No indeed, 'tis I who am at fault. Mr. Adrian delayed me."

"You were a trifle later than usual in descending to breakfast," Bates said respectfully, "but it was five o'clock before you returned this morning, M'Lord."

"I am well aware of it, Bates," Lord Manville cried, "my head feels as fogged as a November day. Tell Taylor I will ride in an hour. That should clear away the cobwebs."

"An assured remedy, M'Lord," Bates said.

He was an old man who had served Lord Manville's father and the present Baron since his inheritance. He watched His Lordship appreciatively now as he ran up the staircase and thought that there was not a more handsome nobleman in the length and breadth of Great Britain.

It was less than ten minutes later that Lord Manville walked into the Salon to where his grandmother was waiting. Now he was elegantly arrayed in a cut-away riding-coat of superfine cloth, his necktie sporting a pearl tie-pin above a yellow waistcoat which matched the yellow carnation in his button-hole.

"Grandmama!" he exclaimed, walking towards the elderly lady seated on one of the satin sofas. "You must forgive me for keeping you waiting but I had not anticipated such an unexpected pleasure."

The Dowager Duchess of Thorne let him raise her rheumaticky old hands in their black mittens to his lips. She looked him over appreciatively, as lifting the tails of his coat he sat down beside her on the sofa.

"What brings you to London?" Lord Manville asked.

"Her Majesty, who else?" the Dowager replied. "I

can assure you, Silvanus, I would not make the arduous journey over muddy roads for any other reason."

As the Dowager Duchess was famed for turning up in London unexpectedly at all seasons of the year, and was known to have what her children called an 'itching foot', Lord Manville merely smiled.

"You know you adore coming to London, Grandmama," he said. "How else would you know the latest scandal if you buried yourself in the country for too long?"

"There is plenty for me to learn from all I hear," the Dowager replied sharply. "Her Majesty asked me when you were to be married. It is a pity I could not give her a proper answer."

"Do not speak to me of marriage," Lord Manville pleaded. "I have heard enough about that tiresome state this morning to wish the whole Institution abandoned."

"Is that what Adrian came to see you about?" the Dowager enquired with a sudden light in her eyes. "I met him on the door-step in a fit of the sullens, and I thought perhaps you were responsible."

"Grandmama, I can see that you are dying with curiosity as to why Adrian was visiting me," Lord Manville said. "Well, you are correct. He wants to marry some obscure parson's daughter he has met at Oxford."

"And you forbade him to do so?" the Dowager asked.

"Naturally," Lord Manville replied. "Can you imagine a worse mésalliance when he is only twenty?"

"Adrian has always been a sentimental, romantic creature," the Dowager said. "I expect you were right, though your forbidding him to marry would, I should have thought, have made him more determined to defy you."

"It is hard to defy anyone without money," Lord Manville remarked.

"So you threatened to cut off his allowance?" the Dowager said.

"What I love about you, Grandmama," Lord Manville exclaimed, "is that no one ever has to dot their i's and cross their t's where you are concerned. You are always one jump ahead in the conversation. I wish there were more like you, it makes life so very much easier."

"The world is full of fools," the Dowager said scathingly. "But having disposed of Adrian's troubles, what about your own?"

"Have I any?" Lord Manville asked innocently.

"Now, do not try to pull wool over my eyes, boy," his grandmother said. "You know as well as I do that you are the talk of the town. Even Her Majesty must have heard something, and she took her mind off the Prince Consort long enough to enquire when you were to find yourself a wife."

"Her Majesty is so excessively happy in her marriage," Lord Manville said, "that she wishes all her subjects to participate in the same blissful state of 'one man for one woman'."

"Not much likelihood of that where you are concerned!" the Dowager ejaculated. "But you are right about the Queen. She can talk of nothing these days but the virtues of Prince Albert. If all men were like him I should have remained a virgin."

"Now, Grandmama, be careful what you are saying," Lord Manville admonished, his eyes twinkling with laughter.

"I was never careful what I say," the Dowager replied sharply. "I do not belong to this hypocritical era, thank God. It is gloomy enough at Buckingham Palace to bring on the vapours. When I think of the gay times at Carlton House, when the Prince Regent was throwing money about like water, it makes me think that life must be very dull for the young people today."

"We still manage to amuse ourselves," Lord Manville said.

"Oh you do, you are different," his grandmother remarked. "Besides you are a man, and your sex can always find someone to titivate their fancy, like 'the Pretty Horse-breakers', eh, Silvanus?"

"Now, Grandmama, who has been telling you things like that?" Lord Manville asked. "You should not even know the expression, let alone speak it."

"Do not be so nonsensical," the Dowager snapped. "Do you never read the newspapers? Why, *The Times* had an article about them the other day. I must say I was somewhat surprised. It was not the sort of thing that one expected to find in *The Times*. And Lady Lynch sent me a cutting on the subject from *The Saturday Review*."

"What did that say?" Lord Manville asked curiously.

"It said," the Dowager replied, "that nowadays nobody used the phrase 'prostitute' or 'street-walker'. Pretty euphemisms are found which make, presumably, their profession sound more genteel. 'Pretty Horse-breakers' indeed! In my day a strumpet was a strumpet."

Lord Manville laughed.

"Grandmama, you are incorrigible!"

"That's as may be," the old lady replied, "but let me hear about them—these 'Pretty Horse-breakers'."

"What do you know about them for a start?" Lord Manville asked.

"Lady Lynch has three marriageable daughters," the Dowager replied. "I admit they are an unprepossessing lot, but virtuous, of good blood and undoubtedly the type which, if they had the chance, would make a well-behaved wife and a good mother. But, Her Ladyship tells me, they never get the chance."

"You mean no one proposes to them?" Lord Manville said. "And whose fault is that?"

"Apparently it is the fault of the 'Pretty Horse-breakers'," the Dowager replied. "The Lynch girls are taken to balls, bazaars, breakfasts, concerts, the opera, Ascot and the Crystal Palace, but all in vain. The eligible young men dance with them, even flirt with them, eat their parents' food and drink their claret; but for amusement they return to the 'Pretty Horse-breakers'."

Lord Manville laughed until the tears came into his eyes.

"Grandmama, you will be the death of me," he declared. "Never have I heard such a sad story! But what can be done? If the girls are not attractive enough, whose fault is that?"

"Yours and your friends'," the Dowager retorted, "making fools of yourselves over a lot of common creatures with pretty faces. Do you suppose that anyone would think twice about them if you did not pay for their smart clothes and their dashing hats, their well-fitting habits and, of course, their fine horseflesh. If you doll them out in their furbelows and make them appear so alluring externally, then no one bothers if they do not have a brain the size of a peanut or an ounce of common-sense."

"Dearest Grandmama," Lord Manville argued, "I assure you there have been Delilahs from the beginning of time. Nothing you or I can say will prevent men from finding their amusement amongst the little doves who flutter so alluringly, but who do not insist that those who admire them must be shackled to their side for ever with a gold ring. Don't tell me that you were not aware that such creatures existed in your day."

"Indeed they did," the Dowager replied, "but they were either doxies or women of our own class, such as the ladies with whom the Regent flirted. The doxies were creatures apart, unspoken of and kept out of sight.

Why, Lady Lynch tells me that in the Park now if a man is talking to one of these well-mounted Amazons he will take off his hat and bow to his hostess of the night before, or indeed his mother, should she happen to be passing by. In my day we should have ignored his very existence."

"We must move with the times, Grandmama," Lord Manville said. "Some of the young women in whom you are so interested are quite well born; many come from a far higher stratum of society than the doxies of the beginning of the century.

What you have to realise is that the girls from Belgravia, or wherever Lady Lynch lives with her unmarried and virtuous daughters, do little to attract modern man other than to imitate, quite ineffectively, the mistresses he chooses because they amuse and beguile him!

No man is such an idiot as to wish to pass his whole life with a woman who can do nothing but amuse. It would indeed be like dining endlessly on sugar candy. But I have yet to find in society any girl who is not an incredible bore after a short dance, let alone after any length of time spent in her company."

The Dowager reached out and put her hand on her grandson's arm.

"Tell me, Silvanus," she said in a very different tone of voice, "you are not still wearing the willow for that

49

chit who treated you so ill when you first came to London?"

Lord Manville rose to his feet.

"No indeed, Grandmama, I had a lucky escape, did I not? I thought myself in love and found that in the matrimonial stakes a Marquess is several fences ahead of a mere Baron."

"I know you were hurt at the time," the Dowager said, "but I could not have believed it would have lingered with you so long."

"I have forgotten the incident long ago," Lord Manville protested, but his grandmother, giving a little sigh, knew that he lied.

"There must be some nice and intelligent girls around who would interest you," she suggested.

"Do not worry about me, Grandmama," he replied, "I am perfectly content with my Anonymas, my Danaës and my Venuses. Call them 'Pretty Horse-breakers' or harlots; they still contribute a great deal of amusement, a great deal of beauty to a man's life."

"I would like to see you married before I die," the Dowager said plaintively.

"That gives me another twenty years, at least," Lord Manville said with a smile. "Stop worrying about me, Grandmama, you are becoming a bore, like the Queen."

"I suppose all people who are in love are bores," the Dowager said. "To concentrate on one person exclusively may be heaven for oneself, but it makes those who have to listen to such tales of bliss yawn and yawn again."

"Then for the moment I will not make you yawn," Lord Manville said, crossing to the mantelpiece to ring the bell. "I am now going to ask you to drink a glass of port with me, or would you prefer champagne? I know your doctor has forbidden you both, but I am convinced you never heed his advice any more than you listen to mine."

"I will have a glass of champagne," the Dowager cried. "You are right, Silvanus, never let people persuade you into doing something you do not want to do. Life is short and you are a long time in the grave, you might as well enjoy yourself while you can."

"Which you have always done, Grandmama," Lord Manville smiled.

A footman appeared and his master gave him an order and crossed the room to sit down again beside the old lady.

"Tell me, Grandmama," he said, "what really brought you to see me? I cannot believe that you really thought that you could persuade me into marriage! There must have been another reason."

"I wanted to see you," his grandmother replied. "You may be a reprobate, but I have always liked you better than my other grandchildren. Well-behaved creatures they may be, but I find it hard to stomach much of their company."

"And what else?" Lord Manville prompted.

The Dowager hesitated a moment and then she said bluntly:

"They are talking of you and Lady Brompton."

" 'They' being the usual busybodies who stick their noses into everything!" Lord Manville said.

"Exactly," the Dowager replied, "and you cannot expect not to be talked about when you are a person of such consequence and Lady Brompton is an acknowledged beauty. Besides it is well known that she and her husband live separate lives."

"Then I will make you happy, Grandmama," Lord Manville said, "by telling you the affaire is finished. Just for a moment—but only for a moment, mark you—I was tempted to flaunt the conventions and ask her to come away with me. She is a wild, irresponsible creature and life with her would be tempestuous, but entertaining. But I was never really serious and nor was she. Lady Brompton has now decided to live abroad. Rome society appreciates her somewhat unusual personality."

The Dowager gave a sigh which seemed to come from the very depths of her body, a sigh of utter and of deep relief. She put her hand on her grandson's arm.

"I am glad, boy," she said. "You belong to an old family and a proud one. I would not have let your Mother marry your Father had I not known the Manvilles were worthy of being joined with the Thornes. There has never been a scandal all down the centuries;

51

there has never been a traitor, a thief or a divorcee amongst us; and I would not let it happen now."

"It will not happen as far as I am concerned," Lord Manville said seriously, "you can rest assured of that, Grandmama. It was just a midsummer madness."

"I think that was perhaps why Her Majesty sent for me," the Dowager said. "She knew that if I came to London I would see you. But she could not bring herself to refer to such a scandalous 'chit chat', knowing there was nothing positive of which she could accuse you."

"There is nothing positive of which anyone can accuse me," Lord Manville asserted. "I too am very conscious, Grandmama, of our family history, and I promise you that when I eventually do get married, if I ever do, it will be to someone of whom you will approve."

"I suppose I should be very pleased by that filial speech," the Dowager said, "but I would much rather hear you say that when you do get married it will be to someone you love."

"I think that is unlikely in the extreme," Lord Manville replied.

He rose as he spoke and walked across the room to ring the bell. The Dowager watched him with an expression of sadness in her old eyes. She knew, as no one else did, that the wound that title-seeking girl had inflicted so heartlessly over ten years ago still festered.

"Her Grace's carriage," Lord Manville said to the footman who answered the bell. "I would rather go on talking to you, Grandmama, but my horse will be waiting, and as he is so excessively fresh, the grooms will be hard put to it to hold him."

"Thank God you like them spirited, as I did!" the Dowager replied. "I never could stand those perambulating rocking-horses and four-legged mattresses on which the usual society wench disports herself in the Park. Give me a horse that is a horse and a man that is a man, that was all I ever asked of life."

"You are a bad example to me, Grandmama," Lord Manville said affectionately. "If I listened to you I should get a worse reputation than I have already. Even Adrian told me that he was ashamed of what his friends said about me at Oxford."

"Ashamed!" the Dowager exclaimed sharply. "Silly young popinjay!"

"Adrian informed me that they have a nickname for me," Lord Manville said, "do you know what it is?"

"Of course I know," his grandmother replied. " 'The Heart-Breaker'! There is nothing much wrong with that, it shows you have got a bit of spirit about you."

"As I have already said, Ma'am, you are a bad example," Lord Manville laughed. "I gather you are now returning to the country. If I find the heat of London too exhausting I will come down and stay with you."

"Better spend your time at Manville," the Dowager suggested. "I do not like to think of the house empty. Besides, when the master is away the servants get out of hand."

"I shall heed your advice," Lord Manville said.

"And what is more," the Dowager went on as they proceeded slowly down the stairs towards the Hall, "do not leave Adrian sulking at Oxford too long without seeing him. Remember there is only one antidote for a love affair, and that is another."

Lord Manville's laughter echoed round the Hall. Then he said quite seriously:

"I will write to him tonight to come and stay at Manville as soon as the term ends."

"Get some girls there to amuse him," the Dowager advised. "A 'Pretty Horse-Breaker' should be able to take his mind off the parson's daughter."

"You are the wisest woman I know," Lord Manville said as he helped the Dowager into her carriage.

It was old-fashioned, comfortably padded, with a coachman and two footmen in their brightly-coloured liveries and crested buttons who had grown grey in the Dowager's service.

They greeted Lord Manville with a beaming smile when he asked how they were and remembered to enquire after their wives and children. Then he stood back and the coach rolled off, the old lady waving her mittened hand to him from the window.

The coach was no sooner out of sight than the grooms appeared leading Thunder, a spirited stallion with white markings who was prancing, rearing and bucking just to show his independence.

The butler handed Lord Manville his top-hat and riding-whip. There was a little difficulty in getting into the saddle, but once he was there, Thunder seemed to settle down, and they set off towards the Park.

Lord Manville had a lot to think about as he trotted down Hill Street. He ignored a salute from several friends before he reached Park Lane, and entered the Park through Stanhope Gate. As he did so he heard Big Ben strike and realised that despite the interruptions this morning and his unexpected visitors, he would still be on time to meet Lais, who would be waiting for him at the Achilles Statue.

The cynical twist of his mouth lifted a little at the thought of her. She was very alluring with her dark hair and slanting eyes, which seemed somehow to have a hint of mystery in them. Lord Manville had not yet found out the truth of her birth or her antecedents. It always took a little time before women were honest about themselves. Anyway, he was not interested.

The one thing which was irrefutable was that she could ride amazingly well. Already he had decided that he must buy her a horse which was worthy of her looks and which would be the envy of her friends. He remembered she had already told him of one she liked, but he couldn't recall where she had seen it. Perhaps it was at Tattersalls.

"I must remember to have a look at the catalogue," he said to himself.

He would, he thought, enjoy spending money on Lais. She was a new acquisition—and already she had shown her gratitude very prettily for the diamond earrings he had given her. He knew it would not be long before he would have to add to the collection.

Money was unimportant; he was rich, he could afford to spend, and if a woman amused him he was only too willing to pay for his entertainment. He remembered the anxiety in his grandmother's face as she had spoken of Lady Brompton.

"That is the last time," he told himself, "that I will get involved with someone of my own class. It always means trouble."

Nevertheless it had been exciting while it lasted and rather intoxicating, because it had flouted the established conventions. But now there was Lais with her slanting eyes and inviting red mouth, excluded by no social barrier.

The thought of seeing her again was pleasing. Lord Manville gave Thunder a little flick with the whip and trotted towards the Achilles Statue.

4

As Candida entered the Park on Pegasus by way of Marble Arch, she looked about her with interest.

On her left was Park Lane, where she had already learnt were the houses of the nobility; and in the Park, moving amid the beds full of colorful flowers and under the great trees with their spring leaves, were the aristocrats themselves, travelling in shining carriages drawn by splendid horseflesh or walking over the smooth grass.

Candida stared entranced at the gentlemen in their top-hats carrying gold-topped malacca-canes, and at the elegance of the ladies whose crinolines swayed seductively as they moved.

"This", she thought excitedly, "is London!" This was the gay world of which she had heard so many people talk, but which until now, she had never seen.

Yet she had now lived in London for three weeks, and it had been the strangest three weeks that she had ever spent. Mrs. Clinton had said to her the night she arrived:

"You understand, dear, you cannot see anyone or meet anyone until you are properly dressed."

"Does that mean I cannot ride Pegasus?" Candida had asked quickly.

"Of course not," Major Hooper interposed. "There is a great deal of grooming to be done to Pegasus by my stable hands, but you must keep him fit. I will arrange for you to ride very early in the morning. People are not usually about until the world is well dusted."

She had laughed at the joke and Mrs. Clinton had joined in.

"No indeed," she agreed, "and Candida will find that

the programme I have planned for her may be dull, but well worth the effort."

Candida had no idea what Mrs. Clinton had meant at the time. She had thought at first that she would be confined to the house except when she was riding, and hoped she could somehow obtain books to pass the hours. She need not have worried; for she found that practically every second of the day was filled, and by the time she did have a few moments to herself she was almost too tired to read.

She was called at five o'clock, and at 5:30 a.m. Major Hooper took her from the stables, sometimes alone, sometimes accompanied by the grooms on other horses, into Regent's Park.

Pegasus could canter to his heart's content, and Candida loved the pale mist rising over the water; shrubs bursting into bloom; the fragrance of lilac and the ground sprinkled with pink and white cherry blossom.

"I had no idea London could be so lovely!" she exclaimed not once but a dozen times, and Major Hooper had smiled at her enthusiasm.

By the time the streets were growing busy with drays, the high butchers' carts, the milkmen with their sleepy ponies and the muffin-men crying their wares, Candida would be back in the Riding School.

There she helped Major Hooper with the young horses which were not fit for ladies to ride until they had been properly broken in, accustomed to a side-saddle and taught to walk proudly over the cobblestoned roads and not to shy at unfamiliar objects. It was hard work, Candida found, although extremely interesting.

Mrs. Clinton had provided her with a riding-habit which she could wear for her morning rides. Made in dark blue whip-cord with satin revers, it had seemed resplendent to Candida. But Mrs. Clinton said scornfully:

"It is only a working habit, you will want something far different when you go into Hyde Park."

At first, until a new pair were made for her, Candida had to wear her own disreputable, almost out-of-toe, riding-boots. The first morning she appeared in them Major Hooper said:

"I doubt if your boots will hold a spur."

Candida raised her eyebrows.

"I do not need a spur," she protested.

"Of course you need one," Major Hooper said sharply, "all women use a spur."

Candida remembered with a shudder Firefly's bloodstained flanks after Lais had ridden him that first evening when she had been watching from the gallery.

She had also turned away from the Queen's bootmaker, Mr. Maxwell, with a gesture of revulsion when after he had measured her for her riding-boots he opened a box for her inspection. In it, arrayed like jewels on velvet, were a number of spurs.

"I do not know which is your choice, Ma'am," he said respectfully, "but most ladies favour this one."

He had taken out a long, vicious spur of the type which Candida suspected that Lais had worn.

"This," Mr. Maxwell explained, "is a straight-necked spur with a five-pointed rowel. The points are long enough and sharp enough to penetrate the thickest riding-habit should it intervene between the lady's heel and the horse's side."

Candida said nothing and Mr. Maxwell took another spur from the box.

"This is even more popular," he continued, "a long, single spike covered by a spring guard to prevent it tearing the habit. The ladies tell me it is twice as effective as the rowel spur."

"Take them away," Candida said quickly in a tone that for her was almost harsh. "I would never insult any horse with horrible weapons like that."

Now she looked up at Major Hooper defiantly.

"I have never used a spur on Pegasus," she said, "and I do not believe that, if one schools a horse properly, there is any need for such brutality."

"Some women enjoy being severe with an animal," he had said, almost without thinking to whom he was speaking. "The more feminine they may be, the more they enjoy subduing the animal on which they are mounted."

"Then they are not worthy of being called women," Candida cried hotly.

Major Hooper shrugged his shoulders.

"Have it your own way," he said, "but there are a

number of spurs you can borrow if later on you come to realise the need for them."

He had to admit after watching Candida at work for the first three or four mornings that she had been right in saying that she could school a horse without severity.

She seemed to get better results from his horses than any of the other horse-breakers who came in later in the morning and who used the spur vigorously and without compunction, just as they always insisted on riding with a painful curb-bit.

It was impossible for him not to compare the methods of this young, unsophisticated girl he had found in the country and the experienced horse-breakers who were either paid by him for their work or earned the privilege of riding his horses in Hyde Park in return for breaking in the new additions to the stable.

But Candida saw nobody at the Riding Stables except the grooms and Major Hooper. By eight o'clock she was back at Mrs. Clinton's house, eating breakfast and wondering what lay ahead of her for the rest of the day. She did not wonder for long. There were clothes fittings—long, tiring and innumerable.

She had no idea it could be so exhausting to stand for hours having delicate fabrics pinned into place, nor had she imagined she would require so many gowns for what she believed was to be her job of showing off Pegasus to an admiring world.

"Why do I need evening gowns?" she asked Mrs. Clinton.

"I expect you will be asked to parties," was the reply. "Gentlemen who are interested in horses are, I assure you, amongst the richest and the most important in the land, besides being the gayest. You cannot be riding all the time."

"No, of course not," Candida answered, looking at the gauzes, the satins, the laces and the brocades which Madame Elisa had brought for Mrs. Clinton's approval.

There were also quantities of lace-trimmed underwear, stockings, gloves and reticules, hats and sunshades, cloaks and wraps, in fact so many articles that Candida lost count.

"I must ask you," she said to Mrs. Clinton at length,

59

her eyes troubled, "who is going to pay for all this? You know I have no money, I cannot allow you to spend so much on me."

Mrs. Clinton had turned away from Candida's questioning face.

"Do not worry," she said, "leave all those problems to me and Major Hooper. All you have to do is what you are told, and see that your horse is worthy of the admiration Major Hooper has already accorded him."

Candida's face softened immediately.

"I am not afraid of how Pegasus will look," she said, "I am much more afraid that I will let him down, or that you will be sorry you have spent so much on me. You see, I am not used to beautiful things."

"You look well enough in them," Mrs. Clinton said, while Madame Elisa went into raptures.

"Never have I dressed a more beautiful, more elegant young creature," she said to Mrs. Clinton in private, "and so sweet there is nothing my workroom will not do for her. She is too good for those autocratic young swells with their roistering and their drunkenness."

"I do not have a young swell in mind for her," Mrs. Clinton said.

"I am glad about that," Madame Elisa replied, "She is nothing but a child! How did she come to be with you?"

Madame Elisa, with her fashionable clientele, might be a privileged person, but Mrs. Clinton was exchanging her secrets with no one.

"What we have got to do, Madame Elisa," she said, "is to see that Candida is the sensation of the Season, and you know as well as I do how much clothes count when it comes to catching the public eye. That is why I am sparing no expense."

"It is a pity the Prince of Wales is too young to take an interest in her," Madame Elisa smiled.

"There are other men just as important," Mrs. Clinton retorted, "and much more likely to pay their bills."

That was all Madame Elisa could get out of her, but it was enough to make her take even more pains over the gowns until Candida felt she would sink on the

60

floor from sheer exhaustion if she had to stand any longer for the fittings.

Finally, when the wardrobe in her room was filled to overflowing, she began to realise the day of her début into the outside world was getting nearer.

Apart from the clothes, however, there were innumerable other things for her to learn. A dancing teacher came to show her the latest steps, and in the afternoon, when the house seemed very quiet, the servants would roll back the rug on Mrs. Clinton's polished floor and Candida was taught to dance.

This she enjoyed, and it was not long before her dancing teacher, an elderly man with grey hair and a drooping moustache, declared that if all else failed she could become a dancer at the theatre.

"That sounds interesting!" Candida said to Mrs. Clinton. "Do you think I could really become a dancer?"

"Certainly not," Mrs. Clinton said sharply. "I have better things in store for you than that."

"What are they?" Candida asked, but she received no reply.

Candida was rather surprised that her teacher, on Mrs. Clinton's instructions, taught her the polka. She had heard of it, but had understood that it was considered rather middle class. Her father had once called it "Bohemian—the type of thing one would expect from Paris!"

"Gentlemen find it very gay," Candida's teacher said almost apologetically, and he half sang the words to Offenbach's music:

> "Why don't you dance the Polka?
> Won't you dance the Polka?
> Joys of earth are little worth,
> If you don't dance the Polka."

"Oh it's fun!" Candida cried, "and as tiring as a two-mile gallop!"

Mrs. Clinton herself taught Candida how to behave at a dinner-party where there were a dozen of more different dishes and five or six different types of wine. She also instructed her on ordering a menu and seating a table.

61

"Most gentlemen," she said, "like to have the parties which they pay for well arranged. Food and wine are extremely important, never forget that."

"I thought all these sort of things were done by a housekeeper if people were rich?" Candida replied. "And then, of course, my husband would choose the wines, would he not?"

For a moment Mrs. Clinton did not reply. Then she answered:

"A knowledge of how to run a house will be useful sometime in your life."

"Yes, of course," Candida said, "but I expect, really, if I marry it will be somebody quite poor and I will have to look after everything as Mama did."

"Who wants to be poor?" Mrs. Clinton enquired with a sudden edge in her voice. "It is something of which I have always been afraid."

"Have you?" Candida asked in surprise. "It is bothersome when one cannot pay the bills and worrying if you know you owe their wages to servants who are so devoted that they go on working despite the fact you do not pay them. But nothing matters as long as one is happy."

"I cannot imagine it is possible to be happy under those circumstances," Mrs. Clinton said coldly.

"My Mama and Papa were very happy," Candida replied, "and so was I. It was only when they died that there was nothing left and I did not know what to do."

"Then realise now that money is important," Mrs. Clinton insisted. "Save it—be sure that you get every penny to which you are entitled. Do not be extravagant, there is no point in it. Let other people pay for you."

Candida laughed.

"I do not suppose anybody will ever want to pay for me," she said. "Why should they?"

For a moment Mrs. Clinton was speechless, and then she answered:

"You are very pretty, child. You will find that gentlemen who admire you will want to give you presents and perhaps money. If you are sensible you will accept them."

"Surely," Candida answered hesitatingly, "that would

not be right. Mama always said that ladies should never accept money from a gentleman, or even presents, unless she was engaged to him."

Mrs. Clinton said nothing and Candida went on:

"Perhaps I shall be fortunate and fall in love with someone who will be able to afford to give me presents. It would be lovely not to have to worry about the future and know I could keep Pegasus and other horses."

She was silent for a moment; then, in a voice that was strangely moving, she said, clasping her hands together:

"Oh, Mrs. Clinton, you do think Major Hooper will keep his promise and not sell Pegasus? He did tell me so."

"I feel sure Major Hooper will keep his promise if that is what he told you," Mrs. Clinton said, and quickly changed the subject, making Candida add up the housekeeping books for the week.

"Never trust your servants," Mrs. Clinton said as she handed them to Candida. "However loyal they appear, however honest they may seem, keep tight reins over the accounts, otherwise you will find your debts are out of all proportion to what you have consumed."

Obediently Candida totted up the accounts for the butcher, the baker, the candlestick-maker and the grocer. When she came to the wineseller's account she looked at it in astonishment.

"How can Mrs. Clinton have consumed so much champagne?" she wondered, but felt it would show an impertinent curiosity to ask questions.

"It must be all those friends," she thought, "who drop in every evening."

By the time they arrived she was banished to her bedroom at the top of the house. Her room, however, was at the front, and sometimes she would go to the window and look down on the street and see the smart carriages with their restless horses and liveried grooms waiting outside.

"Of course," she told herself, "as Mrs. Clinton is a widow she must find it lonely unless she entertains."

Strangely enough none of the callers seemed to stay to dinner. They came and they went, then others arrived. At first Candida thought it was only gentlemen

63

who came to pay their respects to Mrs. Clinton, but then she saw ladies stepping out of hired carriages, resplendent in huge gowns with jewels round their necks and in their hair.

She often wished she could get a closer glimpse of them, but they went straight into the house and usually, after a short wait, they would come out again, this time with a gentleman as an escort, and drive away in his carriage which had been waiting.

Candida wondered why they did not arrive together. But she was far too shy to question Mrs. Clinton, who seemed at times to withdraw into a silent reserve which Candida found quite awe-inspiring.

What surprised her more than anything were the riding-habits which Mrs. Clinton was having made for her by a habit-maker who, she was told, held the Royal warrant. He certainly knew his job, and she thought at first glance that she had never known anything suit her so well.

Mrs. Clinton had however insisted on the waist being even smaller and tighter, and the material moulded over the breast until Candida felt a little anxious in case it should seem indecent. Because her habit was in a way for Pegasus, she paid more attention and took more interest in its fittings than in any of the others. The thing that surprised her most was the choice of material.

When she had finished dressing this morning to ride in the Park for the first time, she stared at herself in the mirror. She felt shy and embarrassed. Could this really be as Mrs. Clinton meant her to look? And what would her Mother have said? The reflection that stared back at her showed someone quite different from the girl she thought of as herself.

She had not liked to seem ungrateful to Mrs. Clinton by voicing her doubts, but after Major Hooper had helped her into the saddle and arranged her full skirt over her shiny new boots, she said to him in a low voice:

"Do you think I look all right?"

He looked up at the anxious little face and answered: "You look very lovely."

"This habit and my hat—they make me feel shy," Candida whispered.

Major Hooper had already learnt how to deal with Candida. He might prefer horses to women, but he knew how to handle both.

"You show off Pegasus to perfection," he said. "There is nothing like an elegant rider to draw attention to a magnificent horse."

His words had exactly the effect he desired. He saw Candida's chin go up, her shoulders straighten, and she smiled at him confidently as they set off at a trot towards the Park.

In Hyde Park the crowds at the Achilles Statue had been gathering for over an hour. No one quite knew why the "Pretty Horse-breakers"—and more particularly the Queen of them, Catherine Walters, known to everyone as 'Skittles'—had captured the interest and the attention of the general public, but the crowds who waited to see her were increasing day by day.

There was no doubt that she set the fashion not only amongst the other members of her profession, but also amongst the aristocratic ladies of the fashionable world who copied her in every possible way.

If she wore a pork-pie hat, they wore a pork-pie hat; if her paletot was made by Poole, their paletots were made by Poole; if she rode, they searched the livery stables and Tattersalls for horses to rival hers.

When she took to driving a pair of handsome brown ponies, the horse-dealers were being offered five or six hundred guineas for a pair of ponies, as well bred and as high stepping as those driven by Skittles.

No one knew how she would appear every day in the Park, but expectation was raised to its highest pitch as the "Pretty Horse-breakers" congregated at the Achilles Statue. They were all of them exquisitely dressed and well mounted, each one vying with the other to look a little different. There were azure-blue and emerald-green habits, crimson and coral ones, brown and black, and every "Pretty Horse-breaker" tried to have a more intoxicating and amusing hat than her friends.

Some wore orthodox cylindrical beavers with the fashionable flowing veil; others had roguish little 'wide-awakes' or perky cocked cavaliers' hats with floating plumes; while the society ladies passing by in their Victorias and broughams looked for what fashion hints

65

they could find in these dazzling creatures they despised, but often envied.

The crowd, sitting on the grass or standing around staring with open mouths, were this morning waiting for one person and one person only.

"There she is!" a woman exclaimed; and every head turned, only to be disappointed when they saw it was not their favourite Skittles but a Duchess, to them unimportant, or some conventional Marchioness.

"I wonders if she'll ride or drive this mornin'?" a man in a cloth cap remarked in a cockney accent.

The heads were turned yet again as a graceful figure driving a pair of greys passed by in the direction of the Row. Then suddenly there was silence. Even the "Pretty Horse-breakers", chatting with their escorts and laughing a little too loudly or pouting seductively, seemed to grow still. From the direction of Stanhope Gate a horse and rider appeared who must be Skittles.

"Here she is!" a woman cried in an almost hysterical voice.

The rider was mounted on an enormous pitch-black stallion without a single mark of white on him. His coat was polished until it shone like a dark mirror; his mane and tail were meticulously combed and he had an air of majesty about him which made those in the crowd who appreciated good horseflesh draw in their breath appreciatively.

But it was the rider at which the crowd was looking, and which also drew the eyes of the "Pretty Horse-breakers". She was very small and seemed far too fragile to control such an enormous beast. At very first sight, though they could not see her face very clearly, she gave an appearance of fragile grace and beauty, besides being almost sensational in her appearance.

The unknown, whoever she might be, wore a white riding-habit, something no one else had dared to wear in the past—white and as chaste as a lily. Cut to perfection and held in the front by a black pearl button, it showed the delicate, almost immature curves of the rider's young body and was finished at the neck by a tiny ruffle of expensive lace.

As she drew nearer they saw her face—the translucent skin; the soft, rose-bud tinted mouth; the large, rather frightened eyes veiled by dark lashes; while under the black top-hat, with its floating transparent white veil, there was a chignon which filled all the other women with an almost insuppressible envy.

Never had there been hair of such a colour, pale gold run through with little flames of gold!

There was almost silence as Candida reached the Achilles Statue, the crowd staring at her wide-eyed. She suddenly felt apprehensive, her fingers in their long black gloves tightening on the reins.

"Ride straight on," Major Hooper said almost beneath his breath.

She obeyed him, looking ahead and passing the gay and glittering crowd who all suddenly seemed to be open-mouthed like surprised goldfish. As she moved away in the direction of the Row the burble broke out.

"Who is she?"

"Where has she come from?"

"Why have we never seen her before?"

"What is her name?"

"Where has the Major found that?" Lais asked Lord Manville who was watching, like the rest, the great horse with its tiny rider.

"That is a very fine animal," Lord Manville replied.

"Do not forget to speak to Hooper about Firefly," Lais begged. "That is the horse I want, and you promised you would buy me the one I wanted."

"I won't forget," Lord Manville said automatically, and then on impulse he tightened his reins and gave his horse a flick with the whip. "I will speak to him now."

He trotted off in Candida's wake and caught up with Major Hooper before they were halfway down the Row.

"That is a good horse you've got there, Hooper," he said in a slightly condescending tone.

"I thought he would meet with Your Lordship's approval," Major Hooper replied, raising his hat.

"What are you asking?" Lord Manville enquired.

"He's not for sale, M'Lord."

'Not for sale!"

Candida had brought Pegasus almost to a walk. The two men were a little behind her, but she could hear every word that was said.

"That is unlike you, Hooper," Lord Manville continued. "I have never known you not be prepared to sell at the right price."

"This is different, M'Lord; a condition is attached to the sale."

"Indeed?" Lord Manville raised his eyebrows. "And what may that be?"

"I do not think this is the right place to discuss such matters, M'Lord," Major Hooper answered, and his tone was so respectful that it somehow took the rebuke out of his words.

Lord Manville was not pleased.

"Really, Hooper, you are being extraordinarily evasive," he protested.

At that moment Candida urged Pagasus into a trot. Major Hooper raised his hat.

"I'm sorry, M'Lord," he said, and was gone before Lord Manville could say anything else.

It was at that moment a voice he most disliked said:

"Who is the fair Traviata? Have you discovered her name, Manville?"

Lord Manville turned his head to see Sir Tresham Foxleigh, a neighbor of his in the country and a gentleman for whom he had a profound contempt. Sir Tresham was excessively rich, he also possessed an unsavory reputation and was considered an outsider at most of the Clubs in St. James's Street.

"I was interested in the horse," Lord Manville said in an off-hand manner.

"A wonderful combination," Sir Tresham exclaimed, his eyes a little narrowed, his mouth twisted in an unpleasant smile as he watched Candida's progress down the Row. "I hope, Manville, we are not to be rivals in this field as in so many others."

"I hope not indeed," Lord Manville replied, and turning his horse rode back toward the Achilles Statue.

Lais was waiting for him, looking particularly alluring in a new habit of deep crimson velvet frogged with black braid. Her eyes were alight with interest as Lord Manville reached her side.

"You asked him about Firefly?" she enquired.

"I will do so later," Lord Manville replied.

"But you spoke to him?" Lais insisted.

"There was not time to discuss business," Lord Manville explained.

Lais shrugged her shoulders. The "Pretty Horsebreakers" were dispersing. It was obvious that Skittles, unpredictably, was not paying a visit to her adoring satellites this morning.

The crowd was also moving away. They were all asking. "Who was the unknown rider?" Her appearance had certainly captured their imagination. Lord Manville heard their comments as he rode away in Lais's wake.

"Damn it," he told himself, and he was as curious as they were. "Where the dickens could Hooper have found such a horse and indeed such a rider?"

One thing he could not forget. When he had asked the Major the price of the horse, the girl in white had turned her head and looked round. There had been an expression of desperate anxiety on her face which was quite unmistakable.

Then, when Major Hooper had said the horse was not for sale, the expression had changed rapidly. It had been one of almost joyful relief—Lord Manville could find no other words to describe it.

In that brief moment, so brief that it had been but the turn of a head, it seemed to him that the unknown rider was so lovely that he could only fancy that his first impression of her being very young and fragile had been mistaken.

Her skin must owe its perfection to artifice, and yet it seemed impossible that artifice could produce the liquid beauty of her eyes or that strange, unusual, tantalising colour of her hair. There was no dye in existence which could be responsible for that.

But why had she been hidden up till now? If she already had a protector, Hooper would not have been with her. No, he was showing her off, Lord Manville was certain of that, and he had done it extremely cleverly. It had been brilliant stage-craft, of which no one who knew Hooper would have believed him capable.

He was not that type of man—he was dedicated to the sale of horses, and the "Pretty Horse-breakers" who had made his stables the most popular and notorious in town were but an adjunct to his sales. There was something behind all this, Lord Manville decided, and then his thoughts were interrupted by Lais.

"You will go and see Hooper?" she asked. "I know you have offered me the horses in your stables, but it is Firefly I want. You understand how one sets one's heart on a certain horse. I have ridden him once or twice and he suits me. That is all I can say—he suits me."

"I will certainly go and talk to Hooper about the animal," Lord Manville promised, feeling in some inexpressible way he was glad of an excuse to visit the livery stable.

"This afternoon?" Lais asked hopefully.

"Perhaps," Lord Manville replied, and she had to be content with that.

Nevertheless it was with an intense curiosity which Lord Manville could not repress that he drove to Hooper's Stable early that evening. He deliberately waited until he thought the "Horse-breakers" would have taken back their mounts and Hooper was likely to be alone.

He found him, as expected, going round the stalls, inspecting the horses and seeing that they were properly fed. He was not a man who would leave such jobs to his Head Groom, however able. He was not surprised to see Lord Manville, elegantly dressed and almost incredibly handsome, drive his Tandem into the stable-yard.

He had known that he might expect him, and that the fish was rising to the bait. His Lordship's tiger, with his cocked top-hat, jumped down and ran to the horses' heads. Lord Manville sauntered across the cobbles to where Major Hooper was waiting.

"Evening, Hooper. I hear you have a horse named Firefly for sale."

Major Hooper's eyes twinkled for a moment. Then he said respectfully, raising his hat:

"Good evening, M'Lord. Yes indeed, come and have a look at him."

Firefly was in his stable, and as they walked towards it Major Hooper could not help remembering Candida's fury when she had seen the condition in which the horse had been returned. She had just arrived for her morning ride at 5:30 A.M. and was greeting Major Hooper when the Head Groom had come up to them.

70

"I forgot to tell you, Sir," he said to the Major, "that Firefly was returned last night."

"Back again!" the Major smiled "Is that the second or third time?"

"I've a feeling it is the fourth, Sir," the groom replied. "She must be making a small fortune out of that animal."

"Is he all right?" Major Hooper asked.

"His left flank has been over-spurred, Sir, I'd like you to have a look at it."

Major Hooper turned abruptly towards Firefly's stall. Candida followed him wondering. The woman called Lais who had ridden him that first night when she had watched from the Gallery seemed so keen that her gentleman friend should buy the horse.

Candida could not understand why he should have been sent back to the stables. And what did Major Hooper and the groom mean by saying that this was the third or fourth time Firefly had been returned?

They reached the stall and Candida saw the spur-gall which Lais's spur had inflicted. The horse was also in a highly nervous state, fidgeting from side to side.

"Whoa, boy," the Head Groom said, holding Firefly's head while the Major bent down to look at the flank.

"Best get it poulticed," he said.

"That's what I thought Sir, but I wanted you to see him first."

"How could she treat a horse in such a manner?" Candida burst out, feeling it impossible to suppress her indignation any longer.

The Major looked up at her in surprise.

"She?" he questioned.

"I saw a lady riding Firefly the first evening I was here," Candida confessed. "I did not tell you about it because I knew you did not want me to see anyone. They did not notice me: I was in the Gallery watching her take him over the jumps in the Riding School. And the gentleman she was with promised to buy him for her. She seemed so keen and anxious to have Firefly, why did she use her spur on him in this terrible manner?"

"I've already told you that some women are like

71

that," Major Hooper said briefly. "It is a pity because Firefly is a decent horse and well broken. The spur is hardly necessary."

"It was not quite so bad the last time," the Head Groom interposed.

"No," Major Hooper agreed. "And this will knock something off the price. I shall charge for two weeks' veterinary treatment; that will teach her a lesson if nothing else does."

"That's the way, Sir," the groom smiled. "Touch their pockets, it is the only thing they understand."

"Well, I am thankful she has sent Firefly back," Candida exclaimed. "Next time do please find him a kind owner, someone who will not treat a fine horse in such a fashion."

She did not see the glance that was exchanged between Major Hooper and his groom. She only knew as she walked away from the stall that she hated this dark attractive woman who could treat any animal as she had treated the horse who had responded without a fault to all she had asked of him.

Firefly's flank was healed now, Major Hooper noted as Lord Manville entered the stall and the groom pulled off the saddle-cloth.

"Would you like to see him outside, M'Lord?" the Major asked.

"It's not necessary," Lord Manville replied. "If you assure me he is sound in the wind and well schooled. I will believe you."

"I have never sold you a dud one yet, have I, M'Lord?" Major Hooper asked cheerfully.

"You had better not try," Lord Manville smiled. "Well, have him taken round to my stables. What are you asking for him?"

"Only two hundred and fifty guineas, M'Lord."

"That is fifty guineas too much, as well you know, Hooper," Lord Manville retorted. "I will split the difference with you, I am not going to argue."

"Very good, M'Lord. As a valued customer I'm only too pleased to meet you."

"So you should be," Lord Manville said.

He turned as if he was about to go, and then said with a different note in his voice:

72

"What about that animal you had in the Park this morning?"

The two men moved from the stable into the yard.

"As I told you, M'Lord, he is not for sale."

"What is the plot, Hooper?" Lord Manville enquired.

"No plot, M'Lord, it is only that they go together, they are inseparable as you might say, the rider and the horse."

"And I pay a fancy price for the introduction I suppose?" Lord Manville said. "Well, Hooper, I am not interested—not at the moment."

"No question of waiting, M'Lord," Major Hooper said, "there have already been a large number of enquiries, as you can imagine."

Lord Manville glanced up at him speculatively.

"And you are waiting for someone like me to come along?" he asked quietly.

"That is the idea, M'Lord," Major Hooper agreed.

"Damn you, I will not be manœuvred!" Lord Manville exclaimed. "I expect the price is too high anyway."

"You might think so, M'Lord," Major Hooper agreed, "but there are others who will not."

"Are you prepared to tell me what it is?" Lord Manville said.

Major Hooper looked up at the stable clock.

"It is nearly half past six, M'Lord. The Riding School will be closed, and if you will go into the Gallery I would like you to see something."

For a moment Lord Manville looked as though he would refuse, then unaccountably he laughed.

"Very well, Hooper," he said, "I will go along with your mystery and your new tactics. They are amusing if nothing else. But I have an engagement for dinner, so do not keep me waiting more than ten minutes."

"I will not, M'Lord," Major Hooper promised.

Trying to appear more languid and bored than he was in actual fact, Lord Manville let himself into the Riding School and climbed up into the Gallery.

He seated himself in the centre on the chair that had been originally arranged for its builder. There was a smell of horseflesh and hay mingled with the dust of ages, and the scent from many female riders had somehow become impregnated into the air.

The sun was sinking and there was a golden glow over the school from its skylight, which gave it an air of mystery, as after only six minutes' wait through the door at the far end came Candida riding Pegasus.

She was wearing her dark working habit with only a crisp white blouse beneath it. She had no hat so that the sunlight caught the gleams of gold in her hair and seemed to halo her tiny pointed face.

"I want you to put him over the jumps," Lord Manville heard Major Hooper say. "I've heightened them a little."

"Yes, of course," Candida replied. "It will do him good after all that polite trit-trotting in the Park today."

Her voice had an unexpected musical quality about it, Lord Manville decided, and he thought he had never seen such an expressive little face as, with her eyes alight and her lips smiling, she took Pegasus over the fences. Round and round she went, increasing her speed a little, but never pushing the horse too hard. Her timing was perfect, it would have been impossible to fault her performance.

"That's enough!" Lord Manville heard Major Hooper say, "If you wait for me in the office I will take you home."

"All right, I will wait," Candida promised, "although I would be quite safe walking back myself."

She smiled at him as she rode Pegasus out of the stable, and the doors closed behind her. Major Hooper stood waiting as Lord Manville came down from the Gallery. The eyes of the two men met.

"All right, Hooper, you win," Lord Manville said. "How much for the horse—and the introduction?"

5

Candida knew as soon as she entered the stable-yard that something was wrong. It was not only the fact that Major Hooper greeted her curtly and did not look at her, but she also saw the stable-boys and the grooms clustered together and then starting apart when she walked towards them. Something had occurred, what was it?

She ran after Major Hooper and caught up with him before he reached his own horse which the grooms were bringing from his stall.

"What has happened?" she asked with anxiety in her voice.

He turned to look at her, but the words in which he would have answered her seemed somehow to die on his lips.

"I know what it is," Candida whispered almost beneath her breath, "you have sold Pegasus!"

There was no need for him to confirm her suspicion; she could read it in the expression on his face.

"How could you?" she asked piteously. "How could you have done such a thing after you promised me that you would not sell him?"

"I promised you when we first met that I would not sell Pegasus at once," Major Hooper replied. "You have had him for three weeks."

"Three weeks! What does three weeks count when he is everything I have got, everything I love?" Candida cried.

There was agony in her voice and tears in her eyes. Major Hooper looked away.

"It is not as bad as it seems," he said, "you go with him."

"With him?" Candida queried. "But how? What do I do and in what capacity?"

"Mrs. Clinton will explain everything to you," Major Hooper said shortly, and walking away from her he swung himself into the saddle.

He was clearly evading her, and Candida knew that it would be useless to question him further. There was a reserve about him, something she had noticed before, which often made it impossible for her to obtain answers to her questions.

She looked round, half expecting to find Pegasus to have gone already. But the Head Groom was leading him towards the mounting-block. She stepped onto it and then into the saddle.

"I'm really sorry about it, Miss," the Head Groom said in a low voice, which Candida knew was not meant to be overheard by Major Hooper. "But he couldn't go to a better owner."

Candida wanted to answer him, but she was fighting back the tears which threatened to overwhelm her. Already Major Hooper and three grooms on other horses were moving out of the yard and there was nothing for her to do but follow them.

They cantered round Regent's Park in silence. All the time Candida was suffering the same agony she had endured that day when she had ridden on Pegasus to the Fair at Potters Bar.

She tried to console herself by remembering that Major Hooper had said that she would go with Pegasus to his new owner, but for how long might that be?

She was suddenly afraid of what lay ahead, afraid not only for herself but for Pegasus. Supposing he was ridden by someone who used a severe spur on him? Supposing he was exploited because he was so gentle and so obedient? Suppose his owner, whoever he might be, was cruel and drove him beyond endurance?

"I would rather see him dead." Candida whispered to herself.

They rode back from the Park towards the stables. When they passed the road in which Mrs. Clinton lived, the Major sent the grooms ahead.

"I will leave you at the door," he said to Candida.

She knew it was because he did not want to talk to her, did not wish to endure her questioning.

"I would rather work at the Riding School," she said, "and I want to take Pegasus over the jumps."

Major Hooper did not answer, and Candida burst out:

"Please, please let me! Can you not understand that it might be for the last time?"

The Major gave in reluctantly, and seeing the acceptance in his face she turned and trotted ahead of him down the mews leading to the stable-yard.

One of the grooms opened the door of the Riding School. Then she put Pegasus at the jumps, feeling him flying over them like a bird, up and over, up and over, again and again, until finally he was sweating as she drew him to a standstill. She saw then that Major Hooper was watching her. She slipped from the saddle and a groom took Pegasus away to rub him down.

"Thank you," Candida said.

"Listen, Candida," Major Hooper said, and his voice was deep. "I know you think I have betrayed you, but there was nothing else I could do."

"Why can I not stay here with you?" Candida asked. "I have been so happy these last weeks. You said that I worked well! Why can I not go on working for you?"

"It is impossible," he answered. "It could not go on for ever."

"Why not?" Candida pleaded.

He walked away from her and she knew he would not answer her question. Then he turned back again.

"Let me give you a word of advice," he said. "Do not fight against life—go with it. You are too young, too vulnerable for this, but what is the alternative? As far as I can see there is none. Learn to accept things as they come; try to adjust yourself; try not to struggle; you'll only get more hurt in the process."

Understanding nothing of what he was trying to say, she could only look up at him, her eyes swimming with unshed tears.

"You have been very kind to me," she said, "but you do not understand what it is like to feel utterly alone, to know that the only one you love—the only one that matters to you—is being taken away."

Major Hooper shook his head and, as if he could bear no more, he walked abruptly from the Riding School out into the yard.

"You'd best go back to the house," he said over his shoulder.

Candida wanted to run after him to say good-bye and thank him for letting her ride his horses, but she knew she could not say it. She no longer felt bitter against him; for she knew that he had in his own way, however strange it might be, been honest with her.

She believed him when he said there was nothing else he could have done, and though she could not understand what had happened she could not hate him.

Slowly, looking utterly dejected, she went from the stable and down the mews. She did not hear the Head Groom say to Major Hooper:

"I knew she'd take it hard, Sir. She loves that horse!"

"He will be in good hands," Major Hooper said automatically, then replied: "Don't look at me like that, man. Don't you know that I feel as though I've committed a murder?"

He walked away and dressed down a stable hand for some minor offence in such a furious manner that the boy was white and shaking when he had finished with him. Then he went into his office and slammed the door.

Candida reached Mrs. Clinton's house and went upstairs. She went to her room, took off her habit, washed and put on one of the simple but fashionable morning gowns which Mrs. Clinton had bought her during the first week of her arrival.

It was very quiet and still. No one was allowed to make a noise in the house first thing in the morning because its mistress slept late. Candida had soon learnt that, owing to the amount of champagne Mrs. Clinton habitually consumed during the evening, she was usually heavy-eyed and irritable until lunch-time. So when possible, she contrived to keep out of sight.

Taking off her slippers she crept downstairs in her stockinged feet to the Dining Room, where breakfast was waiting. She thought if she ate anything she would be sick, but she sipped a cup of weak tea and sat trying to visualise what lay ahead for Pegasus and herself.

She was surprised when the door opened a little while later and Mrs. Clinton, fully dressed in her bonnet and shawl, came into the room. She was obviously in a very good humour.

"Good morning, Candida, my dear," she said. "Did you have a good ride? It must have been nice in the Park."

Candida twisted her fingers together.

"Major Hooper told me that you would tell me about Pegasus—being sold," she said in a voice that trembled.

"Of course I'm going to tell you about it," Mrs. Clinton replied. "You're a very lucky girl, very lucky indeed."

Candida said nothing. She only waited, her face very pale. Mrs. Clinton tried to smile.

"Do not look so tragic, child. You are going to be pleased, very pleased, when I tell you what has been planned for you."

"Major Hooper promised me that he would not sell Pegasus," Candida said in a low voice.

"Do not be so ridiculous!" Mrs. Clinton said sharply. "You cannot go on working at a livery stable for the rest of your days. I did not dress you and make you the sensation of London for that."

"If only they had not seen Pegasus yesterday," Candida murmured. "If only we had not gone into the Park! That led to someone wanting to buy him, did it not?"

"Of course it did," Mrs. Clinton agreed, "and the fact that you were riding him. You made a magnificent pair, all London is talking about you."

Candida made a little gesture with her hand.

"I do not want to hear about it," she said, "I only want to know what is happening to us, Pegasus and me."

"Then I will tell you," Mrs. Clinton said.

She looked away as she spoke, and Candida had the idea that she was choosing her words carefully. She was right about this, in fact Mrs. Clinton had been cogitating as she dressed what she should say.

Candida was ridiculously innocent, and it was almost

impossible to cope with a girl who never thought of herself but only of the horse she loved.

It was not surprising that Mrs. Clinton was in a good mood. It had been a moment of supreme triumph in her life when the previous evening John had come up-stairs to tell her that Lord Manville had called.

This was what she had been waiting for, this was what she had planned: it seemed almost incredible that what she schemed so cleverly with Major Hooper should work out exactly as she had intended it to do.

"Show him up, John," she had said, trying to repress the note of triumph in her voice.

She was standing in front of the mantelpiece in the Drawing Room when Lord Manville entered. She had seen him often enough, but she had not realised until now how tall he was, how devastatingly handsome, how square his shoulders.

"No wonder," she had thought, "he is known as The Heart-Breaker. It would be a very strange woman in-deed who did not fall in love with him."

She realised as he came into the room that he had come to call on her only because he was compelled to do so. He had deliberately restrained from knowing her in the past, and she knew that now the fish was hooked she must play him carefully.

"Good evening, M'Lord," she smiled, dropping him a curtsy. "This is a great honour. I have hoped for a long time that we should meet."

"I have heard about you, Mrs. Clinton," Lord Man-ville said, and his voice was cold, "but I have had no need of your services until now. Major Hooper, how-ever, has persuaded me that only you can contrive the introduction which is necessary in this instance."

"Major Hooper was speaking the truth," Mrs. Clinton said. "Will you not sit down, M'Lord, and have a glass of champagne?"

"I thank you, no," Lord Manville replied decisively. "This is a business matter, Mrs. Clinton, and one I would wish concluded with all possible speed."

"Very well, M'Lord. What you need from me is the introduction to Miss Candida Walcott."

"That is correct," Lord Manville agreed. "I have al-ready given Major Hooper my note of hand for two thousand guineas. An exorbitant sum, but the horse is an exceptionally fine animal."

"You will also find his rider exceptional," Mrs. Clinton said softly.

"I hope I will," Lord Manville said, "I hope so indeed. I understand there are other moneys you require in payment for clothes."

"Yes indeed, M'Lord," Mrs. Clinton replied. "The girl came to me without . . ."

Lord Manville put up his hand.

"Spare me the details, I am not interested in the history of the young lady," he said sharply. "All I require to know from you is what money you require and whether the person in question can be ready the day after tomorrow to proceed to Manville Park."

"She will be ready," Mrs. Clinton promised. "Would you like me to send for her now?"

"That is quite unnecessary," Lord Manville replied curtly. "The luggage-wagon will conduct her baggage about nine o'clock. I myself will be here at 10:30 A.M. if that is convenient to you both."

He made the words sound as though it was more of a command than a request.

"Candida will be waiting," Mrs. Clinton assured him. "And the sum which is owing to me, M'Lord, is in the region of two hundred pounds."

"It will be sent to you during the course of the day." Lord Manville said.

He turned towards the door. He reached it and inclined his head.

"Good-day to you, Madam."

"Good-day, M'Lord, and thank you," Mrs. Clinton replied in what she hoped was a voice as cool as his.

The door shut behind him and she heard him go down the stairs. Then she put her fingers to her mouth to stifle a laugh. The imperiousness and the insolence of him!

Yet what a man he was! She could not help running across the room to watch from behind the lace curtains as he crossed the pavement and climbed into his Tilbury. He picked up the reins, the long whip in his right hand, and the tiger, releasing the leader's bridle, ran to the back, scrambling aboard just as the tandem set off down the street.

Mrs. Clinton's eyes followed Lord Manville until he was out of sight. Top-hat at a slight angle, his almost classical features, the sharpness of his jaw-line, the width of his shoulders—all made him a man that any woman would yearn over, even one as old as herself.

And she had now brought him to heel! She had made him visit her! All these years he had eluded her, though she had entertained nearly all of his friends.

Well, she had won. It was her brains and her cleverness that had achieved what might have seemed the impossible. She had captured the attention of The Heart-Breaker and forced him to make use of her service.

Everyone would learn about it sooner or later, which would be greatly to her advantage.

But how was she to explain her victory to Candida? That was a question that perturbed her even in her moment of triumph. She told herself she was being nonsensical. Never before had she worried about the feelings of any of her women.

They had just been names, she could list them on her books, and the mere fact that they existed brought her in a considerable and ever-increasing income.

But Candida was different—how different she did not like to explain even to herself. Now she picked her words with great care one by one.

"It is Lord Manville who has bought Pegasus," she said, and half expected Candida's face to light up at the name.

"He is a true gentleman," she went on as the girl did not speak, "and Major Hooper thinks he is the finest judge of horseflesh in the length and breadth of the land. Pegasus is indeed a fortunate horse to be included in his stables."

"Major Hooper said I was to go with him," Candida said. "What am I expected to do?"

Mrs. Clinton paused a moment.

"I think I must leave it to Lord Manville to tell you that," she said slowly. "He is coming to collect you tomorrow morning to take you to his country-seat. I am told Manville Park is a magnificent place. Now I have to visit Madame Elisa and pay what I owe her. So I suggest that you go upstairs, Candida, and start packing. You had best do it yourself; Rose is not good with gowns, being too heavy-handed."

"I have not any baggage to put them in," Candida said.

"Oh dear, did I not tell you?" Mrs. Clinton asked. "I bought some trunks a few days ago. I will tell John to bring them down from the attic."

"You bought some trunks?" Candida exclaimed. "Then you expected me to go away. Why? What have I done? I like being here with you."

Mrs. Clinton's face softened.

"I know, dear, and I like having you," she said. "But you could not stay here for ever, it would be impossible. I have never had a girl in the house before, and besides . . ."

She paused.

"Besides what?" Candida asked.

"Oh never mind," Mrs. Clinton said sharply. "I cannot stay here talking all day. You must leave it to me, Candida, and trust me to do what is best for you."

"Will I never see you again?" Candida asked.

"Of course you will," Mrs. Clinton replied. "You will be back—they always come back. But then things will be different.

She was talking almost to herself and Candida looked at her in perplexity.

"I do not understand," she said. "If only you would explain to me."

"I've not got the time," Mrs. Clinton replied crossly. "If I do not get to Madame Elisa's now, she may have gone to visit a client. Run upstairs, Candida, like a good girl and start packing. It will take you some time. And you might change the satin cushion in the Drawing Room. That tiresome Lord Lindthorp upset a glass of port over it last night. Why he cannot drink champagne, which does not stain, I cannot think. But you will find another cover in the linen cupboard."

"I will change it," Candida said.

Mrs. Clinton had not waited for her answer. She was already walking down the Hall and John was opening the front door for her. Slowly, as though every step was an effort, Candida made her way upstairs.

In her small bedroom she sat down on the bed, asking herself over and over again what it all meant. Why did nobody explain things to her? What would Lord Manville want her to do?

He was very wealthy, that was obvious, perhaps he had a Riding School. She knew such an idea was ridiculous, and yet it was something to realise that she did not yet have to say good-bye to Pegasus. It was bad enough to part from Major Hooper and Mrs. Clinton, of whom she had grown fond these last few weeks. Mrs. Clinton was sometimes unpredictable, but she had been kind in her own way.

Candida knew that Mrs. Clinton had taught her a lot. If for instance Lord Manville asked her to arrange a dinner-party she would be able to do that. She knew how to deal with the household accounts, and what duties the servants were expected to perform in a large house. Also due to Mrs. Clinton that she knew how to dance, what type of curtsy she should make to different people, even to a Prince of the Blood—one piece of information, she thought, she was very unlikely ever to need.

Yes, Mrs. Clinton had been kind, and so had Major Hooper. It had been a wonderful experience to school his horses, teaching them to walk collectedly and obediently round and round the stable yard so that they would be safe for a nervous rider. Then she had been able to ride Pegasus every morning, to take him over the jumps in the Riding School.

She wanted to cry at the thought of leaving it all, but the tears would not come. . . . She was disturbed by John carrying in the new trunks, round topped in shiny black leather. He fetched five of different sizes and set them down on her bedroom carpet.

"That's the lot," he said with a grin. "It's sorry I'll be to see the back of you, Miss."

"And I have no wish to leave," Candida answered miserably.

"My Ma used to say what can't be cured must be endured," John told her. "Keep your pecker up, Miss!"

A little comforted Candida packed for nearly an hour until, feeling as if her back was breaking, she thought she would go downstairs and change the cushion cover in the Drawing Room before Mrs. Clinton returned.

She fetched the fresh one from the linen cupboard. It was in pale pink satin embroidered with forget-me-nots, and Candida thought with a little smile that her Mother would have thought it in bad taste. However, it smelt of the neatly stitched lavender bags which Mrs. Clinton put amongst all her linen.

Candida went to the Drawing Room and found the cover on which His Lordship had left a large purple stain of port wine. She took the cushion and was just beginning to replace the cover when she heard voices.

One was loud and aggressive, although she could not hear exactly what was said. She could however hear John expostulating.

"It must be one of Mrs. Clinton's gentlemen friends," she thought, "but it is strange that they should call at this hour. They never come before the evening."

Then to her astonishment the voices grew louder and suddenly the door of the Drawing Room burst open.

"I've told you, Sir, Mrs. Clinton is not at home," John almost shouted.

"Don't worry about that, my young fellow," the gentleman replied as he forced his way into the room, "this is the young lady I want to see. I have no need for Mrs. Clinton's presence."

As the gentleman spoke he pushed the door to with his hand, shutting John out. Candida stared in surprise at the large, florid, middle-aged man, with an expression on his face which instantly made her feel shy. According to her teaching she dropped him a curtsy.

"I am afraid Mrs. Clinton is out," she said quietly. "If you would like to wait for her I do not think she will be long."

"I'm in no hurry for her return," the stranger replied. "I've been trying to see you, my dear, since yesterday morning, and I've been circumvented at every turn. But now I have succeeded. Let us introduce ourselves."

"I am sorry," Candida said quickly, "but I have things that require my attention upstairs. Be so kind as to excuse me."

"I'll do nothing of the sort," he answered smiling.

"I do not think Mrs. Clinton . . ."

"Damn Mrs. Clinton!" he interrupted. "Must we go on talking about that boring woman when I want to talk about you? Now, let us start again. I am Sir Tresham Foxleigh, and you—what is your name?"

"Candida Walcott," Candida replied.

"A very pretty name for a very pretty person," Sir Tresham approved. "Now, let us get down to brass tacks, shall we? I saw you yesterday and knew that you were exactly the sort of filly I've been looking for. I've a cosy little villa not very far from here which will suit you admirably, and as for horses, well my stable is at your command. If there is anything else you particularly like I'll buy it for you."

"It is very kind of you," Candida said in a bewildered voice, "but . . ."

"Kind? Of course I want to be kind!" the stranger asserted. "And you'll be kind to me, won't you? I assure you that I'll appreciate someone as lovely as yourself, far better than those feckless young bloods you associate with. What is more I shall see that you have the right setting for your beauty. Every woman wants that. There's no one so beautiful that they don't need a frame, and a frame is what I'm willing to give you."

"I am afraid I could not accept presents from a stranger," Candida said quickly.

Sir Tresham put back his head and laughed.

"Admirable," he said, "nothing could be more attractive—the unsophisticated, the ungreedy! You're as clever as your appearance yesterday on that great black monster. God knows where Hooper got it from!"

Candida stiffened. The gentleman was obviously deranged, she was sure of that; at the same time he had no right to disparage Pegasus.

"I am afraid, Sir, I have really some important matters to which I must attend," she said, moving towards the door.

Before she could get there he was in front of her.

"No, you're not going to run away from me like that! I'm frightening you, am I? Very well, we'll take it slowly. I'm a blunt man, I know what I want and I go for it bald-headed. But if you want to play it another way we'll do what you wish. May I, my dear, pretty, adorable Miss Candida, have the privilege of taking you out to lunch or, if you prefer, dinner?"

"No, I . . . I am . . . afraid not," Candida said.

"Already engaged, are you?" Sir Tresham smiled. "Well then, tell him you're no longer interested! For I assure you, my dear, I'm going to look after you and no one else."

There was no doubt that the gentleman really was crazy, yet he stood between Candida and the door. She had an idea.

"Let me get you some refreshment, Sir."

She tried to pass him but his arms went out and held her.

"No," he said, "I need no refreshment but you. Come, my dear, a little kiss to start our acquaintance, and then we can go on from there."

Candida gave a cry and struggled against him. To her horror she realised that he was extremely strong and was only amused by her struggles. He drew her nearer . . . Then, as she screamed, the door opened.

"May I ask what is going on here?" Mrs. Clinton enquired.

Sir Tresham turned and his grip on Candida slackened. With one lithe movement she escaped him and pushing past Mrs. Clinton in the doorway ran out of the Drawing Room and up the stairs. Her cheeks were burning and she was breathing quickly as she reached the sanctity of her bedroom. She shut the door and locked it.

"How could any man behave in such a manner?" she asked aloud.

How could he dare to speak to her in such a crazy way and then try to kiss her?

She was shocked and disgusted; she was at the same time convinced in her own mind that Sir Tresham was mad. Only a madman would want to give presents to someone they had never met before. Besides this there had been something rather horrible about the way he had looked at her.

She could not explain it, she only knew she felt an instinctive repugnance for him. She was ashamed that she had stayed so long in the Drawing Room.

Downstairs Mrs. Clinton was saying:

"You have no right to force yourself into my house, Sir Tresham. John told you I was not at home, and your behavior is not that which I expect from a gentleman."

"Now, do not get hoity-toity with me," Sir Tresham smiled, installing himself comfortably in one of the easy-chairs. "You know why I am here, and the sooner we start coming to terms the better. I'm a good client of yours, as you well know."

"Do I?" Mrs. Clinton said. "That is a surprise to me! You remember the last girl to whom I introduced you. She was apparently not to your satisfaction."

"I do not know what you mean by that," Sir Tresham replied.

"I think you do," Mrs. Clinton answered. "You promised me not only one hundred guineas for the introduction, but fifty pounds for the clothes I had bought her. But you may recall that when she had moved into your villa you said they were not new and had been used on other occasions. So you did not pay me."

Sir Tresham looked uncomfortable.

"I'm a rich man, Mrs. Clinton," he said, "but I do not like being had for a mug. That girl, as I subsequently discovered, had been seen at Cremorne and Kate Hamilton's in half the gowns that you told me you had purchased entirely for my delectation. As a matter of fact, I meant to pay you. I kept her for six months and she turned out to be quite amusing."

"Nevertheless, I am still waiting for that money," Mrs. Clinton said.

"And you shall have it," Sir Tresham replied. "I will write a cheque now, or would you prefer bank-notes?"

As he spoke he drew a great wad of ten-pound notes from the inner pocket of his coat. He counted out five of them and held them out. Mrs. Clinton took them and placed them in a drawer in her desk. Then she said:

"And now, good morning, Sir Tresham, I do not do business at this hour."

"Now, look here, Mrs. Clinton," he protested. "I called here at three o'clock yesterday afternoon and was told you were not at home. I called again at five and again at seven—I received the same answer. I want that girl, and the horse if necessary, and I'm prepared to pay for them."

Mrs. Clinton smiled.

"I am sorry, Sir Tresham, you are too late."

"Too late, damn it!" he exclaimed. "Who was here before three o'clock?"

"That is my business," Mrs. Clinton replied.

"I am not allowing any whippersnapper to get ahead of me," Sir Tresham said. "Who has got her? Is it Manville?"

"You know me well enough, Sir Tresham, to be aware that I never give away my clients' names or discuss their personal business," Mrs. Clinton replied. "And now, if you will excuse me, I must ask you to leave. If you wish to call upon me again this evening at the proper hour, I shall, of course, try to accommodate you. There is a very pretty young widow I do not think you have met."

"I do not want a pretty young widow," Sir Tresham bellowed. "I want that girl Candida, and I'm going to have her."

Mrs. Clinton shook her head and at the same time pulled the bell-rope hanging beside the mantlepiece.

"You are not going to do this to me," Sir Tresham said angrily as John opened the door.

"Sir Tresham is leaving, John," Mrs. Clinton said in a cool, unflustered voice. "Please show him downstairs to his carriage."

"Damn it, this is the last time you get the better of me, woman," Sir Tresham snarled.

Nevertheless he left the room and preceded John downstairs. Mrs. Clinton gave a little sigh but looked far from distressed. She was used to handling men like Sir Tresham Foxleigh. They always made scenes if they did not get what they wanted; but she was confident that, although they might sulk and stay away for a few months, they would come back in the end.

There was no one else in London who could even begin to rival her position when it came to supplying the very best quality goods.

At the same time she hoped he had not upset Candida. There was no knowing what a girl as sensitive and unsophisticated as Candida might do. She might run away, she might refuse even to go to Lord Manville's.

With an anxious expression on her face, Mrs. Clinton went upstairs. She knocked on Candida's bedroom door.

"Who is it?" There was no mistaking the fear in Candida's voice.

"It is only me, dear," Mrs. Clinton answered.

She heard Candida run across the room and unlock the door.

"Has he gone?" she asked breathlessly.

Mrs. Clinton walked into the room and looked around her.

"I see you have been getting on with the packing," she said. "That is splendid. I am sorry you have been perturbed by Sir Tresham. He had been drinking, of course, and when he has had a few glasses of wine he talks the most utter nonsense. I hope he did not upset you."

"I was frightened," Candida explained. "He wanted to kiss me."

"How disgracefully he must have behaved," Mrs. Clinton said sympathetically. "But he gets like that, it is because he is such a lonely man. His wife became a chronic invalid soon after they were married, and so he has never had any children. One cannot help being sorry for him. And as I said, when he has been drinking he really does not know what he is doing. Tomorrow he will not remember what he said to you or, for that matter, if you even exist."

"Are you sure?" Candida asked.

"I have know Sir Tresham for years," Mrs. Clinton answered. "Now, do not think about it any more. I gave him a good talking down for calling at this door, when I am unlikely to be at home. I gather that he had seen you in the Park and got it into his head that he admired you very much. Did he offer you anything?"

"He talked about giving me a house and horses," Candida said. "I could not understand what he meant."

"He didn't mean anything," Mrs. Clinton told her soothingly. "He is a very, very rich man and he is always throwing his money away on all sorts of people. Why I heard only the other day that he gave a ten-pound note to a crossing-sweeper. The man nearly fell dead from the shock. But that is Sir Tresham—very unpredictable, but a kindly soul at heart."

Candida laughed.

"I quite understand," she said. "It was silly of me to be frightened, but he would not let me go to the door, and when he wanted to kiss me I thought how repulsive he was."

"You are quite right, he is," Mrs. Clinton agreed, "but I suppose I am used to him as an old acquaintance. Do not think about him again, it is very unlikely your paths will cross. Next time I see him I am sure he will have forgotten that you ever existed. As I said, that is what he is like when he has had a few drinks."

"I . . . I understand," Candida said. "I suppose I have not had much experience with men, so I do not know how to handle them."

"You will learn," Mrs. Clinton prophesied. "And now, dear, try and finish off your packing. There are all the bonnets to be put into the boxes, and they need special care."

"I know," Candida agreed, "but do you think I could go round to the livery stables later this evening when everyone has gone? I want to see that Pegasus is all right."

Mrs. Clinton, who had walked towards the door, paused a moment.

"I do not think there is any point in your doing that," she said. "I met Major Hooper just now and he told me that Lord Manville's groom had just left with Pegasus. He is on his way to Manville Park, and you will see him tomorrow."

She saw the expression on Candida's face and went from the room quickly.

"God knows what will happen to that child," she said to herself beneath her breath as she went downstairs. "I ought not to have taken her in the first place."

6

At exactly 10.30 a.m. Lord Manville drew up outside
Mrs. Clinton's house. He was driving a D'orsay Curricle
with a groom behind and a hood which could be used if
the weather was wet.

The sunshine was gleaming on the silver-crested har-
ness of the magnificent pair of chestnuts and on the
high polish of His Lordship's hat. The brass accoutre-
ments of the Curricle were shining as if they were
mirrors.

Mrs. Clinton, who had been peeping between the
curtains of the Morning Room to watch for his arrival,
said:

"I have never seen such an elegant turn-out. No girl
could fail to be thrilled by being fetched in such style."

"Is he really here?" Candida asked in a low voice.

Her lips felt dry and her fingers trembled a little. Mrs.
Clinton turned from the window to look at her.

"Don't be so nervous, child," she said soothingly.
"You look very charming, and His Lordship will think
so, I promise you that. Now remember all I have told
you and you will find everything will be done to make
you happy."

"I will try and remember," Candida answered.

The door of the room opened and Mrs. Clinton
looked up expectantly. It was only John who stood
there.

"His Lordship's compliments, Ma'am, and as his
horses are restless he would be obliged if Miss Candida
would join him outside."

Mrs. Clinton pressed her lips together. She was well
aware of the reason for Lord Manville's sudden solic-

itude for his horses: he had entered her house once and he did not wish to do so again.

However, what did it matter? She had achieved her ends, she had got what she wanted.

"Come along then, Candida," she said with a forced smile. "You must make your curtsy on the pavement because there is no going against a man who is fidgeting about his horses."

As she stepped slowly down the steps in the wake of Mrs. Clinton's crinoline, Candida felt unable to raise her eyes to look at Lord Manville. She had had no more than a fleeting impression of him in the Park when he had spoken to Major Hooper, and she could not describe later whether the man she had seen as she had turned her head was dark or fair, thin or fat.

She knew that whatever he was like, he now held her destiny in his hands, and try as she would she could not force herself to look up at him.

"Good morning, M'Lord," she heard Mrs. Clinton say.

"Good morning, Mrs. Clinton," a deep, resonant voice replied. "I must crave your apologies for not leaving my horses to a groom, but they are a spirited pair and I would be away as soon as possible."

"I quite understand, M'Lord," Mrs. Clinton said soothingly. "And now, may I present Miss Candida Walcott? Candida, this is Lord Manville."

As Candida rose from a curtsy she looked up and found herself staring into Lord Manville's eyes. There was something curious, at the same time critical, in his expression, and then it seemed to her that as they looked at each other something passed between them.

It was an experience so transitory, gone almost before she realised it had happened, so she felt she must have imagined it. Then her eyes dropped again as Lord Manville, steadying his horses, said:

"It is delightful to meet you, Miss Walcott. I hope you have no objection to riding in an open vehicle."

"No indeed," Candida answered shyly.

"Good-bye, my dear," Mrs. Clinton said, when as Candida would have turned towards her to clasp her hand or kiss her cheek, she turned and walked back into the house. Candida looked after her in perplexity.

"Let me help you, Miss," John said respectfully at her side.

He helped her spring up into the Curricle, arranged the skirts of her gown and put a light rug over her knees, tucking it in round her small feet.

"Thank you, John," Candida said gently, "and thank you for all you have done for me. I am afraid I have no money, otherwise I would have given you some."

She spoke in a low voice but Lord Manville overheard.

"No money?" he queried. "That is something I must remedy, of course."

He put his hand into his vest pocket.

"Do you wish to give him one guinea or two?" he enquired.

He held them out on his gloved hand. Candida, looking down at the shining coins, felt a sudden dislike of taking them from him. The words rose to her lips to refuse, but she realised it was John who would suffer because of the instinctive scruple which told her she should not take money from a gentleman.

"It is kind of you," she said in a shy voice, "and perhaps you would be gracious enough to give the money to John yourself."

Lord Manville raised his eyebrows, but he said loudly to John, who was standing back on the pavement:

"Here, my man, this is for your trouble."

A golden guinea flashed through the air and John caught it deftly.

"Thank you, M'Lord," he grinned.

Lord Manville tightened the reins, flicked the chestnuts with his whip, the groom ran to the back of the Curricle and they were off, moving, Candida noticed with delight, with a smoothness and a rhythm which could only be achieved by a really experienced driver. As they turned north Candida said shyly:

"Thank you for giving John the money."

"I should have thought of it myself," Lord Manville replied, and added: "What did he do for which you were so grateful? Did he bring you *billets-doux* from your many *beaux?*"

Candida shook her head.

"I have no beaux," she answered.

94

Lord Manville, intent on his horses, smiled a little cynically.

"So that was to be her line, was it?" he thought to himself. "Well, it was in keeping with her appearance—a young, unsophisticated maiden!"

He only hoped she would keep to the role: it would suit his plans if she played the part well. At the same time she was not likely to deceive anyone as experienced as himself. He had seen all the pretences and play-acting of the "Pretty Horse-breakers". They were usually as efficient at this as they were at their riding, and no man could ask more.

One thing that pleased him, he had not been mistaken in his impression of Candida. She was as elegant and attractive off a horse as on one. For one moment, as she had come down the steps following that scheming harridan, Mrs. Clinton, he thought with quite unusual sentimentality that she looked like a rose-bud.

Mrs. Clinton had, in fact chosen Candida's gown with care. It was very pale pink, with a crinoline skirt tucked and frilled in a material which Madame Elisa had sworn had come from Paris. With it Candida wore a tight-fitting little coat ending at the waist, which was made of just a slightly darker shade of pink and fastened with tiny buttons reaching to the neck.

Her bonnet was of pink straw, simply trimmed, and the only contrasting note of colour was provided by the satin ribbons which tied round her chin. They were of forget-me-not blue and seemed to accentuate the fairness of her skin and the burning gold of her hair.

They had journeyed for some way before Lord Manville spoke again, and then he noticed that Candida was bending forward to peer at the horses.

"What do you think of my pair?" he asked.

"They are magnificent," Candida answered, "and I have never seen such a perfect match. Are they twins?"

"No," Lord Manville replied, "there is a year between them. Naturally they are both from the same dam and sired by the same stallion."

"It is very unusual to get such a match," Candida said. "Pegasus's dam, so I understand, has never had another foal which is entirely black."

"He is certainly a very splendid piece of horseflesh," Lord Manville said. "Have you ridden him for long?"

"I have had him since he was a foal," Candida answered.

Lord Manville looked surprised. He thought Pegasus had been one of Hooper's finds and that he had been clever enough, with Mrs. Clinton's help, to discover a girl who would show the horse off to advantage.

However, by this time they were out of London, but as the roads were still somewhat crowded he was fully occupied in tooling his horses in and out of the traffic until they were clear of loaded drays, family landaus and tradesmen's carts.

The Royal Mail came speeding towards them, four horses full out at the gallop, a guard blowing his horn. It was filled with passengers and piled high with luggage.

"It is overloaded!" Candida said almost as if she were speaking to herself. "It is wrong that they should treat the horses so badly."

Lord Manville looked at her in surprise.

"Most people complain that the mail does not travel quickly enough."

"They do not have to pull it," Candida replied. "Do you know that those horses only have a life of three years? After that they are broken in wind, and for some there is nothing left but the knacker's yard."

She spoke with such feeling in her voice that Lord Manville said:

"I can see that you have a real feeling for horses. And I agree with you, the long-distance coaches are often shamefully overloaded."

"And the new short-distance omnibuses which carry nearly ten passengers," Candida cried. "Why do you not do something about them? Someone like yourself who sits in the House of Lords could raise such matters and perhaps get an Act of Parliament passed to protect the animals which cannot speak for themselves."

"I can see you are a reformer," Lord Manville said drily.

Candida felt the colour flush in her cheeks and she remembered too late that Mrs. Clinton had spoken to her most earnestly before she left.

"Remember," she said, "that a woman's job is to look attractive and be entertaining. Whatever Lord Manville asks of you, Candida, you must agree, if you want to stay with your horse. If you are difficult or if you make scenes, there is no doubt at all that he will send you away. Gentlemen dislike scenes more than anything else, and they dislike women who do not do what is asked of them. Try to be accommodating, my dear, it will make life much easier for you."

"I will try," Candida promised, wondering in what way she would be asked to accommodate Lord Manville.

"Things are not always what we expect," Mrs. Clinton went on, not looking at Candida but fidgeting with the morning paper which was beside her on the breakfast table.

"But I do not know what to expect," Candida complained.

"In which case you will undoubtedly be surprised at a lot of things," Mrs. Clinton replied, "and that is why I am begging you, Candida, for your own good, to do what you are asked to do with the minimum amount of fuss."

"Why should I make a fuss?" Candida enquired.

"Oh, some women like to prove their importance," Mrs. Clinton said quickly, "others have very preconceived ideas of what they expect of life. Many are just thoroughly tiresome."

"I will try and make you proud of me," Candida smiled. "You must not think I am not grateful, for indeed I am. You have done so much, taught me so many things, given me all these wonderful clothes. No one could have been kinder, even if you had been a relation.

She had a momentary feeling that Mrs. Clinton was embarrassed, and she could not think why. Then she thought that perhaps she was the type of person who did not want to be thanked for her generosity.

"You have been a very good pupil," Mrs. Clinton said. "But do remember what I have told you, Candida. It is not going to be easy for you to adjust yourself to the society into which you are now moving. Just remember what I have said—gentlemen want to be amused!"

Now as the ground sped away beneath the horses' hooves, and the sunshine gleamed in her eyes, Candida chided herself for being so foolish.

"I must try to be amusing," she said to herself, and wondered how one could be amusing with someone she had never met before and of whom she knew nothing, save that he was a good judge of a horse.

"We must talk about horses," she thought, "at least there we shall be on common ground. But I must not force my opinions on him."

It was some miles later that Lord Manville spoke again.

"You have a very unusual name for a girl," he said.

"Voltaire was one of my Father's favourite authors," Candida replied.

"And what do you think about it?" he asked, referring to her name.

"I find him very stimulating," she replied, speaking of the author. "It is extraordinary, though, to realise what a commotion he caused in France. Now we are quite used to people being outspoken."

"I did not know there was a translation of *Candida*," Lord Manville said.

"I do not think there is," Candida replied. "I have never heard of one."

Lord Manville's eyebrows went up again. So she had read the book in the original French. He had heard that many of the "Pretty Horse-breakers" were supposed to be well educated, but perhaps in his acquaintance with them he had been unfortunate. Most of the ones in which he had taken any interest had many attributes, but education was not one of them.

The ones to whom he had extended his patronage were usually more like Skittles—exquisite to look at, expert on horseback, but with a Rabelaisian manner of speech. Skittles' oaths and profanity were the rage amongst the young bloods, and many of the "Pretty Horse-breakers" copied her. Lais was perhaps one of the exceptions.

She did not swear often, but she had a sharp wit which Lord Manville found most entertaining, and she made no pretence about being ready to bestow her favours to the highest bidder, whoever he might be.

Lais was a relief and a relaxation after the turbulent emotions he had experienced in the company of M'Lady Brompton. Never again!—he told himself—no more entanglements, no more surreptitious assignations, no more clandestine rendezvous, no more journeying about dark passages in the middle of the night!

He was free—free to enjoy himself if he wished, and all he asked for his comfort and his delectation was a "Pretty Horse-breaker" who would please his eye with her equestrian prowess and grace his bed with the same sophisticated expertise.

One good thing about this pretty little thing he had picked up was that she did not chatter. He disliked chattering women, because the Lord knew they had very little to say without making a great noise about saying it.

They journeyed quite a number of miles before Lord Manville spoke again.

"We will lunch at Beaconsfield. We should be there about noon. And we will have only about an hour's journey to Manville after the meal."

"Do we change horses?" Candida asked.

"No," he answered. "My groom will give them a rest, and they will carry us as far as Manville Park, although actually I have my own change of horses on most of the main roads out of London."

Candida looked surprised.

"Is that not rather extravagant?" she enquired.

"I consider my convenience more than the expense," Lord Manville replied casually. "I do not wish to travel with the type of animal one gets at a posting-inn."

"No indeed," Candida agreed, "but what happens to your horses if you do not journey that way for perhaps a month or two?"

"They have their grooms with them," Lord Manville replied. "They look after them well, I assure you."

There was a hint of laughter in his voice, and she said quickly:

"I am sorry if I sounded impertinent just now, I did not mean to."

"Do not apologise," he said, "it is interesting to find

99

a young woman such as yourself who is really concerned with the treatment of horses. Most of them are themselves very severe on their animals."

"Unnecessarily severe!" Candida exclaimed, thinking of Lais.

She wondered if she should say how much she disliked the use of the spur, but decided this again would be controversial. So she kept quiet.

As the clock in the tower of Beaconsfield church sounded the hour of twelve, they drove into the village with its flowering chestnut trees, black and white houses and bow-fronted shops. Lord Manville drew up outside the inn. Ostlers hurried forward to take the horses, and Candida was helped from the Curricle by His Lordship's groom.

Inside the Landlady appeared and took Candida up some old oak stairs to a bedchamber, where there was warm water to wash her hands and a mirror in which she could see that the wind had disturbed the neatness of her hair. She took off her bonnet to tidy herself and the Landlady exclaimed:

"What beautiful hair you have, Ma'am if you'll excuse me for mentioning it."

"Thank you," Candida smiled, smoothing the wayward curls back into place. "Do you think it would matter if I lunched without putting my bonnet on again?"

"No indeed, Ma'am," the Landlady replied. "No one will see you but His Lordship. Luncheon is arranged in the private Parlour, as is usual when His Lordship drives this way."

"Does he often come here?" Candida asked.

"I believe this road leads to His Lordship's estate," the Landlady answered. "We're always glad to have the honour of his company. He's a fine gentleman, not like some that travel the road and expect more than we poor inkeepers can provide them with."

"It must be very difficult to keep an inn," Candida said sympathetically.

"It is indeed, Ma'am. You never know who will come barging in asking for this or that, finding fault or making trouble. 'Tis a hard life but we're happy enough, my husband and I. We inherited the inn from his father, and although I says it, it's been much improved in our time."

"I am sure it has," Candida answered. "And now that I am ready, would you be kind enough to show me downstairs."

"You are a very pretty young lady and no mistake." the Landlady said admiringly. "His Lordship has brought many ladies here, but none of them could hold a candle to you."

"Thank you," Candida said again a little shyly, and followed the buxom woman, with her white cap and spotless apron, down the ancient stairway.

The Landlady preceded Candida along a little passage and opened the door.

"Lunch'll be served at any moment, M'Lord," she said as Candida went into the room.

It was a small Parlour, low ceilinged with heavy oak beams. There was a round table in the window on which lunch was laid, and two big wing-backed armchairs in front of the hearth. The smell of age, tobacco smoke and wine mingled with the sweet scent of lavender and honeysuckle. The latter came, Candida found, from the garden which lay outside the open window.

"What a pretty place," she exclaimed enthusiastically.

Lord Manville, who had been leaning against the mantelpiece, moved towards the table in the window.

"Will you not sit down?" he asked. "The Landlord assures me that he has an excellent luncheon for us, so I hope you are hungry."

"I am," Candida replied simply. "I was too nervous to eat any breakfast."

"Of what were you nervous?" he asked, seating himself opposite her.

"Meeting you," she answered truthfully.

"Am I so awe-inspiring?" he enquired.

"Everyone is so impressed by you," she replied. "You could not expect me to be anything else."

He laughed at her seriousness, thinking how much her shyness became her and how skilfully she managed to portray the nervous young girl going out into the world for the first time.

He wondered how much of this clever acting was due to her own inspiration or to Mrs. Clinton's tutelage. He was well aware that Mrs. Clinton was a shrewd woman whose introductions were eagerly sought. Her women were well behaved, and there was no question of blackmail or disagreeableness when a liaison ended.

But His Lordship could not believe she often produced a girl who could act the part as well as this one. Mrs. Clinton obviously had a better idea of stage-craft than anyone had given her credit for.

The Landlord came bustling in with pigeons roasted on the spit, a prime leg of mutton, a hot veal and ham pie and a cold collation, which made Candida think there was enough to feed a regiment of soldiers rather than two passing travellers. She chose a little of the veal and ham pie, and noted that His Lordship was prepared to sample not one but quite a number of the dishes.

"Your wife is a good cook," he said to the Landlord, "convey her my compliments and tell her she never disappoints me on my various visits."

" 'Tis my mother, M'Lord, who does the cooking. She used to be in service before she married my father, and she still knows how to tempt the palate of a gentleman like yourself."

"She does indeed," Lord Manville smiled. "And now, what wine have you brought me?"

"Your favourite claret, M'Lord."

"Will that please you?" Lord Manville asked Candida. "Or would you prefer a white wine? If you prefer champagne, I expect there is a bottle tucked away somewhere in the cellar."

"I will have water," Candida replied.

Lord Manville looked amused.

"I hardly think that is necessary," he said. "A little wine will do you good."

"I have sometimes had a glass in the evening," Candida said, remembering the times when her Father's sales had allowed them to celebrate, "but I do not think I should drink at lunch-time."

"As you wish," Lord Manville said indifferently.

This was carrying the game to extremes, he thought, but he would let her have her way. She would soon get tired of it, he was sure of that!

The Landlord withdrew from the room. Lord Manville made a few unimportant observations and Candida contrived to agree with him. Then when he had finished eating, he leant forward in his chair and said:

"There is something I want to say to you, Miss Walcott. I hope you will not misunderstand or be annoyed by what I am about to propose."

He was surprised at the expression of concern on Candida's face and the apprehension in her eyes as she fixed them on his face. He did not know that for one terrible moment she thought she had failed and he was going to send her back.

"It is like this," Lord Manville went on, obviously choosing his words with difficulty. "I have not asked you to come to Manville Park for my . . ."

"He was going to say "amusement", but changed it.

". . . for my companionship. It is for someone else that I have asked you, and I hope you will help me where he is concerned."

Lord Manville was not really a conceited man, but he was complacently used to seeing an expression of admiration in the eyes of women who looked at him. He was also well aware that if he took a "Pretty-Horsebreaker" from London to Manville Park, she would expect that his interest in her was personal.

It was therefore with surprise that he noticed that, as he finished his sentence, Candida's expression of anxiety changed to one of relief. For a moment he could not credit it, but there was no doubt that, while she was still listening to him intently, she seemed not as anxious as she had been a few seconds earlier.

He even fancied a little colour had come back to her cheeks. It was extraordinary, something for which he would like an explanation, but he continued:

"I need your help, Miss Walcott, or now we know each other better, may I call you Candida?"

"Yes, of course," Candida agreed.

"The young man I am talking about," Lord Manville continued, "is my Ward, and he has been the source of a great deal of worry to me lately."

"Is he a child?" Candida asked, thinking perhaps that this was the reason why Lord Manville had asked her to come to Manville Park. She had never been a governess, but she felt certain she could be one.

"No indeed," Lord Manville said quickly, dispelling

her idea almost before it was formed. "Adrian is twenty years of age and a charming person when he is in his rightful senses."

He saw Candida's expressive eyes widen and added quickly:

"I do not mean he is deranged, it is just that he imagines he has fallen in love."

Candida smiled.

"Is that not very romantic?" she asked.

"No it is not," Lord Manville said sharply, "He has not only fallen in love, but he wishes to marry the girl. How can anyone at twenty know if he has chosen the right person, or if his love is not just an illusion?"

"I expect really you disapprove of his choice," Candida said shrewdly.

"I have not seen the lady in question," Lord Manville said crushingly. "I understand she is entirely respectable. Her father is a parson at Oxford, where my Ward is supposed to be pursuing his studies. Last week I received the information that he has been rusticated until the end of the term."

"I expect he was caught climbing in," Candida said. "That is what a man is usually rusticated for, is it not?"

"You seem to know a great deal about it," Lord Manville answered disagreeably. "When I was at Oxford I climbed in practically every night of my life, but I was never foolish enough to be caught."

"Perhaps you were also very lucky," Candida observed.

"Well, to continue about Adrian," Lord Manville went on, "I am absolutely determined that he shall not marry this girl. And I thought it would help matters a great deal if you were to try to persuade him that there are other attractions in life besides the undoubtedly worthy charms of the lady from the vicarage."

"What exactly do you want me to do?" Candida asked.

"Well, I think your own common-sense will tell you that," Lord Manville replied. "Try to make Adrian see that at the moment he knows nothing of life and that there are all sorts of amusements waiting for him before he need settle down and take life seriously. Tell him about London—make him curious about the Casinos, the Argyll Rooms, Mott's, Kate Hamilton's, or any of the places which are amusing in the evening. Ask him to take you out to dinner at Cremorne Gardens and you can dance the polka under the stars."

Candida made a small sound and His Lordship stopped and asked:

"Did you say anything?"

"No . . . n . . . o," Candida replied.

"Tell Adrian too," Lord Manville continued, warming to his theme, "what fun the music halls and theatres can be, not forgetting the ballet. He will find that irresistible when he gets to know some of the pretty dancers."

He stopped, seemingly to consider what other instructions he should give Candida, then almost apologetically he went on:

"Adrian has never seen anything of the gay life. Make him understand that it is part of the experience of growing up to sample these delights before he takes on the responsibility of a wife and family."

Candida was aghast at what Lord Manville was asking of her. How could she possibly explain to him that she had never heard of any of the places of which he was speaking? How could she convince him that she had no knowledge of London except Hooper's Livery Stable and her one sortie into the Park?

She realised there had been some extraordinary mistake, that Lord Manville thought she must know of all these places and be a part of them. Then she remembered Mrs. Clinton's advice. If she told the truth there was no doubt, exasperated by her ignorance, Lord Manville would dispense with her services and instantly send her back to London. There was only one thing she could do—pretend to carry out what he asked and hope by some miracle he would not find her out.

"Now, will you do this for me?" she heard him say, and answered quietly:

"I will do my best."

"That is exactly what I hoped you would say," Lord Manville replied in satisfaction. "Adrian is a strange young man. I really do not understand him, but I am sure that with your help we can wean him away from this marriage—which would be quite disastrous, I am sure of that."

"Suppose he really loves her," Candida asked.

"Love! What does a boy of that age know about love?" Lord Manville retorted. "Besides, love can be a snare and an illusion at any age."

Candida wanted to argue that love was something which just happened, you could not prevent it. Just in time she checked herself and said nothing. It seemed to her that Lord Manville was well satisfied and now was ready to proceed on their journey.

He threw some notes on the table, and quickly Candida tied on her bonnet in front of the old mirror in a walnut wood frame which hung on the wall.

Then she found herself starting off again for Manville Park and knew that His Lordship was in a good temper. She did not realise that he had, in fact, been quite worried as to whether she would, as he put it, "cut up rough" at being palmed off on Adrian.

"She is being jolly sporting about it," he told himself, "and I will see she does not suffer in consequence. Adrian will not be able to provide for her, but I will do all that is necessary. With any luck we shall hear no more about marriage. Candida is pretty enough to put the thought of any other woman out of his stupid young head."

It had been worth coming away in the middle of the Season, Lord Manville decided, to sort out Adrian's affairs, even though last night, when Lais had pleaded with him not to go, he had felt incensed with the boy.

May was the best time in London—there were routs, balls and masques every night; there was the theatre and ballet; and there was always the amusement of watching the "Pretty Horse-breakers".

Lais had told him last night that Skittles was breaking in a new horse this morning. All his friends would be there, while he had to post to the country just because Adrian was making such a fool of his young self. To be rusticated nearly a month early from Oxford, on top of everything else, was enough to make any guardian lose his temper!

But everything was working out splendidly! Adrian would gain experience with Candida, and when he came down from Oxford he would take up the life of a fashionable young man about town.

"No one could say," Lord Manville told himself with satisfaction, "that I am not a proper sort of guardian. God knows I did not want to be saddled with the boy, but he is my responsibility and I shall certainly do my best for him."

He glanced down at Candida in satisfaction.

"It was Grandmama's idea," he thought, "and she will be amused to hear how well it is working out."

It now almost seemed unnecessary to have told Lais that he wanted three days alone at Manville Park before she joined him. He had asked Lais to come down on Sunday, and by then, if Candida had done her part well, he ought to be able to return to London.

He wondered if he should say anything to her about being recompensed in hard cash for turning her attentions to Adrian rather than himself.

After some consideration he decided against it. It was not as though she seemed the greedy type, and he was still somewhat piqued by the look of relief on her face when he started to explain to her that it was Adrian on whom she could bestow her favours.

"Could she," he asked himself almost in consternation, "have taken a dislike to me?"

It did not seem possible, they had met only that morning. But still, one never knew with females, they were unpredictable. Nevertheless, it was a sobering thought. Well, today was Wednesday, Lais would arrive on Sunday and he would be glad to see her.

One compensation was that, however boring it might be to be shut up with only Adrian and Candida for company, there was a great deal to be done at Manville. He had rather neglected it while he had been so engrossed with Lady Brompton.

He was quite aware that his Agent would be looking forward to seeing him, and two of the tenant-farmers had requested months ago that he would make it convenient to see them. Time would pass quickly, and what was more attractive than spring at Manville?

Candida was to think the same thing as after passing along a high wall the horses swung in through a big stone gateway surmounted by heraldic lions, with a long avenue of oak trees sloping downhill. Then suddenly she saw Manville Park.

It was not what she had expected. She could not have imagined anything so big and impressive—the great colonnaded front, the wings square and solid, the urns and statues on the roof silhouetted against the blue of the sky. It was as overwhelming as its owner, and yet at the same time it was lovely.

She must have given an audible little gasp because Lord Manville looked down at her and said:

"Do you like my house?"

"It is so big," Candida answered. "Yes, it is beautiful."

It was built of grey stone, and yet it had a kind of luminous quality about it. The house was set almost in a hollow with a lake at its foot, and parklands stretched away on each side towards the horizon wild, green and verdant.

"Does it all belong to you?" Candida asked.

"Almost as far as the eye can see," Lord Manville replied. "On the right my neighbour is the Earl of Storr, on the left—you cannot see his boundary I am glad to say—lives Sir Tresham Foxleigh."

He did not notice the start Candida gave or the expression of distaste on her face, but a moment later she had forgotten what had been said as they drew near the house and she saw the gardens.

She was not to know until later that the gardens had been there for centuries, or that the house had been built by Lord Manville's grandfather in 1760, just one hundred years earlier. But the lilacs, purple, mauve and white, the trees covered in pink almond blossom, and the lawns, smooth as green velvet, were the result of care and toil over generations of devotion.

The park was ablaze with daffodils stretching down to the lake, blowing golden in the breeze, and the bushes of fragrant white syringa and the laburnum trees weighed down with golden blossom were lovely beyond words.

"How can you ever leave such a place?" Candida asked.

"You make me feel I should come home more often,"

Lord Manville replied, and she knew that he too was moved by the beauty of the spring at Manville.

The horses drew up at the front door. Footmen in claret-coloured livery came hurrying to help Candida to the ground and greet their master.

"Nice to see you, Bateson," she heard His Lordship say to a very imposing major-domo. "Everything all right?"

"Yes, M'Lord. Mr. Adrian is in the Library, shall I fetch him? I do not think he will have heard your arrival."

"No, I will go and find him," Lord Manville replied. "Come, Candida."

He led her through an imposing Hall with a marble floor, life-size statues of Greek gods, the walls in pale apple-green, before they proceeded down a wide passage on which were hung many fine portraits.

She and Lord Manville were reflected in the mirrors which stood above gilt console-tables. She thought how tall he looked, and how tiny she was in comparison.

He walked swiftly and without speaking. At the far end of the passage were double mahogany doors. The footman following them was too late. His Lordship opened the door himself and they passed into the most amazing room Candida had ever seen.

There were books from floor to ceiling, books as colourful and beautiful as the painted ceiling or the valuable furniture with which the room was embellished. In the centre of it was a large desk and seated writing at the desk was a young man, his fair hair falling forward over his forehead as he wrote.

"Good afternoon, Adrian," Lord Manville said. "I want to present you to Miss . . ."

Before he could finish the sentence his Ward had risen to his feet behind the desk, staring at him angrily.

"I will not have it," he said. "I know just what you are about and I will not meet her. Take her away, take her away immediately!"

As he spoke he flung his quill pen down on the desk, and walking across to the window stood with his back to the room looking out on the sunlit garden. Candida stared at him in astonishment. Lord Manville stepped forward towards the desk.

"Adrian!" he said, and his voice was like a whip. "You will oblige me by turning round immediately and allowing me to present you to Miss Candida Walcott. This is my house, and while you are here as my guest you will behave with propriety to a lady who has honoured me by her company."

Lord Manville's voice seemed to ring out round the great room, and then slowly, with a reluctance that Candida thought was very obvious, Adrian turned to look at her.

7

Adrian stood staring at Candida for a moment. Then the expression on his face changed and with a smile he came from the window saying:

"My apologies . . . I did not realise . . . I thought you were . . ."

"Adrian!" Lord Manville interrupted in a voice of thunder, and then added in a quieter tone: "Candida, may I introduce my somewhat eccentric Ward, Mr. Adrian Rushton? Adrian—Miss Candida Walcott."

Adrian bowed, Candida curtsied, and then there was a moment of embarrassing silence until Lord Manville, moving towards the mantelpiece, said:

"Perhaps, Adrian, you would care to explain to me why you have been rusticated from Oxford."

"I was caught climbing in at two o'clock in the morning," Adrian answered.

"Careless of you to be caught," Lord Manville said good-humouredly. "I only hope the party justified it, or should I say the lady?"

"You should say neither," Adrian replied in a somewhat sulky voice. "I had been alone."

"Alone!" Lord Manville ejaculated. "And what in Heaven's name could you have been doing at two o'clock in the morning?"

Adrian did not answer, and His Lordship continued:

"Well, where had you been?"

"I was in the churchyard, if you must know," Adrian replied.

His Guardian stared at him incredulously.

"You never fail to surprise me, Adrian," he remarked at length. "However, we can discuss it on another occasion. Now, I shall be obliged if you will entertain Miss Walcott. I know that my agent is waiting to see me, and at least half a dozen people will be insisting that I give them my full attention after so long an absence. I expect you young people will have a great deal to say to each other."

Lord Manville went from the room while he was still speaking. Candida stood a little shyly in the centre of the room, her pale pink dress and elegant bonnet making her appear even younger than she was. Adrian, however, was not looking at her. He was staring at the door through which his Guardian had disappeared and said in an exasperated tone:

"There! Is that not just like him? If I had said that I was at some drunken party, had beaten up the Watch or smashed half the windows in the College, he would have been delighted! Or if I had told him what he really wanted to hear, that I had been with some . . ."

He suddenly seemed to realise to whom he was speaking. The words died on his lips and he turned petulantly towards the desk, covering over the paper on which he had been working as if he thought Candida would read what he had written.

"It may seem rather impertinent of me," Candida said in her soft voice, "but I am curious to know why you were in the churchyard."

"Do you really want to know?" Adrian asked somewhat aggressively. "Very well then, I will tell you. I was writing a poem."

He did not wait for Candida's reply but continued in the same hostile voice:

"Now laugh! You will think that a really despicable, foolish thing to be doing, when I might have been dangling after some flashy female or proving myself to be a drunken fop. But, as it happens, that is the truth."

As he spoke the last words he stared at Candida as if he were ready to bear the brunt of some cynical comment or a peal of laughter.

"But of course I understand," Candida said gently. "When one is writing a poem one becomes lost to everything—the time, one's surroundings, hunger, even the need for sleep."

112

"How do you know that?" Adrian asked in a very different tone.

Candida smiled.

"My Father was a poet," she said simply.

"Your Father?" Adrian ejaculated.

Candida nodded.

"Yes," she said. "He was Alexander Walcott. I do not suppose you have heard of him."

"Not the Alexander Walcott who translated the *Iliad?*" Adrian asked incredulously.

"Yes—he was my Father," Candida smiled.

"He was at Christ Church," Adrian cried, "where I am now. My tutor told me only last term to read Walcott's edition of the *Iliad;* he thought it might help me."

"I am so glad Papa is not forgotten there," Candida said softly.

"Forgotten? Of course he is not forgotten! We are very proud of him in Oxford," Adrian replied.

Candida clasped her hands together.

"Oh, I wish he could have heard you say that," she said.

Adrian walked from behind the desk towards her.

"You mean your Father is dead?" he asked.

"Yes, he died only last month," Candida answered with a little break in her voice.

"I am sorry," Adrian said quietly. "Of course I did not realise that he was alive until now; I mean . . . I had no idea what age he was. I just know that I enjoyed reading the *Iliad.*"

"He did translate it beautifully, did he not?" Candida asked. "Have you read any of his other books?"

"No, but you must tell me about them," Adrian replied.

"And you must tell me about your poetry," Candida said shyly.

"Of course I will," Adrian agreed, a new light in his eyes. Then he glanced towards the door. "But promise me that you will not mention it to my Guardian."

"Why not?" Candida asked.

"He would not understand," Adrian explained. "You see, he wants me to be a fashionable young blood. He wants me to take an interest in what he thinks are the

113

right occupations for someone in my position, someone, in fact, who is his Ward."

"Surely he would not mind your writing poetry?" Candida said.

"He would be furious," Adrian declared, "and would despise me even more than he does at the moment."

Candida was about to protest when she remembered what Lord Manville had said to her at the Inn while they were having lunch. The writing of poetry certainly did not fit in with the pursuits in which he had asked her to interest his Ward—the casinos in London, the other resorts of which she had never heard, and the Cremorne Gardens which she had once seen described in a newspaper.

Adrian was undoubtedly right. Lord Manville would not approve of his preoccupation with poetry.

"You will not tell him, will you?" Adrian begged.

"No, of course not," Candida promised.

"And you will let me read you what I write?" Adrian went on.

"Perhaps I will be able to help you," Candida said tentatively. "I used to help my Father."

"In what way?" Adrian enquired.

"Well, I know a little Greek."

"You can read Greek?" Adrian exclaimed.

"Not as well as he did," Candida replied. "But he used to say two heads were better than one when he found it difficult to find the word he wanted or to scan a line. And I too have read a great deal of poetry."

"This is the most wonderful thing that has ever happened to me!" Adrian declared. "I never believed I would find anyone who would be interested in what I was doing, let alone help me."

"Well, I expect there are lots of books which will be of assistance in this magnificent library," Candida said, looking round.

"I expect there are," Adrian said indifferently, "but what I really want to do is express my own ideas. I know it is a good exercise to translate the classics, but there is so much I want to say which I feel can only be expressed in verse."

"That is right!" Candida said, clapping her hands

114

together. "Papa always used to say 'A poet must bring out what lies dormant inside him'."

"Did your Father really say that?" Adrian asked. "I thought I was the only person who had discovered what poetry could mean."

"I think a lot of people," Candida suggested, "have found it can help them as nothing else can."

"I have got quite a lot of my poems upstairs," Adrian said. "I will not bring them down now in case my Guardian comes back; but if we can get away somewhere alone, then I will read them to you."

"I should like that," Candida said. "It will almost feel like being at home with Papa again."

"It is very queer that you, being a girl, should like poetry," Adrian went on. "Lucy does not care for it at all, although she tries to understand it for my sake."

"Lucy is . . . ?" Candida asked, a little hesitatingly.

"The girl I want to marry," Adrian explained, reverting to his hostile tones. "I expect my Guardian has told you about that."

"And are you going to marry her?" Candida enquired, ignoring the reference to Lord Manville.

"He will not let me," Adrian said crossly. "Oh, he pretends I am too young and all that sort of thing, but what he really means is that she is not grand enough. Besides, the Heart-Breaker is not interested in marriage as an institution."

"What did you call him?" Candida asked curiously.

Adrian had the grace to look ashamed.

"I ought not to have said that," he replied apologetically, "it just slipped out. It's his nickname. Everyone calls him the Heart-Breaker."

"Does he break so many hearts?" Candida asked innocently.

"By the dozen," Adrian said extravagantly. "You can see how good-looking he is. And since he is also rich and important, the women flutter round him like stupid moths round a lighted lamp. And then, when he will not marry them, when he is tired of their hanging round his neck, they go away weeping bitterly with broken hearts."

"How pathetic!" Candida exclaimed. "I did not think

115

of him like that—he seemed so awe-inspiring and rather frightening."

"I am frightened of him too," Adrian said confidingly. "That is why I do not want to annoy him any further. He is annoyed enough already. Please promise me you will not say anything about my poems."

"No, of course not," Candida agreed. "I have given you my word and I will not break it. But why do you not do what Lord Manville wants?"

"Because I want to marry Lucy," Adrian said crossly. "I do not want to go to London; I do not want to rush about with a lot of stupid young dandies, whose only idea is hunting a fox, shooting game-birds or riding a breakneck race blindfolded in their night-shirts, or something equally nonsensical."

"Do you not like riding?" Candida asked quickly.

"Of course I like riding," Adrian asserted, "but I do not want to do it in the middle of the night, or for a bet, nor to hurt my horses by taking them over jumps that are too high for them."

"Of course you do not!" Candida said enthusiastically. "Gentlemen who exploit their horses just to amuse themselves are as thoughtless and horrible as the women who use their spurs so severely."

"I see we agree on a lot of things," Adrian said. "You will help me, will you not?"

"With your poems?" Candida asked. "You know I will."

"Not only with my poems," Adrian explained, "but to make my Guardian understand me a little better. You see, the trouble is that he controls all my money until I am twenty-five, which means that if I do not do exactly what he wants, he can cut me off meanwhile without a farthing."

"But I am sure he would not do that," Candida said.

"He would," Adrian answered grimly. "He has already threatened to do so if I marry Lucy."

"But that seems wrong!" Candida cried impulsively, and then remembered that her task was to try to prevent Adrian from making a marriage of which his Guardian disapproved.

"Of course it is wrong," Adrian said hotly, "but he knows he has got the upper hand and there is nothing

I can do about it. I cannot ask Lucy to marry me without a penny-piece on which we can live. And she is such a pretty girl—if I do not marry her there are dozens of other chaps at the University who would only be too willing to engage her affections."

"I do not think that is likely," Candida interposed.

"Why, what do you mean?" Adrian enquired.

"Well, if Miss Lucy really cares for you," Candida explained, "surely she would not fall in love with someone else just because you have to wait a little while!"

"Do you really think that?" Adrian demanded.

"I am sure of it," Candida said. "If one really loves another person, then it does not matter what difficulties are in the way, or how long one has to wait."

Adrian was silent for a moment before he said in a low voice:

"Lucy did not seem very pleased when I came back from London after having talked about our marriage to my Guardian. I think she expected me to offer for her, and when I did not . . ."

His voice trailed away, and Candida said quickly:

"I expect she felt piqued, or just disappointed. I dare say you let her believe that everything would be all right once you had spoken to Lord Manville."

"I suppose I did," Adrian admitted.

"Perhaps he will reconsider his decision," Candida said comfortingly, "when he realises how serious your intentions are."

Adrian gave a short, unhappy laugh.

"That does not sound at all like His Lordship," he said. "He is as hard as nails, and once he has made up his mind nothing anyone might say could make him change it."

He paused and looked at Candida.

"You might do it," he suggested. "You are very pretty, and naturally the Heart-Breaker likes pretty women."

"Do not call him that," Candida said.

"Why not?" Adrian asked.

"I do not know," Candida replied, "it just sounds rather cheap and unpleasant. I think that if you are a poet you ought not to say or think unkind things about anyone. It must affect what you write."

"You do know a lot about it," Adrian said admiringly. "You are right, of course you are right! I do not want my poetry to be tarnished with the resentment that I feel towards my Guardian, or the jealousy that I cannot help feeling about Lucy."

"Papa used to say that a poet should be like a priest —dedicated to his profession and untainted in any way by the world in which he has to live," Candida said. "But of course he did not live up to that—he loved my Mama and they ran away together."

"Did they really?" Adrian asked. "How thrilling! That is what I thought of doing."

Once again he looked over his shoulder.

"I should not tell my Guardian about your parents," he warned her. "He thinks it is utterly and completely despicable that any gentleman should persuade a lady to elope with him."

"He has no good reason to think that," Candida said stiffly, feeling suddenly angry that anyone should say something that could impugn the honour of her Father.

Then, quite sensibly, she realised that Lord Manville had very likely said this to discourage Adrian from eloping with the Vicar's daughter. Remembering the task that had been laid upon her she said hastily:

"I do not think it is wise to elope unless in very exceptional circumstances."

"And what are they?" Adrian enquired.

"The two people concerned," Candida answered, "must love each other so much that they are prepared to sacrifice everything—their comfort, their social position and all that has been familiar to them in the past."

"Is that what your Father and Mother had to do?" Adrian asked.

Candida nodded.

"We were very, very poor," she said.

"It must be terrible trying to live with no money," Adrian said.

"Papa earned some, of course," Candida replied, "but it was rather spasmodic. Sometimes we felt quite rich, then at other times, when one of his books had not been a success, or we spent faster than he could write, things were very difficult."

"But he did make some money," Adrian insisted.

"Yes, of course he did," Candida said, "and I always hoped that perhaps one day he would suddenly become famous."

"It would be wonderful if I could do that!" Adrian cried. "It really would be the answer to everything. I would not have to depend on my Guardian, I would have money of my own—money over which nobody else had any control."

"Why do you not try?" Candida asked softly.

Adrian gave a laugh of sheer delight.

"Why not?" he asked. "I should like to read you what I am writing now."

He picked up some papers from the desk and brought them to Candida.

"I have just got stuck for one particular line," he confided, "I am sure you will be able to help me."

Nearly an hour later Lord Manville came into the Library and saw two fair heads very close together. They were sitting on the sofa, and he thought with a little twist of his lips that she had not taken long—the Pretty Horse-breaker—in getting down to work.

As Candida and Adrian heard him come into the room they started apart almost guiltily, and he wondered why, instead of being pleased, he felt a sudden irritation at the expression on their faces.

"They're concocting something between them," he thought.

"Have you finished your business with the agent?" Adrian asked in what his Guardian thought was a somewhat affected voice.

"I have," Lord Manville said abruptly. "I came to see if there was anything you would like to do."

"Nothing . . ." Adrian began, but Candida interrupted:

"Oh, please, Lord Manville, would it be possible for me to see Pegasus? I know he came here yesterday."

"Of course," Lord Manville replied. "I was thinking of going to the stables myself. Are you coming with us, Adrian?"

"Yes, Sir, of course, I should like to do that," Adrian replied.

Lord Manville thought he detected a glance passing between Candida and Adrian.

"She has told him to toady me," he thought. "Oh well, it's a step in the right direction."

Candida picked up her bonnet which lay discarded on one of the high-backed chairs, and Lord Manville saw her glance at it uncertainly.

"There is no need for any formality here," he said. "There is no one to see you if you would rather not wear that obviously Bond Street piece of headgear."

"I need not? That is splendid!" Candida cried. "I hate anything on my head."

"Nothing should hide the loveliness of your hair," Lord Manville said.

Candida blushed at the compliment. He looked at her approvingly.

"She really is incredible," he said to himself. "If one did not know from which stable she has come, both metaphorically and physically, one would really believe she had never received a compliment before."

They went out of the house into the warm sunshine. The fragrance of lilacs seemed to fill the air, and Candida, looking across the park with its golden carpet of daffodils, thought that this was the type of country-gentleman's Estate of which she had always dreamt.

This was the right home for Pegasus; this was the sort of place, given the right master, which could be a paradise for any horse. They turned towards the stables.

"Who is Pegasus?" Adrian asked curiously.

"He is my horse," Candida said impulsively, then added: "I mean, he now belongs to Lord Manville. He is the most wonderful horse in the world, there has never been another like him."

"Why did you call him Pegasus?" Adrian enquired.

"I think you know the answer to that," Candida replied.

"Of course," he answered. "The famous winged horse of Greek mythology."

She smiled at him, and then, in case Lord Manville should think they were being too poetical, asked:

"Has Your Lordship a lot of horses here?"

"Quite a number," he replied, "and I hope to purchase some more very shortly. Perhaps you would like to help me break them in."

"Can I do that?" Candida asked eagerly, her eyes sparkling.

"You look too small and weak to break in a really spirited horse that has never been schooled," he answered.

"I have been helping Major Hooper," Candida said. "He says I am as good as, if not better than, any horse-breaker he has ever known."

"And Hooper is, of course, an expert," Lord Manville said, a somewhat sneering note in his voice.

"His horses are fine animals," Candida said, "and they are well broken. I am sure he must have the best livery stable in the whole of London."

"It is certainly the most famous," Lord Manville said.

"I thought it must be," Candida replied in all sincerity, but although he glanced at her mockingly he said nothing.

They reached the stables and Candida gave an exclamation of delight at the beauty of them. They were very well laid out—the stables themselves being of old, mellowed red brick, with the doors of the stalls painted a bright, cheerful yellow.

There were a great number of them, she noted, and the horses with their heads over the half doors looked, as she had expected, worthy of the man who had been spoken of as one of the finest judges of horseflesh in the country.

The Head Groom came hurrying up as they approached.

"Afternoon, M'Lord, it's a great pleasure to see Your Lordship."

"Thank you, Garton," Lord Manville replied. "Candida, this is Garton, who has been at Manville since I was a boy."

"That's right, M'Lord, thirty years next Michaelmas," the Head Groom said.

"Miss Walcott is particularly interested in horses, Garton."

"Then I have plenty to show you, Miss," the Head Groom said proudly.

"Can I see Pegasus first?" Candida asked, unable to wait for anyone else to make the suggestion.

At the sound of her voice there was a sudden stamping in one of the stalls.

"That'll be Pegasus, M'Lord," the Head Groom exclaimed. "He seemed a bit restless, so I shut him in."

"Will you please let him out?" Candida asked. "There is no need for anyone to hold him."

The Head Groom looked at her in surprise, then at Lord Manville for instructions. Lord Manville smiled.

"Do as the lady says, Garton," he commanded.

"Very good, M'Lord," the Head Groom replied, but he was muttering beneath his breath as he went towards the stall.

Candida stood waiting. The noise of Pegasus stamping his hooves was plain to hear. Then, as the bolts were drawn back and the door swung open, she gave a little whistle. The Head Groom stood to one side as if he expected a tornado to come tearing into the yard. But Pegasus came out slowly. He was looking magnificent with his shining coat and tossing head.

"Pegasus!" Candida called.

He gave a little whinny as if in sheer delight, bucked to show his independence, and then came trotting towards her.

"Pegasus," she said softly. "How are you, my love?"

She put up her arms as he reached her side and the great stallion nuzzled his nose against her neck.

"Are you well?" she asked. "Are they looking after you properly? Oh, my dear, I missed you this morning."

She had no idea what a picture she made, or indeed that every stable hand was staring in astonishment, but she heard Lord Manville's voice say:

"You see, Garton, Miss Walcott knows how to handle horseflesh."

"I can see that, M'Lord."

Adrian moved to Pegasus' side to pat his neck.

"Pegasus is the right name for him," he said quietly to Candida. "He looks exactly as I expected him to look."

Candida smiled up at him.

"I thought you would say that," she said.

Lord Manville had not missed the exchange between them. Now he strode away down the line of stalls.

"Oh please wait!" Candida cried, feeling instinctively that something was amiss. "May we not come too?"

"If you are not otherwise engaged," he replied indifferently.

"But I want to see all your horses," Candida said. "If I seemed preoccupied with Pegasus just now it was because I have not seen him for so long."

"Since yesterday!" Lord Manville retorted.

"It seemed a long time to me," she answered.

He looked down at the small, pointed face with its big eyes and at Pegasus standing quietly beside her.

"Come and tell me about my horses," he said in a more friendly tone. "I feel I have a lot to learn about them."

"Major Hooper says you know more about horses than anyone else in the country," Candida said.

"It is a good reputation to have," Lord Manville answered, "I only wish it were the truth. However, I am always ready to learn. Tell me how you taught your horse to come when you call him."

"He has always followed me everywhere," Candida said, "there is no need for him to have a bridle. Wherever he may be in the fields, I have only to whistle and he comes to my side."

"Do you hear that, Garton?" Lord Manville said. "I expect your stable-boys spend hours in the morning trying to catch a horse that does not want to be saddled."

"That's something you can't teach, M'Lord," Garton replied.

"You are right there," Lord Manville agreed. "Come, Candida, what do you think of this mare? I bought her three years ago as a foal, and I think you will admit that she is worth today a great deal more than I paid for her."

They wandered around the stables for over an hour. Candida enjoyed every minute, talking with a knowledge of horses which seemed to surprise not only Lord Manville, but even Garton.

She told them what herbs were best for poultices, she went into the stall of a horse of which all the stable-boys were afraid, and he let her pat his neck and was quiet and well behaved as long as she was with him.

"We will ride tomorrow morning," Lord Manville said

as they left the stables. "Do you mind getting up early, Candida?"

"No, of course not," Candida replied, "I am used to it. In London we left the stables at 5.30 a.m."

"You must have found it hard burning the candle at both ends," Lord Manville smiled. "Most ladies like to lie in bed in the morning after a gay evening on the town."

Candida opened her lips to say she had never had a gay evening on the town; then she remembered what was expected of her.

"I expect I am very strong," she said instead.

"You would need to be if you led that sort of life for long," Lord Manville snapped, and she wondered why he sounded so disagreeable about it.

They went back to the house, where Lord Manville sent for the housekeeper—an austere old woman in rustling black silk who, Candida thought looked at her disapprovingly.

"Mrs. Hewson, this is Miss Candida Walcott," Lord Manville said. "Will you please show her to her bed-chamber and give her every possible attention. I expect by now her luggage has been seen to."

Mrs. Hewson gave Candida the very briefest possible bob, then answered respectfully:

"Indeed it has, M'Lord. The housemaids have un-packed everything."

Lord Manville looked at his watch.

"Be down in an hour," he said, "and, Adrian, try to contrive not to be late. If there is one thing I dislike, it is infuriating my chef by spoiling his dishes."

"Have you brought down your London chef?" Adrian asked. "That is good news. I had no idea you planned on doing any entertaining."

"I do not," Lord Manville replied, "but I felt that good food and drink are essential to my own comfort, as well, of course, as yours."

Only Adrian guessed that something lay behind Lord Manville's smooth reply. And even he would have been astonished if he had realised what a sacrifice his Guardian was making on his account.

"If I go to the country," Lord Manville had said to his Major-domo in London, "I am damned if I am going to have country food. It is irksome enough to leave London at this particular moment, without adding to my discomfort by being badly fed."

"Mrs. Cookson is not a bad cook, M'Lord," the Major-domo replied. "She is, of course, not in the same class as Alfonse. At the same time, you know what these Frenchmen are. I have a feeling that he, like Your Lordship, will not wish to leave London at this particular moment."

"Tell Alfonse I am relying on him to support me during what I have reason to believe will be a very tedious and irksome three days," Lord Manville said.

"If that is Your Lordship's message, I feel quite sure Alfonse will do his best to relieve the situation," the Major-domo replied.

To Lord Manville's surprise, it was not only the dinner which was delectable and an epicurean dream, but he found Candida and Adrian far more entertaining company than he had imagined possible.

He thought he had forgotten that the young have a natural gaiety all of their own. He had grown used to the destructive and razor-like wit of his contemporaries, and the artificial blandishments of the ladies to whom he proffered his affections.

It was one thing to flirt brazenly with a *double entendre* behind every sentence, something very different to listen to two young people teasing each other, to find himself laughing at things which at other times he would have thought merely common-place and boring, to find incredibly that the childish card games he had not played for twenty years were just as amusing as the gambling for the high stakes in which he indulged at White's Club.

"There is a very good game we used to play at home called Word-Making," Candida said, and then proceeded to beat both Lord Manville and Adrian.

"You are too good," Adrian said accusingly, "but it is only because you have played it more often than we have."

They ended up with Consequences, laughing so much at the ridiculous situations they conjured up that Lord Manville found himself still chuckling after both Candida and Adrian had gone up the Grand Staircase with lighted candles in their hands.

"Good-night, M'Lord," Candida said before she left, dropping him a curtsy. "I will not be late tomorrow morning. You did say seven o'clock, did you not?"

"We will make it later if you prefer," he said.

"I think it is Your Lordship who will be sleeping late in the good country air," she replied.

"We will see," Lord Manville replied. "And we will see too how you manage on Pegasus outside the Riding School or the confines of Hyde Park."

"Pegasus much prefers to be free of conventions, restrictions and pomposity—as I do," she answered.

She smiled at him, then lifting the front of her evening gown ran up the stairs after Adrian.

"I beg you also to be on time," Lord Manville heard her say to his Ward in a low voice, "and do not sit up late. It will not help if you are heavy-eyed."

"No, I will try to sleep," Adrian answered.

Lord Manville stood staring after them in perplexity. Help what? What were they talking about? And why did he suddenly feel out of it?

They had both been so friendly and gay at dinner, and he had been grateful to Candida for charming Adrian out of the sullens and making everything so easy. In fact he had positively enjoyed himself—quite contrary to his expectation.

Now he was suspicious. Of what and why he did not know, but he felt something was going on behind his back and he did not like it. Then he shrugged his shoulders. These "Pretty Horse-breakers" doubtless had their own way of doing things. The girl was doing what he had asked of her. He ought to be grateful, he ought to be pleased.

He could not help remembering that unmistakable look of relief he had seen on her face when he had told her that he—personally—was not interested in her. What could it have meant? Her attitude towards him was frank and friendly, and he realised that by dinner-time she had lost some of her shyness.

When they had been playing games she treated him in exactly the same way as she treated Adrian. She had teased them both a little for their stupidity in not finding the right words.

She had laughed with a spontaneous and infectious gaiety, and what at any other time he would have sneered at as a childish joke, had seemed to him— because it had amused Candida—something quite exceptionally funny.

There was no doubt he had picked a winner as far as Adrian was concerned. He had never seen the boy more animated or apparently more sensible: if he was not out of love with the Vicar's daughter and in love with Candida by the end of the week, he would be very much surprised.

She was an amazing creature, almost as amazing in her own way as that enormous black stallion she loved so dearly. Then he remembered Hooper saying much the same thing, and his lips tightened.

Seeing who she was, seeing from where she came, was she putting anything over on him? Was she being so clever that he was being tricked without realising it?

Lord Manville went back into the Drawing Room and poured himself a glass of brandy. Then he walked across the room to stand at the open French window looking out into the garden. It was a starry night with a half moon creeping up the sky.

The scent of night-stock was fragrant in his nostrils; a warm breeze was soft on his cheeks, and around him was the quietness of the sleeping house and the great empty parkland stretching away across the silver lake.

Lord Manville suddenly felt as though the beauty of his own possessions gripped at his heart and held him as they had never done before. Manville Park was the one place that would always be his home, the place in which he had his roots, the place in which he had been brought up.

Almost mockingly, it seemed to him, he saw the face of the girl he had wanted to marry all those years ago, the girl whom he had planned to be mistress here, his wife and the mother of his children.

He had loved her whole-heartedly and, though there had been other women in his life before her, she had been the only one he wished to marry. He could now hear her saying in that light, unfeeling voice:

"I am sorry, Silvanus, but Hugo has so much to offer me that you have not."

"You mean," he replied almost incredulously, "that because he is a Marquis, while I have not yet inherited, you love him more than you love me."

"It is not exactly that I love him more," she replied a trifle uncomfortably, "it is just that we would have to wait for so long, Silvanus. Your Father is not yet old, and if I marry Hugo I shall be the bride of the Season and a Lady-in-Waiting to the Queen. There are lots of other things too which he can give me, things which matter, however much one thinks they do not, in a girl's life."

"But my love for you and yours for me," he had insisted, "does that not count?"

"I do love you, Silvanus," she replied, her voice softening for the moment, "but it is no use, you must see that. I have got to marry Hugo, there is nothing else I can do. I shall always remember you, and I hope you will remember me, but it would be foolish for us to be married, it would really."

He could remember at the time feeling as though someone had dealt him a sharp blow on the head. He felt numbed, almost as though he could not comprehend what had happened.

Then later had come the pain and the anger, even the hatred, that someone could have hurt him so cruelly.

He had never forgotten her, and he had never wanted to marry any other woman. He had made love to dozens of them and they had loved him, perhaps trying all the harder to capture him because he eluded them.

There was always something, even in the closest hours of passion, which made them know he was not their captive, not completely in their thrall.

"Why do you stand aside and watch yourself?" one woman had asked him as they lay together very close, with only the gentle flames of a dying fire to light the room.

"What do you mean?" he had asked.

"You know exactly what I mean," she replied. "You are always a little aloof, a little apart, never really one with me."

He had known exactly what she meant, and though

128

she loved him desperately and he had been very fond of her, she was one of the lovely women whom he had left with a broken heart.

He could not help it, there was something in him which made him despise and almost hate a woman while he held her in his arms. There was some part of his brain which told him jeeringly.

"This love is not enough, it will never be enough, you will never be completely one with anyone."

He asked himself now if it was possible for him ever to find a woman who was as beautiful as Manville, who could hold him because their love for each other was enough?

Then he laughed cynically at the thought and, putting down his untouched brandy on the table, turned from the beauty outside because it hurt him so intolerably and went upstairs to bed.

Candida heard his footsteps coming up the stairs; for her room opened off the landing at the top of the Grand Staircase. Her room was in darkness and she lay tense and excited in the big four-poster bed, which one of the housemaids told her had been slept in by a Queen.

She had been thinking of Pegasus, but now as she heard Lord Manville coming to bed she thought of him.

"He was nice tonight," she told herself, "and not at all awe-inspiring. I think he means to be kind, both to Adrian and to me, but there is just something that stops him."

She wondered what it was and thought that it must have been a woman. Someone had hurt him—and she knew instinctively that she had stumbled upon the truth.

He was like a horse that had been injured or perhaps cruelly treated, and had never forgotten it. He was rather like Pegasus, big, strong and handsome, and yet at the same time wanting love.

"Perhaps . . . I can make him . . . forget whatever it is that he has . . . suffered," she thought sleepily.

And when she slept Pegasus and Lord Manville were indivisibly mixed in her dreams.

8

Riding with Lord Manville on one side of her and Adrian on the other, Candida thought she had never been so happy. The sunshine was warm on her face and the beauty of Manville Park had never ceased to thrill her. Now, after three days, she realised she had begun to love it deeply.

She had found, Candida thought, a freedom and a gaiety which had seemed enchanted since that first evening when they had played childish games after dinner. Lord Manville no longer appeared to be aloof or awe-inspiring, and he had even ceased to be cynical.

And it was not only Lord Manville who had stopped frightening her. The formidable army of servants who ministered to their comfort in the great house had become people she could talk to as easily as she had talked to old Ned.

Mrs. Hewson had soon lost her look of disapproval, and Candida had been told all about her niece, who was consumptive, and her sister, who was a housekeeper to the Duchess of Northaw.

Candida learnt that Bateman the butler, who looked like an Archbishop, had rheumatism in his right leg when the wind was in the east, and that Tom, the youngest pantry-boy, suffered from chronic toothache.

As she had dressed this morning, knowing with a little thrill of excitement that they were going off immediately after breakfast to ride over the parkland, she thought to herself how lucky she was to have found so many friends at Manville Park, and to feel in some strange way as if she herself belonged there.

The three of them had spent the previous day visiting

the various farms on the estate, and she had been entranced by the big oak-raftered kitchens with sides of bacon and haunches of pork hanging from the ceiling.

She had noticed how easily Lord Manville adjusted himself to sitting down to a tea of newly baked bread, fresh eggs and slices of ham cured by the private recipe which every farmer's wife believed was better than that of her neighbours.

Candida had listened to him talking to his tenants and realised they not only had a respect for him as their landlord, but a feeling of admiration and what might be almost termed affection. One farmer had said to her as they left:

"His Lordship not only be a nobleman, but he be a man, and a fine upstanding one at that."

Candida too felt an increasing admiration for Lord Manville as she watched him control Thunder, who was in one of his more difficult moods, prancing, behaving skittishly, and even attempting to break unnecessarily into a gallop. It took a strong man and a really experienced rider to hold him that morning.

Candida knew she had never seen anyone who sat a horse better than Lord Manville, or who looked more as if he were one with the animal he rode.

Adrian was somewhat silent, and she knew without being told that a new idea for a poem was forming itself in his mind. Already, with her help, he was getting a better sense of style, and a poem he had read to her on the previous evening before Lord Manville came down for dinner had been so good that she felt that even her Father would have approved of it.

"That is indeed splendid!" she exclaimed. "The very best you have done!"

He flushed a little at her praise, but his expression changed when she added:

"Why do you not show it to your Guardian?"

"No, no," he answered quickly, "His Lordship would not approve, and I would not wish to disturb his unprecedented good humour."

He slipped the poem back into the inside pocket of his evening coat just as Lord Manville came into the room, at the same time giving Candida a warning glance in case she should feel compelled to betray trust.

131

She had given him a smile of reassurance and Lord Manville, advancing towards them down the Salon, wondered once again with an irritation which he could not repress what it was they were keeping from him.

This morning, however, there was no cloud on the horizon and he was laughing at some light remark Candida had made as they turned their horses towards the house.

"The Riding School will be ready this afternoon," he said. "Shall we put Pegasus through his paces?"

"Oh, could we?" Candida asked. "That would be wonderful!"

She had already found that Manville Park not only contained an indoor Riding School, but also one which had been constructed outside and which almost resembled a miniature racecourse.

When Lord Manville's father grew old he was afflicted with such severe rheumatism that he was no longer able to ride. This did not prevent him from supervising the schooling of his horses, and he would never allow any horse to be broken-in except under his own surveillance.

The two Riding Schools had been a joy in the last years of his life. In the winter he directed his grooms indoors; and in the summer the charming little School laid out at the back of the house beyond the stables was a place where he spent many hours a day, schooling not only his horses but those who rode them.

"I have had the jumps remade," Lord Manville said, "and Garton tells me that the old water-splash has been re-dug and filled especially for our amusement."

"That will be something new for Pegasus," Candida said, "he has never jumped water before. I shall be mortified if he fails."

"I am sure he will not fail," Lord Manville declared.

Candida's face was turned towards him, her eyes alight with excitement, her lips parted, and he thought then, as he had thought so often in the past few days, that she was one of the loveliest women he had ever seen.

He had watched her, and without really consciously planning it he had set traps for her to see if her sweetness, and her kindliness were only a façade. But like her horse she appeared to be faultless.

"There must be good blood in her somewhere," he thought, and it was impossible not to compare her with the thoroughbreds she rode so fearlessly and with a grace that was unsurpassed by any of the other "Pretty Horse-breakers", however skilled and efficient they might be.

One thing Lord Manville found very surprising was that, despite Candida's gentleness towards the horses she rode, they never seemed to take advantage of her.

He had watched so many women ride, and he had begun to believe that the "Pretty Horse-breakers", in their attitude of almost cruel severity to their horses, were using the correct method of breaking and schooling. Now he had begun to be doubtful.

"Was it not some strange, exotic quirk of their characters," Lord Manville had asked himself, "that their sweetness and subjection in bed should be set in direct contrast with what sometimes amounted almost to persecution of the animals they rode?"

Candida was different, so different that he could not express even to himself what he felt about her. She had done everything he had asked her: she had indeed made herself so charming to Adrian that he could not believe the boy was not already deeply in love with her.

Yet somehow he was not satisfied—why he could not explain.

He found himself watching her, listening to her, thinking about her, and for all that she seemed so open, so frank, so child-like he was convinced that she was in fact deceiving him. He told himself he was almost on his guard against her, and then laughed at the ridiculousness of the idea.

She was only a girl, and only such was suitable in every way for Adrian. Again and again he congratulated himself on being so clever as to have found such "a Pretty Horse-breaker" for his Ward, and wondered why the plan, now it was fulfilled, gave him so little pleasure.

They reached the house, and Candida dismounted and went upstairs to change her habit. There was an hour and a half to wait before luncheon would be served, and they were not to ride again before two o'clock.

Her maid had prepared a bath for her, as was usual after riding. It was scented and the bath-towels smelt of lavender. As Candida dried herself she thought that never before had she lived in such luxury.

Not only did she enjoy the comfort of it, but the loveliness of Manville seemed to tug at her heart.

There were the gardens ablaze with blossom; there was the beauty of her bedroom with its huge fourposter bed and embroidered hangings, which had been stitched in the reign of Charles II; the mirror with its gilt cupids; the furniture inlaid and polished with beeswax from the still-room; the vase of pink rose-buds standing by her bed—the first roses of summer.

"I am happy! I am happy!" Candida said aloud, and she suddenly had an urgency to find Lord Manville again, to be with him.

She did not attempt to explain the feeling to herself, she only knew she must hurry. Somehow the sands of time were running out, she must not miss one second of this strange enchantment which she found in herself.

Her maid hooked her into a gown of pale green silk with innumerable lace flounces on the wide skirt. There was lace too on the tiny puffed sleeves and round the somewhat décolleté neckline.

When Candida had complained because Madame Elisa cut her bodices so low, Mrs. Clinton and Madame Elisa had merely smiled at her protests. Now she wished the gown was higher, then thought no more about it.

She wanted to go downstairs, she wanted to see Lord Manville; and almost before her maid had finished tidying her chignon of red-flecked gold she had left the bedroom and was speeding down the Grand Staircase towards the Library.

She opened the door and could not suppress a little throb of disappointment because the room was empty. Perhaps he had gone out again, she thought, and then remembered she had promised Adrian she would try to find a book of Greek poems that they were quite convinced would be found somewhere in the Library.

Neither of them could remember the name, but Candida knew she would recognise the cover the moment she saw it.

She glanced along the closely filled shelves. At the

top, high up, she thought she saw the book she was seeking, and with some difficulty she fetched the tall mahogany ladder from the other side of the room.

She climbed up it and drew the book from the shelf, only to find it was not the one she sought yet was nevertheless interesting.

She was turning over the pages when she heard the door behind her open and looked down to see Lord Manville, also changed and exceedingly elegant, come into the Library. She felt her heart give a sudden leap of excitement, and holding the book in her hand she started to climb down the ladder.

"What were you expecting to find so high up?" Lord Manville asked, a hint of amusement in his voice. "Is it that the sweetest fruits are always out of reach?"

Candida was halfway down the ladder. She turned her head to smile at him and as she did so lost her footing. For a moment she swayed, and then half fell, half slipped into his arms.

"You should be more careful," he scolded, "you might have hurt yourself."

Then he looked down into her face. Candida was suddenly conscious of the strength with which he held her and the closeness of him. Her head just reached his shoulder, and as she looked up their eyes met.

Quite suddenly the world vanished and they were alone. Something magical and exceedingly strange passed between them, so strange that Candida drew in her breath and felt she could not breathe again.

His arms tightened and she was tinglingly conscious that his lips were very close to hers.

Then she must have moved, because she heard a tiny sound which broke the spell between them and distracted her attention. It was the lace of her dress which had caught on the ladder. Quickly, because she was shy and afraid of her own feelings, Candida struggled and was free.

"Oh, I have . . . torn my . . . gown!" she exclaimed breathlessly, and her voice sounded strange even to her own ears.

"I will give you another one."

His eyes were on her face and he spoke almost auto-

135

matically as if he was not thinking of what he was saying. Candida disentangled her dress from the ladder.

"I could not . . . let you do . . . that," she replied. "it would not be . . . correct."

"Why not?" Lord Manville asked with a smile. "There was no difficulty about my paying for the one you are already wearing."

Candida turned to him and the expression on her face astonished him.

"You . . . paid . . . for this . . . gown?" she asked, the words coming slowly from between her lips.

Lord Manville was just about to reply when they were both startled by the sound of voices and of laughter. It seemed as though a hundred tongues were speaking all at once, and a second later the Library door burst open.

There was a sudden vista of laughing faces, feather-trimmed bonnets, flashing jewels, of silk and lace, tarlatan and velvet, of crinolines so large they had to be manipulated through the door.

Then one person detached herself from the crowd—a live, graceful little figure with a magnolia skin and dark slanting eyes swept across the room towards Lord Manville.

"Lais!"

Candida heard him ejaculate the name, and then two arms were round his neck and a gay voice was crying:

"Is this not a surprise? Are you not pleased to see us? We could not allow you to rusticate any longer."

Lord Manville looked over Lisa's feather-trimmed bonnet at the women crowding behind her into the Library. He knew them all. There was Fanny, who came from a Liverpool slum, but whose brilliant riding had made her one of the most famous, and certainly the most expensive, of the "Pretty Horse-breakers".

There was Phyllis, the daughter of a country parson, who had fallen in love with a married man who had taken her under his protection for several years. Then he had returned to the bonds of matrimony, and so she had become one of the notorious "Pretty Horse-breakers", and it was considered fashionable to be seen in her company.

There was Dora, with her baby face and blonde curls, who was known to be so severe in breaking a horse that

136

the skirt of her habit always had bloodstains on it, while to make love to her was like sinking into a bowl of thick, rich, cloying cream.

There was Nelly, Laurette and Mary Anne, all pretty witty and gay, all women who had amused and beguiled him, whose company he had found infinitely preferable to the respectability of Belgravia. Now, for some unknown reason which he could not even explain to himself, he did not welcome them at Manville Park.

Behind them came their escorts, three officers of the Household Cavalry—the Duke of Dorset, a rather oafish, red-faced young man who drank more than was good for him; Captain Willoughby, who had run through one fortune before he was twenty-five and had accumulated another on the gambling tables; the Earl of Feston, who gave the most expensive parties the Argyll Rooms had ever seen, which usually ended by his paying for the whole place to be redecorated.

Behind them, sauntering slowly, with a smile on his rather florid countenance, came Sir Tresham Foxleigh.

"We are all staying with Foxy," Lais was explaining shrilly above the noise of the "Pretty Horse-breakers" who had clustered round Lord Manville to greet him. "He invited us and we brought some horses with us. He has the perfectly splendid idea of a competition in your Riding School this afternoon, so do not tell us that you will not give us luncheon first as we are already famished with hunger."

It was difficult for Lord Manville to reply. He had not seen how Candida, at the sight of Sir Tresham, had stiffened and looked round to see if there was any escape except by the door through which everyone had entered.

There was none, and there was nothing she could do but watch and listen and know that Sir Tresham's eyes were on her and her only as he came across the room.

It was then that Lord Manville, above the turmoil and clamour made by his friends, heard Sir Tresham say:

"Miss Candida, you must believe me that I wish only to apologise to you, and ask that you will forgive me."

With a sudden almost unreasonable anger Lord Manville asked himself how it was possible that Candida knew Sir Tresham, or what reason he could have for offering her his apologies. He wanted to hear her reply, but Lais's voice in his ear made it impossible, and only Sir Tresham heard Candida say:

"I have nothing to say, Sir."

"But you must believe me," Sir Tresham persisted, "that I am deeply grieved that I should have upset you, and I am indeed humbly contrite."

Candida did not reply, and he said insistently:

"See, I throw myself on your mercy. You cannot be so hard-hearted as not to forgive a very contrite sinner."

"Then I accept your apology, Sir," Candida said in a low voice, "but now, if you will excuse me . . ."

"No—wait!" he pleaded.

But already she had slipped past him, finding the way clear to the door, and running from the Library and out into the Hall she met Adrian halfway down the stairs.

"What has happened?" he asked. "What is all this noise?"

"A lot of people have arrived," she answered, "and that man—that horrible, beastly man! I had hoped never to see him again."

"Who is it?" Adrian enquired. "And why has he upset you?"

Candida did not answer and he said:

"Tell me, what has he done to you that you should feel like this? Why, you are trembling! Who is he?"

"His name is . . . Sir Tresham Foxleigh," she stammered.

"I've heard about him!" Adrian said with scorn. "I believe he is a complete outsider. Do not have anything to do with him!"

"I will not if I can possibly help it," Candida replied miserably. "But why is he here? Lord Manville told me that he lived nearby but that he disliked him."

"I do not suppose he will stay long," Adrian said soothingly. "What has he done to frighten you?"

"He forced himself into Mrs. Clinton's house in London," Candida answered in a low voice. "I was there . . . alone."

She gave a little shiver at the memory and then said almost beneath her breath:

"He . . . tried to . . . kiss . . . me . . . It was . . . frightening."

"I told you he was an outsider!" Adrian exclaimed. "But he cannot hurt you here in this house."

"I do not want . . . to speak to him, I do not want him to come . . . near me," Candida said almost wildly.

"He will not," Adrian declared, "I will be near you and keep him away."

"You promise?" Candida asked.

"I promise," he replied with a smile. "Don't worry, Candida."

She tried to smile back at him, but her eyes were troubled.

"Lunch will be ready in a moment," Adrian continued, looking at the grandfather clock. "I suppose they will stay, but I hope they will leave afterwards."

"I hope so too," Candida said, thinking of what they had planned for the afternoon.

Her hopes were, however, to be dashed. At luncheon Lais, who had seated herself as if by right on Lord Manville's right, announced the plans they had made before their arrival.

"It was Foxy's idea," she said, "that we should have a competition to see who can ride the best. And what do you think? He has offered one hundred guineas as the prize."

"That's right," Sir Tresham's voice boomed from the other end of the table, "a hundred guineas, Manville! Are you prepared to match it?"

Lord Manville looked at him coldly.

"As the competition is to take place on my property, I feel that would hardly be appropriate," he replied. "My prize will be two hundred guineas."

There was a little gasp and several "Pretty Horsebreakers" clapped their hands. For a moment Sir Tresham's eyes narrowed. He looked truculent and Candida guessed he was the type of man who would hate to be bettered at anything. Then he smiled.

"I'll have a side wager with you, Manville, that my choice will beat yours, whoever it may be."

"What stakes are you suggesting for that?" Lord Manville enquired, and there was no mistaking the distaste in his expression and his voice.

"Let us make it worthwhile," Sir Tresham suggested, and the under-current of rivalry in his tone was very apparent. "Why not five hundred guineas? Or is that too expensive for you?"

"On the contrary," Lord Manville answered coldly, "I am surprised you are so moderate. May I ask who you are selecting as the lady of your choice?"

"But certainly," Sir Tresham replied. "Who else but Lais."

There was a little gasp round the table. It was quite obvious Sir Tresham meant to be provocative. The eyes of the two men met, and Candida saw that, while there was an expression of defiance on Sir Tresham's face, Lord Manville gave no indication of what he might be feeling, or if indeed he had registered the full impact of the insult.

"In which case," he said coolly after a moment's pause, "my choice will be Candida."

Again there was a little flutter of surprise, and Candida realised that the whole table had turned to look at her. Just for a moment she felt a sudden panic creep over her, then she realised that it was not she that Lord Manville was backing but Pegasus. Pegasus would show them all what a horse could do!

"I declare it is too bad," Lais cried, "that Foxy should choose me. I meant to ride for you, Silvanus, I have even brought Firefly with me."

"I wonder who arranged that," Lord Manville said, one of his most cynical smiles just lifting the corners of his mouth.

"There is something behind all this," Candida thought to herself.

She felt as if it was all part of a play, that it had all been planned. Who was Lais, who was so familiar with Lord Manville and who seemed to have a special place by his side? And why should Sir Tresham Foxleigh be behaving in what was obviously, even to someone as ignorant and uninformed as herself, a manner which was both aggressive and rude?

Lord Manville had said he disliked Sir Tresham, but it appeared that Sir Tresham had an even deeper distaste for Lord Manville. It was all very bewildering, and then beneath the table she felt Adrian's hand touch her reassuringly.

"Do not worry," he said almost beneath his breath, "they are old enemies."

There were so many questions she wanted to ask, but it was impossible. Chattering and laughing, the ladies rose from the table and she heard Lais say to Lord Manville:

"We will go and change. Foxy has seen to everything, and we are convinced you will wish us to stay for dinner. We could dance and gamble afterwards. That would be fun, would it not?"

"Have I any say in the matter?" Lord Manville enquired.

Lais, her red lips inviting, bent forward to whisper something in his ear. Suddenly Candida felt as though the whole room had gone dark and she was alone.

She followed the chattering throng of "Pretty-Horse-breakers" out of the Dining Room, across the marble Hall, and started up the Grand Staircase. Then, when one of the women would have spoken to her, she fled, holding up the skirt of her gown to run helter-skelter up the rest of the stairs into her own bedroom.

What she was escaping from or why, she had no idea. She only knew that everything had changed—the happiness had gone, the feeling of being almost at home at Manville Park had vanished. She was alone, utterly alone in a strange place with strange people she did not understand. What was wrong? She could not find an explanation; she only knew she was desperately unhappy.

There came a knock at the door. Candida felt herself stiffen.

"Who is it?"

"It is I, Miss," answered her maid.

"Come in," Candida said.

The girl came into the room, closing the door behind her.

"I understand, Miss, you are changing into riding things."

"No, I am not riding," Candida replied—then she remembered the bet.

How could she let Lord Manville down, how could she refuse to ride Pegasus? For if she did not ride, would he not lose five hundred guineas to that odious Sir Tresham Foxleigh?

"No, no," she said quickly, "give me my riding-habit."

She must go through with it, there was nothing else she could do. At least Pegasus would show them that all their horses were inferior to him.

She would not think about Lais with her lovely face and slanting eyes; she would not think about her relationship with Lord Manville, whatever it might be; she would not think about Sir Tresham Foxleigh with his horrible, insinuating smile. She would think only of Pegasus, who was a king amongst horses.

It was only when she was actually mounted on Pegasus and moving down with the others towards the outdoor Riding School that Candida realised she was wearing a habit she had never worn before.

Of periwinkle-blue it made her skin seem very white, her hair almost like flames of fire. The little velvet hat which went with it had an ostrich feather of the same colour which curled under her chin.

She knew that she looked elegant, and she would not have been a woman if she had not been glad that she need not feel ashamed of her appearance amongst the colourful and expensive habits of the other women. Then she saw Lais, and was no longer satisfied with herself.

Lais was wearing a scarlet habit frogged with black braid and a high top-hat trimmed with a scarlet veil. She looked not only incredibly smart but extremely seductive. She was riding Firefly beside Lord Manville, and only Candida noticed the little movement beneath her skirt which meant that even at the walk she was using her spur on Firefly.

"I hate her!" Candida whispered to herself. "I hate her for her viciousness to that poor horse!" But she knew there were other reasons for her hatred.

Sir Tresham Foxleigh appeared to have planned the whole competition down to the last detail. Each lady was to ride in turn, and the gentlemen could lay their bets with one another or with him.

"I am prepared to challenge the field," he said grandiosely.

Then last of all there would be a competition between

the rider of his choice and the rider of Lord Manville's. As he had it all cut and dried, there were no protests or arguments.

Dora's horse was playing up and so she insisted on going first over the jumps, using, Candida noticed, not only her whip with quite unnecessary severity, but at the same time thrusting in her heel with its long, pointed spur. Candida had got a glimpse of it as Dora walked up the steps of the mounting-block, and the mere sight of that long, vicious point had upset her.

The Duke of Dorset was backing Dora against Phyllis, who was the next rider. He collected two hundred guineas, and Phyllis's sponsor shrugged his shoulders good-humouredly and paid without a murmur.

Correspondingly large bets were placed on Fanny, on Mary Ann, Laurette and Nelly, and then finally, almost too quickly it seemed to Candida, the moment came when Lais, after a whisper aside with Lord Manville, took Firefly to the starting point.

There were ten fences, all quite high, and then the water-splash, which consisted of a blind hedge with quite a wide ditch at the other side. The horse, not knowing it was there, had to stretch out in mid-air if he was to miss the water.

Nelly had already had a refusal, punished her horse severely and forced him to take the jump again. He had, however, misjudged the distance and his hind legs splashed water over himself and his rider.

Nelly's sponsor lost two hundred and fifty guineas on this, and Nelly was looking sullen and disagreeable as she rode back, making her horse pay dearly for his obstinacy with her armed heel.

Lais was very confident, and there was no doubt that she was an extremely fine horse-woman. Firefly was also a very good horse. Her timing was perfect; Firefly seemed faultless in the way he took every fence and cleared the water-splash.

Then, when Lais had finished, instead of riding off, she took Firefly round the center of the School, making him walk slowly, high-stepping with a precision and a grace which drew exclamations from everyone watching.

"That horse is unbeatable," Sir Tresham declared loudly, "and so is its rider. Do you not agree, Manville?"

143

"The competition is not yet ended," Lord Manville answered coldly.

There was a fresh burst of applause as Lais came from the enclosure to join them.

"Bravo!"

"Well done!"

"Are you pleased with me?" Lais asked, but she looked as she spoke not at Sir Tresham but at Lord Manville.

He looked away from her.

"Now, Candida," he said, "let us see what Pegasus can do."

It was his asking for Pegasus' prowess, not her own, Candida thought, which made it easier than it otherwise might have been. She was no longer afraid for them to see her ride, no longer shy of those strange women watching her or even of Sir Tresham Foxleigh.

"Steady, boy," she said softly to Pegasus, "do not rush it."

There was no need to tell Pegasus what was expected of him. He took every fence with a foot to spare, and treated the water-splash with contempt. Round he went, not once but twice, and then Candida took him into the middle of the School, even as Lais had done. She walked him round high-stepping, just to show Firefly that what he could do, Pegasus could do better.

Then Pegasus did all the tricks she had shown Major Hooper in that field at Potters Bar, and half a dozen more besides. He knelt down on his front legs, he sat down, he waltzed, he walked, he did everything almost, it seemed, without a touch of the reins or heel, clearly enjoying every moment, with the grace and expertise of an animal that has been taught not by cruelty but by love.

When finally he bowed low, his head right, to the left and to the centre, there was no one watching who did not cry out spontaneously at the sheer brilliance of the performance.

Candida trotted slowly towards the assembled throng. She had eyes only for one person, and when she saw the admiration and satisfaction in Lord Manville's expression, she knew it was all she had asked for and more.

"Well done!"

He spoke softly above the cries of the other people who now were clustering round Candida asking questions, exclaiming with delight.

"What a wonderful horse!"

"Where did it come from?"

"How do you teach him to do those things?"

"Can you show us how it is done?"

Then suddenly, before she could answer, there was Lais, her voice shrill above the others.

"I will ride him, let me show what he will do for me."

Without waiting for a reply, Lais dismounted from Firefly and a groom ran to his head. She came up to Candida, forcing her way through the others to stand at Pegasus' side.

"I will ride him," she said again. "Dismount and I will show you some new tricks."

"No," Candida answered softly.

"You cannot say no," Lais protested, "he is not your horse."

She turned towards Lord Manville.

"You have always told me, Silvanus, that any horse in your stable was mine. Well now, you must keep your promise. Let me ride this one and I will show you something worth seeing."

"No," Candida said again, and now her hands tightened on the reins.

Pegasus felt that something was wrong and he started to fidget a little, making the spectators move away from him. Lais however stood her ground.

"Get down," she said furiously, 'you are not going to prevent me from riding one of His Lordship's horses, not you or anyone else. You may think you are a horse-breaker, but you are inexperienced. This horse will work better under me, I assure you. So give him to me."

She saw the defiance in Candida's face, and almost instinctively she raised her whip. Whether it was to hit Candida or Pegasus, there was no knowing, because, with a little cry of protest, Candida moved. She rode Pegasus forward, forcing Lais out of the way, and then, before anyone could move or speak, she was gone, and leaping a post and rails was riding wildly across the parkland. Urging Pegasus to a full gallop, she had almost vanished between the trees before anyone realised what was happening.

She thought she heard someone call her name, she had the idea it was Lord Manville's voice, but she had only one desire, one thought, and that was to save Pegasus, to prevent him coming under the spur of Lais—a woman she loathed with every nerve in her body.

9

Candida had galloped nearly a mile when from behind her she heard a voice calling. She turned her head again and saw that the gap between herself and Lord Manville had now narrowed, but he was still some distance away.

Nevertheless she could hear him, and though she tried not to listen his cry was insistent.

"Stop—Candida—it is dangerous—you will kill yourself—and—Pegasus!"

It was the last two words which made Candida reluctantly, but because she dare not disobey, draw in the reins. It was quite difficult to stop Pegasus; however finally she drew him to a standstill and turned defiantly, but at the same time apprehensively, to face Lord Manville. He came nearer, slowing Thunder down from a gallop to a trot, and finally drew level with her.

"There are gravel pits just ahead," he warned her. "They are not easy to see, and if you fell into them there would be no hope for either of you."

He spoke in quiet tones, but, as he faced her, Candida replied hotly:

"I would rather we were both dead than that Pegasus should be ridden by that fiend! She is cruel, cruel, do you hear me? She spurs, not merely to control the horse, but because it gives her positive pleasure!"

"Listen Candida . . ." Lord Manville began, only to be silenced as Candida continued, her eyes blazing, her whole body trembling with the intensity of her feelings:

"I have seen Firefly when she has sent him back to the stables, not for the first time, but for the third and fourth, his left flank bady spur-galled! I have helped poultice him and hated the rider who should treat any horse in such a brutal manner."

"I understand . . ." Lord Manville began again—but his words were to be swept away once more as Candida went on:

"It may seem amusing to you—and gentlemen like you—to applaud the women who ride effectively and show off to advantage in the Park or in Riding Schools. But have you ever thought of the suffering that is caused by these horse-breakers who rely on their spur to punish an animal until he obeys them because he is afraid? Who even when he does what is faultless continues to get the spur without reason. It is cruel, cruel I tell you! I will have no part in it!"

Candida paused a moment and then she added, and her voice was low and broken:

"I could not even bear to think of Pegasus being subjected to treatment like that."

Her anger was now spent and she was very near to tears. Her head dropped forward and her hair, loosened from its chignon, fell in a great golden wave on her shoulders.

"I swear to you," Lord Manville said quietly, "that Lais will never ride Pegasus."

Candida raised her face.

"Nor any woman like her?" she asked.

"Nor any woman like her," he repeated.

He saw her relief show itself in her face, and now that the tension was gone it seemed as if she might collapse in the saddle.

"It is very hot," Lord Manville said. "Let us give our horses a rest and sit in the shade."

He pointed to where, about fifty yards to their right, was a small silver birch wood. The young green of the leaves was vivid in the sunshine, which strove to pierce through to the banks of primroses and violets flowering beneath.

Without a word Candida moved in the direction in which Lord Manville had pointed. When she reached the wood she slipped from the saddle, caught her reins over the pommel, patted Pegasus and walked into the shade of the trees. Lord Manville, having also dismounted, wondered whether he dare let Thunder free.

There was the chance he might not catch him again. But he counted on the two horses staying together, and knotting his reins so that they would not get entangled in Thunder's feet he followed Candida.

The wood grew on a slope, and there was a bank beneath the trees exactly the right height on which to sit. Mauve and white violets were peeping from beneath their rounded leaves, and Candida sat down gently as though she hated to hurt them.

Then, because she was warm, she slipped off her coat and threw it on the ground at her feet.

She was wearing a white lawn blouse inset with lace, and she raised her arms instinctively towards her hair. She had long since lost her hat, and with her gesture the last remaining hairpins fell from her chignon and her hair tumbled loose over her shoulders, reaching to below her waist.

Nervously she would have swept it into some sort of order, but Lord Manville was beside her and caught her hands.

"Don't," he said insistently, "don't touch your hair! If you only knew how much I have wanted to see it like this."

She looked at him in surprise, while the touch of his fingers made her quiver in an unaccountable manner.

"I have to apologize," she began, the fire gone from her tone; she showed instead an anxious humility which was infinitely pathetic.

"No, you did what was right," he answered. "It is I who should apologize for being so thoughtless."

"Then you understand what I feel about Pegasus?" Candida asked.

"Of course," he answered. "I would not wish Thunder or any of my horses to be treated in such a way. I have always believed that a spur is essential in a side-saddle, but you have convinced me it can be unnecessary."

A smile lit her face, then she was conscious he was still holding her hands and that he was very near her. Her fingers moved beneath his.

"I must tidy myself," she murmured.

"Why?" he asked. "Have you any idea how lovely you look?"

There was something in his voice which made her

heart turn over in her breast, and it was impossible for her to move.

"Candida!" Lord Manville asked hoarsely. "Candida —what has happened to us?"

She could not reply, and after a moment he said:

"Will you not look at me? It cannot be that you are afraid of me."

"N-not . . . really," she whispered, and forced herself to turn her head and look into his eyes.

His face was very close and drawing nearer still he put his arm round her shoulders. He felt her tremble, then his lips were on hers. He could not have believed that a woman's lips could be so soft, so sweet, so yielding, until, with what was almost a little cry, she turned her head away.

"Why do you turn away from me?" he asked, and his voice was deeply moved. "Can it be that you are still angry with me?"

"No," she whispered, "it is not . . . that."

"Then what?" he asked. "You cannot still be afraid of me."

She shook her head and murmured:

"Not of . . . you but . . . of myself . . . I think."

"But why, my darling?" he asked. "I do not understand."

"You . . . make me feel . . . strange," she stammered. "I cannot explain it . . . it is just that when I am . . . close to you . . . like this I feel as if I cannot . . . breathe, and yet . . . it is very . . . wonderful."

"Oh, my sweet!"

He took her hand and covered it in kisses.

"That you should say such a thing to me touches me more than I can express. Do you not realise, my dearest, that this was meant to happen? I think I knew it would when you stood on the steps—in your pink gown— looking so small, so absurdly young."

"I was . . . afraid," Candida said.

"I knew you were," he answered. "Your eyes are very expressive, Candida, and yet when I told you that I wanted you to amuse Adrian you looked relieved. I cannot tell you how often that has worried me. Tell me why?"

"You are so . . . grand, so . . . important," Candida replied, "I was afraid of . . . failing . . . you."

"Oh, my dearest dear," he said, a smile on his lips, "was there anyone so entrancing, so captivating as you? Candida, we shall be so happy together, there is so much I want to show you, so much I want to teach you. When did you first know you loved me? Tell me, I must know!"

There was a masterfulness about him which was irresistible.

"I do not think I realised it until . . . this very moment," Candida replied, "it was just that I always . . . wanted to be with . . . you. A room seemed . . . empty when you were not . . . there, and the house . . . very quiet."

Lord Manville gave a smile of utter happiness. Then, holding her closer to him, he lifted her little chin in his free hand and turned her face up to his. This time she did not turn away. The gentleness of his kiss grew stronger and more possessive, and yet she was not afraid.

She felt something awake within her, a flame which seemed to burn through her body so that she was conscious only of his lips, the closeness of him, and the happiness which was brighter than sunshine.

She felt as though the songs of the birds were caught up into a song of beauty and glory which carried them both towards the sky, and now she trembled not with fear but with ecstasy because the wonder and the beauty of it was almost too great to be borne.

How long they sat there Candida had no idea, but at length they drew apart and she said:

"You must . . . return . . . they will wonder what has . . . happened . . . to you."

"And you will come with me?" he asked, and she knew that never in her life had she seen a man look so happy.

"Of course I will . . . if you want me."

"If I want you!" he said in a low voice, and taking her hands he turned the palms upwards and kissed them, first one and then the other. "You hold my heart in those little hands. Come, darling, we must be brave and face the music. What does it matter?"

"They will stay for dinner?" Candida asked in a low voice.

"I am afraid so," he answered. "I could not refuse the hospitality they ask—as it is all arranged. They will leave afterwards and then we shall be alone—alone as we have been before—only it will be different."

"Very . . . different," Candida said softly.

She searched amongst the violets and found enough hairpins to arrange her hair. Lord Manville helped her into her coat, kissing her cheek as he did so, then turning her round once again to seek her mouth.

"This is our wood," he said. "I never knew before that I had an enchanted place on my Estate. Is it real or are you a witch, Candida, who has merely made me believe that this is the most wonderful and magical wood in the whole world?"

Candida looked back at the bank on which they had sat, at the shafts of sunshine piercing through between the trees, the dark blue of the shadows where the sun did not penetrate, the gold of the primroses and the purple and white of the violets.

"Our enchanted wood," she said softly, "our very own."

He lifted her face once again to his.

"You go to my head, Candida," he said, "I feel intoxicated with your beauty, your sweetness and the touch of your lips. I am like a man who has drunk the nectar of the gods and can never again be quite normal."

"I feel like that . . . too," Candida whispered, and hand in hand they went from the wood to find the horses.

Pegasus came the moment that Candida called him, and though Thunder would not come obediently to the command, he at least stood still until Lord Manville reached him. They rode back together slowly side by side. It was almost as if they could not bear to go back into the world and must delay every passing minute.

At length Manville Park stood in front of them, and as they saw the grooms waiting outside the front door Candida said quickly:

"I shall go to my room."

"Come down early for dinner," Lord Manville

begged. "I must have a word with you alone before the others join us."

"I will try," she promised.

But when she reached her bedroom it was to find it was far later than she thought. By the time she had had her bath and her maid had arranged her hair, she knew there would be little time for her and Lord Manville to be alone.

Although she was consumed with an impatience to be with him again, she wanted to look her best.

She took from the wardrobe the gown she liked the most of all those that Mrs. Clinton had bought for her. It was white, and the great hooped skirt was trimmed with folds of soft chiffon caught with tiny bunches of snowdrops.

It seemed to Candida it could not be more appropriate; the flowers, symbolic of the spring, must remind Lord Manville, when he looked at the dress, of their enchanted wood. There were snowdrops too in a bunch between her breasts hidden in the soft chiffon fichu which only partially veiled her shoulders.

"You do look lovely, Miss," her maid exclaimed when she had finished dressing her, "almost like a bride!"

Candida smiled as she looked at her own reflection in the mirror. Soon they would all know, she thought, but for the moment she must say nothing.

"Thank you," she said softly.

"You are the most beautiful young lady who has ever stayed here," the maid went on, "and it is not often there is anyone as kind and as nice to us as you are."

"Manville Park is a very lovely place," Candida said. "Nothing and nobody should ever spoil that loveliness."

She was thinking of Lais as she spoke. Tonight, she thought, was the last time she need ever see that cruel, horrible woman, and she felt that she would have been afraid to go downstairs and face her had she not known that Lord Manville was there and that they loved one another.

She could hardly realise now what had happened that afternoon. He had held her in his arms and he had kissed her. She often wondered what it was like to be kissed by a man, and now she knew. She remembered how his lips had touched hers at first gently, and then become stronger and more possessive.

It was as if he drew her heart between her lips and took it into his keeping. And that, she thought, was exactly what he had done because she had given him her heart irretrievably. It was his and she was a part of him; they belonged, one person for ever.

Now she knew what her Mother must have felt, and why nothing had mattered except that she should marry her Father and they should be together. This was how they loved each other, and Candida knew that if she had to make the same choice as her Mother, she too would leave her home, leave behind everything that was familiar, and go with Lord Manville, penniless and emptyhanded, wherever he might lead her.

What was money or position compared with the ecstasy which made her tremble when he touched her, compared with that look in his eyes and that note in her voice which made her heart turn over?

"I love him! I love him!" she whispered to herself, and thought as she looked in the mirror that she too was transfigured.

The look of anxiety and uncertainty which had been on her face ever since her Father had died had gone. Instead she looked like someone who had suddenly come alive, with her lips parted, her eyes shining. She almost found it hard to recognise herself, and she knew this was what love could do for a woman.

"There, Miss, you are ready," her maid said, fastening the last hook at the back of the tight bodice.

"Thank you," Candida said.

"Oh, one minute, Miss," the maid exclaimed. "I think there are two bunches of snowdrops to go in your hair."

"Indeed there are," Candida replied, "I had forgotten."

"I found them just now with the shoes that match the gown," the maid said. "Let me fix them on either side of the chignon, they will look very beautiful there."

"Yes, please do," Candida agreed, "but hurry, it is getting late."

A few minutes later she sped from her room and she

saw with dismay that it was nearly the hour for dinner and she was unlikely to find Lord Manville alone.

Yet she was lucky. When she entered the Drawing Room where she guessed they would assemble before the meal, he was there waiting for her, looking incredibly handsome in his evening clothes, his white shirt front ornamented only with two enormous black pearl studs set with diamonds.

She stood for a moment in the doorway and then she ran towards him. It seemed to him as she approached that he had never seen a woman's face so warm, so lovely and alive. He caught her in his arms.

"Oh, my darling," he said, "I thought you were never coming. Every moment seemed an eternity while I waited."

"I hurried," Candida explained, "but I wanted to look my best for you."

"You look beautiful," he said, his eyes on her lips, "so beautiful that I want to kiss you."

"No, no," she demurred. "Be careful, someone might come in."

"Are you so shy of what they might think?" he enquired teasingly.

"No, it is not that," she said quickly, "it is just that I would not have anyone know about us . . . for the moment."

He smiled as one might smile at a child.

"It shall be our secret," he promised.

"Only until they have all gone," Candida said. "I could not bear those people to . . . chatter and laugh about . . . our love."

"I understand," he said.

"And another thing I was thinking," Candida went on, "and please do not think it very stupid of me, but could we . . . could we be married very, very quietly . . . in some little church without a crowd . . . without people staring . . . at us?"

Even as she spoke she felt him stiffen, and instinctively she knew she had said something wrong. She looked up into his eyes, and what she saw there made her feel as if an icy hand clutched at her heart.

"Oh, here you are, Silvanus!" a gay voice cried from

155

the door. "Where have you been hiding yourself? I declare you are the worst host in England."

It was Lais who came sweeping across the floor, followed by several of her friends. She was too clever to make a scene, but there was no doubt at all that the look she gave Candida was one of hatred, even while her lips smiled and her voice belied the rancour she was feeling.

Candida noticed nothing. She had backed away from Lord Manville almost as if he had struck her, and she stood bemused and bewildered, hearing neither the clatter of voices nor the compliments that were being paid to her by the gentlemen who had now joined them.

She was conscious only of a dark cloud which had descended upon her, and a constriction within herself, for which she could not find an explanation.

Then Adrian was beside her, talking to her eagerly, telling her how he had spent the afternoon alone and what poetry he had composed. She forced herself to listen to him, and it seemed as though only he spoke in English while everyone else conversed in a foreign language which she did not understand.

"Tell me about it," she heard herself say, and thought her voice sounded strange, like the voice of someone lost in a fog.

Thankfully she found Adrian beside her at dinner.

"Are you ill?" he asked her once. "You look a bit strange, and you are eating nothing."

"I am not hungry," Candida answered. "Go on telling me about your poem."

"It suddenly came to me," Adrian said, "and I knew I had to put it down on paper. That was why I sneaked away after lunch. You were all right, were you not?"

"Yes, I was all right," Candida said.

Was what had happened in the enchanted wood really true, or had she dreamt it all? What was happening now? She wanted to cry out, to beg Lord Manville to come to her through the dark cloud which seemed almost to obscure him from her view.

Yet she could see him sitting at the end of the table, a pretty woman on either side of him, laughing, talking, their voices getting louder and louder.

The whole party seemed to make more and more

noise. She did not realise the men were drinking heavily; that the women were becoming more abandoned in their laughter; that the jokes were getting broader and more lewd. She could not hear most of what was said, and when she did she did not understand it.

Adrian was still talking, and he was like a life-line thrown to her when she was drowning. She could make herself hold on to what he was saying, try to make it seem sense, try to find an answer.

She must have been reasonably successful, and as they rose from the table she managed to say:

"Do you think I can go to bed?"

"Not yet," he advised. "It would annoy my Guardian if you slipped away too soon. Wait and I will tell you when you can go."

"Please do that," Candida begged.

She thought the ladies would leave alone, as was usual, but she heard Lais cry:

"You are not all going to stay here and get foxed. The band is already tuning up, I can hear it. There is money to be won on the tables. Come, Silvanus, we will not leave you to your port, bring it with you. I hope there is plenty of champagne for us poor, frail women! I have a feeling we shall need it."

The men had laughed and followed the ladies into the Drawing Room. While they were at dinner part of the carpet had been turned back and there was a six-piece orchestra playing one of the latest and wildest polkas.

"Do you want to dance?" Candida heard Adrian ask at her side.

She could not help looking towards Lord Manville, but Lais had her hand on his shoulder and his arm was on her waist.

"No," she murmured.

"Then let us sit quietly on the sofa," Adrian suggested. "I have no money for gaming, and I dislike these noisy, jumpy dances."

"So do I," Candida answered, feeling a sudden revulsion against the swinging crinolines, the flushed faces and the noisy shouts of those taking the floor.

It seemed as though Sir Tresham Foxleigh was avoiding her. He made no effort to speak to her before dinner, and she had noticed that he deliberately walked round the other side of the table when they entered the Dining Room as though he did not even wish to be beside her.

She was thankful because she felt she could not have endured the repulsiveness of him had he sought her company.

She sat for a while on the sofa at Adrian's side, seeing that after the first dance Lord Manville had moved from the dance floor towards one of the gaming tables where some of his guests were flinging down piles of golden guineas as though they were mere halfpennies.

"Surely I can go now?" Candida asked.

"You will annoy him," Adrian said warningly.

"It is already quite late," she said despairingly, "dinner took hours."

"I know, it always does on these occasions," Adrian replied. "They all wanted to eat and drink themselves stupid. I must say it is something that has never amused me."

"Do you realise it is nearly one o'clock?" Candida asked, looking at the clock over the mantelpiece. "How long do parties of this sort last?"

"Until three or four in the morning, I expect," Adrian said mournfully.

"I cannot bear it! I cannot!" Candida cried.

As she spoke she saw Lais come from the dance floor where she had been waltzing with Sir Tresham Foxleigh and walk across the room to Lord Manville.

She stood on tip-toe to whisper in his ear, and then drew him insistently towards one of the French windows which gave onto the garden. He seemed reluctant to go with her, but she was pulling him by the arm, persuading him. Candida got to her feet.

"I am going to bed!" She knew that she had reached breaking-point.

"I will do the same in a minute," Adrian said, "it would not be wise for us to be seen leaving together. You know what these people are like."

Candida did not understand what he meant, or care. She only had one desire, and that was to get away, to be by herself. She passed through the Drawing Room door, and as she did so she heard a hated voice beside her.

"Miss Candida, may I crave your indulgence?"

"No," she answered quickly, feeling that to talk to Sir Tresham at this moment would be the final blow in an evening of misery.

"Please," he pleaded, "I have a favour to ask you. I have just been told by my coachman that one of my horses is in considerable pain. He does not know if it is a strained fetlock, or what it might be. Would it be asking too much for you to look at the animal?"

"No, no, I . . . cannot," Candida answered, hardly realising what she was saying.

"That is unlike you, Miss Candida," Sir Treshman protested. "As I have said, the animal is in pain, and though the man is experienced he does not know what to do. I would not wish to inconvenience His Lordship by asking for a replacement from his stable if it can possibly be avoided. Nevertheless it would be cruelty to drive the animal back to The Towers if it is not in a fit state to travel."

"No, that would be . . . wrong," Candida agreed.

"Then please help me," Sir Tresham begged. "It will not take you a minute. The carriage is already waiting outside the front door as I intended to leave early."

"It is outside?" Candida repeated almost stupidly, trying to understand what had been said, trying to concentrate, but longing only to get away.

"The horse I'm talking about is in the courtyard," Sir Tresham told her.

His hand was on her arm, drawing her across the marble floor towards the front door.

"I know you would not wish an animal to be in pain," he went on, "not if it was easy to prevent. Say you will come and see this animal. I assure you it is one of the best in my stable."

"Very well, I will come," Candida consented.

It will only take a few seconds, she thought, and wondered what could be wrong with a horse that its own coachman could not diagnose.

The carriage was standing outside the front door. It was a closed barouche drawn by a pair, with the coachman and footman on the box. Candida would have gone to the nearer horse, but Sir Treshman checked her.

"It is the animal on the off side," he said.

Candida, lifting her dress with both hands, walked round the back of the barouche out of sight of the front door. The footman had dismounted from the box and was holding open the door of the carriage as if he expected his master to be leaving.

Candida would have passed him by, but as she reached the open door Sir Tresham suddenly lifted her in his arms and threw her inside.

She gave a scream of horror and surprise, but even as she fell onto the cushioned seat, a hand came over her mouth, preventing her from screaming again. As she struggled fruitlessly, she heard the door slam and felt the carriage start up.

They were driving away, and though she fought against him with all her strength, it was some minutes before Sir Tresham took his hand from her mouth.

"What are you doing? How dare you!" she tried to say—and heard him laugh.

"You will learn, my pretty Lovebird," he said, "that I always get what I want. I wanted you, my dear, from the first moment I saw you, and by God I've got you!"

"You are mad," Candida cried, and bent forward to rap on the window. "Stop! Stop! Help!"

He laughed again.

"My servants will not listen to you. Indeed they cannot believe that any woman would not be charmed to be in my company."

"Where are you taking me?" Candida asked. "You must be crazed to behave like this! I will have nothing to do with you, you know that."

"You have little choice, my dear," he replied drily, "and now, let us cease this nonsense. I will be very generous to you, as I told you the first time we met. You attract me as I have seldom been attracted by a woman, and what I want—I have."

"Lord Manville will not permit this to happen to me," Candida retorted.

"It is unlikely that he will know of your departure until tomorrow morning," Sir Tresham said suavely, "and I have a feeling, my dear Candida, that His Lordship, having no partiality for me, will not be much interested in you when tomorrow comes."

There was a lantern in the carriage which made it possible for Candida to look at Sir Tresham Foxleigh. With a pathetic little effort at dignity she said:

"If you mean what I think you mean, I can only ask you as a gentleman to let me go. I dislike you; you repel me! Surely that is reason enough for you not to wish for my company."

"On the contrary," Sir Tresham said, "I find a too complaisant woman a bore. It will amuse me to break you, my dear, even as you break those fine horses you ride so elegantly. I like my women high-spirited, they are all the sweeter to the touch when I have taught them who is master."

As he spoke he put out his arm and drew Candida towards him. As he touched her she lost control, fighting and screaming, but knew even as she did so it was hopeless and she was utterly in his power. Slowly and relentlessly he drew her to him and, turning up her face to his, sought her lips. She turned her head from side to side, scratching at him and hearing her dress tear beneath his hands.

Then suddenly, as she realised how helpless she was, she thought she would lose consciousness. But like a ray of light a sudden thought came to her. She ceased to struggle, and as she felt his hand fumbling roughly at her breast she said weakly:

"I . . . am . . . about to . . . faint, could you . . . open the . . . window?"

"Why not?" he asked. "It's damn hot in here."

He loosened his hold on her for one second to bend towards the window at his side to lift the sash and let it down. As he did so Candida moved.

She seized the handle of the door on her side of the barouche, opened it and flung herself out. She heard Sir Tresham ejaculate an oath, felt him clutch at her crinoline which was half stuck in the doorway and heard it tear as the chiffon came away in his hands.

There was a sudden crash as she fell which knocked her almost senseless, and then she found herself rolling down a steep incline, rolling over and over, saved from serious injury to her legs by the mere ponderance of her skirts and hoop. Finally she was checked, caught in the branches of a rhododendron bush.

For a moment Candida lay stunned, unable to move, until she heard Sir Tresham's voice shouting at the coachmen and further on up the drive the horses being pulled to a standstill.

She knew then that she must move; for if she stayed where she was he would find her. Staggering to her feet she started to run between the shrubs, banging into trees, falling down not once but a dozen times, still in a panic of fear, desperately running, running, running . . .

Once she stopped and looked back. She saw lights and knew that Sir Tresham and his coachmen were searching for her. She heard his voice.

"Candida! Candida! Do not be a fool! Come back!"

He waited a moment to see if she would reply, and heard him snarl:

"Find her, you nit-wits. Damn it, the girl cannot be far. Spread out and search for her."

Candida waited no longer. She picked up the tattered remains of her skirts and ran as she had never run before. She was still among trees and shrubs, and the branches whipped across her cheeks, hurting and marking her skin, tearing at her hair and tumbling it over her shoulders. But still she ran on.

Suddenly the ground seemed to disappear beneath her feet and she fell headlong into a deep ditch.

For a moment she must have been unconscious, until as she opened her eyes she could see the stars in the sky and hear the rustle of dead leaves. She knew then she could go no further. Her heart was beating suffocatingly in her breast, her breath was coming wheezily between her lips, and her whole body was tense with fear.

She lay there listening. If he found her now she knew she had no strength to resist him. But there was only silence, and after a long while she scrambled to her feet and crawled out of the ditch.

In the far distance she thought in the pale light of a half moon she could see the drive. There were no lights on it, the horses and carriage had gone.

She sat down on the ground and put her head down on her knees. She was past crying, past everything but a kind of animal instinct to find shelter. She must get back to Manville Park.

Slowly, for her whole body was aching, she dragged herself from the bushes and then saw the lights of the house ahead of her. She had run, she thought, almost halfway across the Park in front of the house. It would be quicker to approach from the other drive rather than by the one on which Sir Tresham had abducted her.

Even so it was quite a long way. But at least there, whatever else awaited her, she would be safe from Sir Tresham. The very thought of him gave some impetus to her feet, but she was too weak to move quickly.

After walking only a very little way she sat down and stared at the house. It was then that the thought of Lord Manville made her aware that the only thing that mattered was to find him again. Long ago—was it only this afternoon?—he had held her in his arms.

She thought of all he had said to her, of his lips on hers, and she knew that her happiness at dinner and during the evening had been absurd. Had he not waited for her in the Library? Had he not said that every minute he waited had been like an eternity?

"I must get to him," she told herself, and yet she was tempted to sit and remember, to feel again that wild ecstasy which had been theirs in their enchanted wood.

A chill wind blowing from the lake made her suddenly shiver. She knew it would be madness to stay where she was in case she fell asleep. She must get back.

Slowly, wearily, conscious that every bruise and wound in her body was beginning to hurt, she struggled to her feet, only to find that one of her slippers was missing.

10

Lord Manville found himself being dragged by Lais toward the French window.

"Do come and look," she begged, "I am sure there is a robber trying to get into the house."

"Nonsense!" Lord Manville declared. "No burglar would attempt to enter a house as brilliantly lit and as full of people as this one."

"But I saw the man, I tell you," Lais said. "He appeared very strange and distinctly dangerous!"

Good-humouredly Lord Manville allowed himself to be dragged towards the window. Outside the night was warm and the sky was brilliant with stars. It was, however, difficult to see much of the garden because of the lights shining onto the terrace from the uncurtained windows.

"He was down there," Lais said, running to the balustrade and pointing towards some large shrubs on the other side of the rose garden.

"I cannot see anyone," Lord Manville protested.

"He is not likely to be waiting there for you to catch him," Lais replied, moving down the stone steps. "Do come and search for him, Silvanus. I swear I am afraid for your valuable silver."

"You are imagining things," Lord Manville replied, but he followed her down the stone steps until they reached the centre of the rose garden where there was a sun-dial. Lord Manville looked about him.

"Now, where is your ferocious intruder?" he enquired.

"He must have run away," Lais suggested, "but it is of no importance. Now at last I have you to myself."

"Is that your excuse for bringing me here?" Lord Manville enquired.

"No, no, I really saw someone," Lais answered. "But, Silvanus—it is a wonderful night."

As she spoke she raised her arms to place them round Lord Manville's neck, but he did not draw her close to him. Instead he said quietly:

"I also want to talk to you, Lais, although I would not have chosen this particular moment."

"Must we talk?" she murmured. "Kiss me, Silvanus, it is a long time since I have felt your lips."

Lord Manville put up his hands as though he would remove Lais's arms from his neck, and as he did so a voice in the darkness cried:

"It appears we are very much *de trop!*"

Lais and Lord Manville turned their heads to see coming towards them Captain Willoughby with Dora on his arm. They both looked somewhat dishevelled. Dora's chignon was untidy and her décolleté considerably disarranged. The erstwhile elegance of Captain Willoughby's pointed collar and wide neck-band was now a crumpled disaster.

"Yes, you are interrupting us," Lais answered coldly, "you should have more tact."

"Then we will withdraw immediately to the house," Captain Willoughby said with a little bow. "We know when we are not wanted."

"We will come with you," Lord Manville said firmly. "I have an overwhelming desire to match my skill at cards against yours, Willoughby."

"It is quite a time since we have played together, and last time, if I remember rightly, you won," Captain Willoughby replied. "So that does not make me particularly keen to encounter you once again."

"How do you know that this evening your luck has not changed?" Lord Manville enquired.

"Perhaps you are right," Captain Willoughby said with a glance at Dora, "although, of course, there is the old adage 'lucky in love, unlucky at cards'."

Dora gave a shrill laugh which seemed to jar on Lord Manville, because he frowned and moved a little quickly towards the house. Lais's hand was on his arm.

"No, wait, Silvanus, I wish to talk to you."

"Not now," he said sharply, "I have to play host to my guests. Surely even you can understand that."

There was a sharpness in his tone which made Lais's eyes narrow for a moment and her mouth tighten ominously. She had a quick temper and Lord Manville was driving her hard. But she was too clever to show her annoyance, and when they went back into the Salon she held out her hand prettily saying:

"Be my banker, please; you and Captain Willoughby are not the only people who wish to test their luck this evening."

Lord Manville gave her what guineas he carried in his vest pocket and turned away. Looking around the room he saw that Candida was no longer there and thought she would have retired to bed. He had known she was unhappy at dinner and he was well aware she had seemed bewildered amongst the noise and jokes of the raffish crowd.

He wished now he had gone straight to her side, as he had desired to do, when they left the Dining Room, but he had been half afraid that if he singled her out too obviously Lais would make a scene. He knew he had to dismiss his mistress; but it was never a pleasant task, and he did not think that this was the right time or place to do it.

"Come on, Manville, I'm waiting for you!" Captain Willoughby called from one of the gaming-tables.

It was with a sense of relief that he need no longer perplex his mind with the whims of females that Lord Manville picked up the cards.

To his surprise after he had been playing a very short while, Lais came to tell him that the party was breaking up. Already several carriages had left carrying the Duke of Dorset, the officers in the Household Cavalry, Nellie, Laurette, Phyllis, Fanny and Mary Ann.

"They told me to say good-night to you," Lais said, "since they did not like to disturb your game in case it should ruin your luck."

"He certainly has the luck of the devil," Captain Willoughby exclaimed ruefully. "That's nearly a thousand guineas I owe you, Manville!"

"Then it is certainly time for me to stop playing,"

Lord Manville said with a smile. "But you shall have your revenge another time."

"I bear you no grudge," Captain Willoughby said. "It has been an amusing day. Shall I see you in London this week?"

"I am not yet certain of my plans," Lord Manville answered vaguely.

"Silvanus!" Lais expostulated.

But already Lord Manville had left the Salon, going out into the Hall in time to hear a carriage roll away down the drive.

"So, I am left to escort two charmers, am I?" Captain Willoughby enquired as a footman helped him into his coat, and Lais and Dora arrayed themselves in capes trimmed with marabou. "You should accompany us, Manville."

"No thank you," Lord Manville replied. "I have not entered The Towers since Foxleigh bought it eight years ago, and I have no intention of doing so."

"I do not blame you," Captain Willoughby said with a twinkle in his eye. "Good-night, and thank you once again."

"Good-night," Lord Manville replied.

He held out his hand to Dora, but she flung her arms round his neck and kissed him on both cheeks.

"It has been a wonderful day," she gushed, "I enjoyed every moment. But I wish I had won the contest. And poor Lais lost two hundred guineas!"

"I will make it up to her," Lord Manville said coldly. "Lais, I will send you the money tomorrow."

"I would rather you brought it yourself," she whispered, and now her arms were round his neck, her lips against his cheek.

She sought his mouth, but in some way she could not explain he was free of her. Then they were outside and he was helping Dora and Lais into Captain Willoughby's lightly sprung and very fast curricle.

"That's a good pair of horseflesh you have there," Lord Manville remarked.

"They ought to be," Captain Willoughby replied, "I paid enough for them."

He flicked the leader with his whip as he spoke, and the Curricle moved off with cries of farewell and the waving of hands. Lord Manville, with a sigh of relief, walked back into the house.

"You can shut up, John," he said to the footman on the door.

"Isn't Miss Candida coming back, Sir?"

Lord Manville, who had already reached the bottom of the stairs, turned back.

"Miss Candida?" he enquired. "Surely she retired some time ago."

"No, M'Lord, she went out about one o'clock with Sir Tresham Foxleigh."

Lord Manville's expression was incredulous.

"You are speaking of Miss Walcott who is staying here?"

"Yes, M'Lord."

"You are quite sure she has not returned?"

"No, M'Lord, I've been on duty ever since, I've not left the door."

"Miss Walcott went—quite—freely?" Lord Manville said, obviously choosing his words with care.

"Oh, yes, M'Lord," the footman answered. "I heard her say to Sir Tresham "Very well, I will come", and then they walked down the steps together."

"The carriage was outside?"

"Yes, M'Lord. I heard the door slam and they drove off."

There was an expression on Lord Manville's face which made the footman suddenly feel afraid.

"I hope I did right in telling you, M'Lord."

"You can go to bed," Lord Manville said harshly, "I will lock the door when the lady returns."

"Very good, M'Lord."

The footman scuttled away and Lord Manville stood where he had left him in the centre of the Hall. After a while he started to walk up and down.

The candles were guttering low and the shadows grew deeper. Still there was no sound of carriage wheels, only occasionally the noises of the night—the hooting of an owl, the barking of a fox very far away.

Lord Manville looked at the clock not once but a dozen times. It seemed incredible that minutes could pass so slowly, and then when it was nearly half past two he walked to the door.

With the lights behind him he stood at the top of the stone steps staring out into the darkness, scanning the emptiness of the drive—the one going east, over which a carriage would travel to reach The Towers.

It was then suddenly from the direction of the west drive that he heard a sound. He turned his head sharply and there below him on the gravel of the courtyard he saw a figure.

She was in the shadow of the house but there was no need for him to ask who it was, and he did not stop to wonder how she could have come so quietly that he had not heard her approach.

"So you have returned!" he said.

His voice, icy and contemptuous, seemed to cut through the darkness and he saw the figure who had been coming nearer to him stop uncertainly.

"I hope you have enjoyed yourself," he went on.

There was an acid cynicism in his words which sounded all the more bitter as he spoke in a low calculating tone.

"Have you been hiding with your friend Sir Tresham in the bushes? Or did he take you further afield so that you could amuse yourselves out of sight of someone like myself who might be inclined to ask awkward questions?"

Lord Manville paused, and as there was no answer he continued:

"I presume you intended to sneak into the house without my knowledge, to deceive me even as you did this afternoon when you tricked me into believing you were different from the other women you pretended to dislike.

"Oh, you have been very clever, I grant you that. Your act has been almost perfect, a superb piece of play-acting which would have deceived almost anyone."

He paused again but there was still no response from the slight figure below.

"Now you have revealed the truth all too clearly," he went on. "I confess I was almost beguiled into believing you meant what you said. It was a very subtle bit of trickery! 'Our enchanted wood'—God! that I should have fallen for such childish twaddle! But you did it well, that I grant you. It only surprises me that you did not carry your plan through and get me, as you contrived to do, up the aisle at your side. That was what you wanted, was it not my Pretty Little Horse-breaker? Marriage—a ring on your finger, a place at the head of my table!"

Lord Manville drew in his breath. Then he said, his voice altering to a tone of utter disgust:

"Curse you, I nearly fell for it! I was very nearly caught by the oldest confidence trick in the world. Well, I have learnt my lesson, you can make sure of that. Now you can go. Get out and stay out! And tell your paramour that I want none of his leavings, I would not soil my hands by touching anything which he has already fouled beyond description. Go, and God damn you! I hope that I never see you again."

For the first time Lord Manville raised his voice, shouting the last words. Then wheeling round he went into the house. He was shaking with anger and he intended to slam the door and bar it. But something compelled him to look back, perhaps to see if the silent figure, who had not moved or uttered the whole time he had been speaking, was still there.

She was there—but no longer standing. She was lying in a crumpled heap on the gravel. He hesitated. Then, his voice still rough, he said:

"Get up—pleading is going to get you nowhere."

As she did not move he added uncertainly:

"It is no use, Candida, the game is up, you must see that. If Foxleigh has gone home, I will send you over to him in a carriage."

Still there was no movement or sound from the crumpled figure, and at last, as if compelled against his will, Lord Manville descended the steps.

"Candida," he said urgently.

Reaching her he looked down and saw that her hair was streaming over her shoulders and there was something in the very limpness of her body which made him suddenly afraid.

"Candida?" he cried again.

He bent down and picked her up, realising as he did so that she was unconscious. Then as he carried her up the steps and into the light he caught his breath, and the exclamation he would have made died in his throat.

It was her chest he saw first, scratched and bruised, marked and bleeding from the branches through which she had run. The bodice of her dress was torn, the chiffon hanging in shreds, one white breast naked and bare. Her arms and her hands were bleeding, and she was barely covered by the tattered and torn remnants of what had once been an expensive gown.

There was mud and blood on her cheeks and her hair was full of dead leaves and twigs.

"Oh, my God!" Lord Manville ejaculated, and carrying Candida quickly up the stairs and pushing open the door of her bedchamber, he laid her down very gently on the bed.

But when he would have taken his arms from her she seemed to come back to consciousness. Reaching out her hands she clung to the lapel of his coat with an intensity born of panic.

"Do . . . not let . . . h-him find . . . me . . . h-help me . . . help me . . ." she murmured through dry lips.

Very gently Lord Manville lowered her against the pillows and took her hands in his.

"It is all right, Candida," he said, "you are safe. He will not touch you."

"He is . . . s-searching for . . . me," she murmured brokenly and opened her eyes.

For a moment she stared at Lord Manville in terror. Then in a less frantic tone she said:

"I . . . am . . . safe?"

"You are safe, I promise you," Lord Manville replied. "But, Candida, I must know what happened—tell me."

She shut her eyes again and for a moment he thought she had not heard him, until in a voice hardly above a whisper she stammered:

"Sir Tresham . . . told me . . . one of his . . . h-horses was hurt . . . I went to look . . . he thrust me in . . . the . . . carriage . . . he said . . . he had always . . . meant t-to . . . have me and . . . y-you would . . . never speak . . . to me . . . a-again."

Her voice died away, but making an obvious effort she continued:

"I threw . . . myself out of the . . . carriage, but he

171

. . . and his s-servants . . . searched . . . for me. They had . . . l-lanterns."

Lord Manville reached out his hand and pulled imperiously half a dozen times at the bell-rope. Candida must have drifted away for a moment, for she gave a sudden little cry.

"He . . . must not . . . find me . . . he must . . . not!"

"He will not, I promise you he will not," Lord Manville said gently.

"It was . . . horrible . . . I am . . . f-frightened," she murmured.

"Forget it," he said softly. "You will never see him again, I promise you that."

He felt her relax, and as she did so the door opened and Mrs. Hewson, the Housekeeper, came hurrying in.

"The bell, M'Lord!" she said breathlessly.

"I rang it," Lord Manville said. "There has been an accident, see to Miss Walcott, she has been injured."

As he spoke he went from the room, hurrying down the staircase and waiting in the Hall only to pick up his hat, his gloves and his riding-whip. Then he went out of the front door and across the courtyard towards the stables.

By riding across the fields in a direct line towards The Towers, Lord Manville arrived at Sir Tresham's country home only a short time after the last of the party. There was still a footman on duty in the Hall, and he stared in astonishment as Lord Manville walked straight past him and into the Salon.

As he had anticipated, the ladies had retired to bed; but the gentlemen were having a nightcap, and as he entered the room they stood and stared. Sir Tresham was in the act of raising a glass of brandy to his lips.

"Manville!" he exclaimed, and put his glass down carefully on one of the side tables.

Lord Manville walked across the intervening space towards him.

"I and my friends have many vices," Lord Manville said slowly, making every word an undisguised insult, "but one thing we do not do is to abduct a woman who is unwilling and assault her."

Sir Tresham gave an affected laugh.

"You have got the story wrong, Manville! The girl was willing enough until she became hysterical."

"So willing that she threw herself out of the coach to escape your odious attentions," Lord Manville said. "And for that I am going to teach you a lesson which you are unlikely to forget. I am going to fight you, Foxleigh. Which do you prefer, fists or pistols? I am not particular."

Sir Tresham tried to look Lord Manville in the face, but his eyes shifted.

"If you think I am going to fight you, Manville, over some foolish little soiled dove," he sneered, "who quarrelled with the amount of money I offered her, you are very much mistaken!"

Lord Manville drew his riding-gloves from his hands, put them together and very deliberately slapped Sir Tresham in the face.

"Now will you fight me?" he asked.

"No I will not," Sir Tresham replied in a high voice, "I will not put myself out for any cheap little prostitute."

He got no further, for Lord Manville with a quick movement of his right arm knocked him down. He sprawled on the floor, but instead of getting up covered his face with his hands.

"Go away," he cried in muffled tones, "get out of my house!"

Lord Manville looked down at him in disgust

"I always thought you were an outsider, Foxleigh," he said, "but I did not know you were yellow-livered as well."

He stepped forward, transferring his riding-whip from his left hand to his right, lifted up Sir Tresham by the collar of his coat and started to thrash him as a man might thrash a disobedient dog.

Sir Tresham was a bigger man, but he made no movement to avoid the blows or indeed to do anything but groan, still covering his face with his hands. Lord Manville used his whip again and again. The satin of Sir Tresham's evening coat was in ribbons, when finally Captain Willoughby said:

"That is enough, Manville, he has learnt his lesson."

His words seemed to break the spell which had held all the gentlemen of the party silent and immobile since

Lord Manville had entered the room. It was almost as though they had been hypnotised. Now they began to mutter among themselves like puppets come to life.

"I, personally, am leaving immediately for London," Captain Willoughby continued, looking at his watch.

"And I will come with you," the Duke of Dorset said hastily.

"Let us send for a servant to order all our carriages," Lord Fenton suggested. "Like you, Willoughby, I have no desire to remain under the roof of a coward."

His words seemed to animate the figure of their host. Drawing himself up into a sitting position he said:

"I beg you, gentlemen, not to leave me."

But almost before he had finished speaking the room was empty.

Lord Manville had already left. He had gone from the Salon and up the stairs. On the landing he encountered a housemaid, who informed him where Lais was sleeping.

He walked into her bedroom without knocking. She was seated at the dressing-table wearing a diaphanous wrap and was in the process of removing from her ears the expensive diamond earrings he had given her. She wheeled round as the door opened and gave a cry of astonishment.

"Silvanus! Why are you here?"

Lord Manville walked across the room and gripped her by the shoulder.

"How much did Foxleigh pay you," he asked sharply, "to keep me engaged in the garden while he took Candida away?"

"You are hurting me," Lais complained.

Lord Manville's grip only tightened as he said:

"Tell me the truth!"

"Very well then," Lais snapped. "I did not want paying, I was piqued because you did not seem to care that Foxy had chosen me to ride in the competition. You left me alone in London, you did not seem pleased to see me when I arrived at Manville today!"

"So you planned it between you!" Lord Manville interrupted. "You planned the whole thing."

"You are hurting me," Lais repeated, and then with a

174

little cry of pain: "Very well then, I did. You belong to me and you have no right to treat me as you did."

"That is all I wanted to know," Lord Manville said, releasing her. "I will send you a cheque in settlement, I have no wish to see you again."

He had left the room, but Lais sprang up from the dressing-table and ran after him.

"Silvanus, you cannot leave me like this! I love you."

"Love me?" he ejaculated and added contemptuously: "You do not know the meaning of the word."

"Nor do you," she retorted losing her temper. "You have no heart—you take everything from a woman and give her nothing—nothing, do you hear?"

But Lord Manville had not waited to listen to what she had to say. Already he was running down the stairs, passing without speaking the gentlemen talking amongst themselves in the Hall, and swinging himself into the saddle he set off for home.

It was not yet four o'clock as he entered his own house and proceeded upstairs to bed. When he reached the landing at the top of the Grand Staircase he paused for a moment outside Candida's room. Should he go in, he wondered, and assure her that she would never see Sir Tresham Foxleigh again?

He was ruined socially and for ever; for cowardice was something the gay set in which he liked to move could never stomach or forget. The only thing left for him would be to take his fortune and his boastful personality abroad.

Lord Manville listened, but there was no sound from behind Candida's door.

"She will be asleep," he thought, "it is the best thing that can happen after all she has gone through."

In the morning he would tell her what had happened, he decided, and with a smile of satisfaction on his lips Lord Manville went to his own room.

Perhaps it was his footsteps, perhaps his mere presence awoke Candida. She had slept after Mrs. Hewson and the Head Housemaid had sponged the dirt and blood from her face, arms and neck and undressed her.

She had been too tired and exhausted even to open her eyes, knowing the utter relief of having to do nothing for herself, merely letting Mrs. Hewson and the housemaid minister to her. Then obediently drinking the warm milk and honey which was held to her lips she drifted away into a dreamless sleep.

Now as she awoke her brain was clear, and though she felt stiff, and her arms were sore and painful, she knew then that no real hurt had been done to her body. It was her crinoline which had saved her, and she knew too that, because she was young and strong through so much riding, the physical wounds she had suffered would soon disappear.

As she awoke she recalled in an agony which seemed to pierce her heart Lord Manville's voice denouncing her from the top of the steps. She had not really understood all he had said, but enough to know that he loathed her for her deception, hated her for what he thought she had done, but most of all despised her for the lies that she had told.

It was not quite clear to Candida what crime she had committed; she only knew that he hated her and that his love for her had gone. This was a misery beyond anything she had suffered the night before when she had striven in terror to escape Sir Tresham.

With difficulty she rose from her bed, and walking across the room drew back the curtains and opened the window. Already there was an opaque dawn creeping up the sky; the stars were receding and soon it would be morning.

"I have to go away," Candida thought.

As she moved about she still felt a little stupid and giddy. There was still some of that terrible, exhausting weakness left which made every step back to the house last night seem as though she walked through quicksands which were pulling her down and down into some deep abyss.

The only thing she was sure of in her own mind was that she must leave. She could not see him again, could not bear to hear him speak to her with that cruel, cynical note in his voice—a voice which had finally seemed to break her so that she had fallen forward into a darkness which had swallowed her up.

"I must go away—go away!" she repeated to herself.

Feverishly, although she knew she was being unaccountably slow, she dressed herself, and then going to

176

the wardrobe pulled open the doors. There was a flutter of chiffons and laces, a sudden kaleidoscope of colour as she revealed all the pretty, expensive gowns Mrs. Clinton had bought for her.

There in one corner was what she sought, the dark riding-habit she had used at the livery-stable in the early morning when no one was there to see her. Mrs. Clinton had called it contemptuously "your working-habit".

She put it on, finding her riding-boots were excruciatingly painful over her bandaged feet, but knowing that the suffering was necessary if she was to get away.

When dressed, she pulled open a drawer of an elaborate inlaid chest with gold handles which stood against one wall of the room. In it was a white bundle, the one thing she had placed there herself, and which she had told the housemaids not to unpack.

Consisting of a white shawl which had belonged to her mother, it held everything she really possessed in the whole world, the only personal things she had left.

Ned had brought all her clothes to London the following day after she had arrived, as Major Hooper had promised he should do. But Mrs. Clinton had thrown everything away, allowing her to keep her bundle of treasures, her precious mementoes of the past.

She took the bundle now to the wide window-sill where she could see what it contained. She opened it. There was the miniature which had been done of her when she was a child; there was a little silver heart-shaped box which contained a few four-penny pieces; there was one of her Father's cuff-links; there was a silver button-hook and a comb engraved with her Mother's initials.

The only other things in the bundle were books—her Father's poems, six slim volumes in green leather which her Mother had read and read again, and which had always stood by her bed. Beside them was a prayer-book.

That too was well worn; for her Mother had carried it every Sunday to church, and ever since she had been small Candida had learnt the collect for the week. She could remember them all.

Now as she touched the book she said almost beneath

177

her breath the collect her Mother had always added to
her prayers ever since she was tiny:

"Lighten our darkness we beseech Thee, oh
Lord, and by Thy great mercy defend us from all
perils and dangers of this night . . ."

As Candida murmured the beautiful words that were
so familiar, so much a part of her childhood, she felt the
tears start into her eyes. She could go no further. She
covered her face with her hands.

"Oh, Mama! Mama!" she cried. "Help me! Where am
I to go? What am I to do? I love him . . . I love him . . .
but he hates me! He no longer wants me here. Help me.
Mama! What will happen to me? I am so alone."

Candida's prayer died away in her tears, and then
suddenly it seemed as if her Mother was beside her. She
felt as though things were no longer so desperate, that
she was no longer lost. She could not explain it, she
only knew she was no longer frightened. She wiped her
eyes. Already the sky was much brighter.

"Perhaps I will find somewhere to go," she thought
to herself.

She put the prayer-book back against the other books
and lifted up the corners of the silk shawl to tie them
all together. It was then she saw beside her Father's
poems another volume, one she did not remember. It
was in red leather, in contrast to his which were bound
in green.

Curiously she looked at it, then picked it up. She
recalled that she had found it in the very back drawer
of her Mother's dressing-table just as the furniture was
being moved by the dealer who had given Candida a
few pounds for the contents of the whole room—money
which had gone to pay their debts.

"I have never seen this before," Candida thought, and
remembered pushing it into the bundle with her Father's
books at the very last moment.

Now she turned it over and saw it was *Romeo and
Juliet* by William Shakespeare. There was a little smile
on her lips as she read the title. She understood now
why her Mother had kept the book, because she could
remember her saying:

"I was very young, Candida, when I met your Father, but I loved him with my whole heart. We were not too young to know how much our love meant to each other. Like Romeo and Juliet we knew that we were meant to meet."

Candida opened the book. On the flyleaf was written in strong, upright writing:

"To my dear daughter Elizabeth on the occasion of her seventeenth birthday, from her affectionate father."

"So that is why Mama kept it hidden!" Candida said to herself, and then she looked at the book-plate inside the cover.

It was a very elaborate, impressive book-plate. As she stared at it Candida drew in her breath—her Mother had answered her prayer!

11

Adrian was sitting at the breakfast table, a far-away look in his eyes and a piece of paper in his hands, when Lord Manville entered the room.

"Good-morning, Adrian," he said as his Ward rose to his feet, hastily thrusting the piece of paper he had been holding into the inside pocket of his coat.

At any other time this obvious gesture of deception would have annoyed Lord Manville, but he was in a good temper this morning.

"It is a fine day," he announced cheerily as he seated himself at the table and Bateman hurried forward with a silver dish of kidneys cooked in wine and cream. As Adrian did not reply His Lordship continued:

"How do you feel after all the gaieties of yesterday?"

"I feel well enough," Adrian answered, "but then I retired early. I thought I heard you come to bed very late, about four o'clock in the morning, but maybe I was mistaken,"

"You were not mistaken," Lord Manville replied, "but by that time I had ridden over to The Towers to teach its owner a lesson he will not forget in a hurry."

"You had ridden where?" Adrian ejaculated. "I thought you had sworn never to go near the place."

"We shall not be seeing Foxleigh again," Lord Manville said with satisfaction, helping himself to another dish. "In fact, my prediction is that The Towers and its estate will soon be up for sale—in which case I shall buy it."

"What has happened?" Adrian asked. "What did I miss last night?"

Lord Manville glanced over his shoulder to ascertain that the servants had left the room.

"You missed," he answered slowly, "Candida returning to the house bruised and bleeding after she had thrown herself from the carriage of a swine who was attempting to abduct her."

"Good God!" Adrian almost shouted. "But whenever did this happen? When Candida left me she went to bed."

"I think that is what she intended," Lord Manville said, "but Foxleigh persuaded her to go and look at one of his horses which he alleged was injured. It was a trap, of course, and she walked into it unsuspectingly."

"Damn it! That this should happen to Candida," Adrian exclaimed. "She hated the man, she was afraid of him. She told me he had forced himself into the house when she was in London and had attempted to kiss her."

"So that is how she met him," Lord Manville said reflectively.

Bateman and two footmen returned to the room with other dishes. Lord Manville looked at the empty place at the breakfast table and said to the butler:

"I expect Miss Candida is breakfasting upstairs. Convey my respects to her, Bateman, and say I should be glad to know how she is feeling this morning."

He paused and added:

"If she is asleep, of course, tell Mrs. Hewson not to wake her."

"I will make enquiries myself, M'Lord," Bateman said.

He left the room and when the footman had also retired Adrian continued:

"I cannot believe that this really happened. Was Candida very upset?"

"As I have told you, she threw herself from the coach," Lord Manville replied. "Had she not had the courage to do so, God knows what would have happened to her."

"If only I had escorted her to her bedroom!" Adrian said rather bitterly. "I might have known that something like this would happen with the sweepings of Piccadilly in the house."

"Is that how you view my guests?" Lord Manville said with a lift of his eyebrows.

"If you want to know the truth, they made me feel sick," Adrian replied aggressively.

Lord Manville said nothing but continued eating in silence. After a few moments the door opened and Bateman returned.

"Mrs. Hewson asked me to inform Your Lordship that Miss Candida is not in her bedroom."

"Not in her bedroom?" Lord Manville ejaculated. "Then where is she."

Mrs. Hewson has already ascertained, M'Lord, that Miss Candida went to the stables about 5.30 a.m. She asked for Pegasus to be saddled, and rode off alone."

"Alone?" Lord Manville said angrily. "Why did no groom accompany her?"

"She wished to be alone, M'Lord, in fact she insisted on it."

There was silence, then Bateman said:

"I think you ought to know, Sir, that Mrs. Hewson noticed that Miss Candida took with her a white bundle."

"A white bundle!" Lord Manville repeated questioningly.

Adrian jumped to his feet.

"I know what that is! This means she has left!"

Lord Manville glanced at his Ward's face and signalled to Bateman to leave the room. When they were alone he asked:

"What do you mean? What was in that bundle?"

"Everything Candida possessed in the world," Adrian answered, "everything she treasured! She has gone, can you not understand, and she will not be coming back!"

"How do you know?" Lord Manville began, only to be interrupted by Adrian saying furiously:

"Something else must have happened last night, something you have not told me about. Foxleigh may have insulted her, but that alone would not have made her leave here."

Lord Manville looked embarrassed. He rose from the table and walked towards the mantelpiece to stand looking down into the empty fireplace.

"I did not know at first she had gone with Foxleigh—

unwillingly," he said slowly, almost as if the words were being drawn from his lips. "When she returned—I was somewhat incensed. But afterwards I thought she understood."

"You were incensed?" Adrian repeated slowly. "You mean that you frightened her with one of your refined rages! How could you have treated her in such a manner when she loved you?"

"How do you know she loved me?" Lord Manville asked quickly.

"She did not tell me so, but it was obvious," Adrian said. "Even you must have realised that."

Then, his voice rising a little higher he said:

"So you were incensed at her, and I dare say that speaking in your icy sarcastic voice which bites through your victim you tore her in pieces. Candida—of whom you know so little that you thought she had gone off willingly with a man whom she loathed, and who made her tremble at the very sight of him!"

Lord Manville did not answer, and Adrian, almost beside himself, continued:

"Well, I dare say you are happy! You have driven Candida away, and unless I am very much mistaken you have broken her heart—the sweetest, gentlest person I have ever known. But as a professional Heart-Breaker you have done it again! You have added another scalp to your collection and I hope it gives you satisfaction."

Lord Manville glared at his Ward with a fury which seem almost to contort his face. Then he turned on his heel and strode from the room, slamming the door behind him.

Adrian did not see him again until it was dark. It was long after dinner-time when he came into the Library and flung himself down into a big armchair. His riding-boots and breeches were covered in mud, and it was easy to see that he was almost on the point of exhaustion. Bateman was hovering solicitously behind him.

"Have you dined, M'Lord?"

"No—and I am not hungry."

"I think you would be wise to have some nourishment, M'Lord. Alfonse has everything ready. He has been keeping various dishes until your return."

"I am not hungry!" Lord Manville snapped. "But you can bring me a drink."

Bateman brought him a glass of brandy and he drained it off like a man whose throat was dry and parched.

"You had best try some soup or something," Adrian advised, speaking for the first time from the other side of the fireplace. "You look all in. Have you eaten since breakfast?"

"I have not, and I do not care," Lord Manville answered. "Bring me anything you like, but do not fuss me."

Bateman instructed a footman in a low voice to remove His Lordship's boots. Another flunkey brought him a smoking-jacket and he pulled his crumpled stock from his neck. When the food came he took a few mouthfuls, then pushed his plate aside.

"I am not hungry," he muttered.

Adrian waited until the servants had left the room.

"You did not find her?" he asked.

"There is no sign of her anywhere," Lord Manville said, and there was a note of anxiety in his voice Adrian had never heard before. "You have got to help me. Where can I look? Where can I go? Where did she come from?"

"Her parents are dead," Adrian replied, "that is why she went to London."

Lord Manville did not say anything but looked across at him intently. There was a little pause.

"Her Father was Alexander Walcott," Adrian continued.

The name seemed to evoke no response.

"Should that mean something to me?" Lord Manville asked.

"You might have heard of him when you were at Oxford," Adrian replied. "He translated the *Iliad,* which became part of every student's curriculum."

Lord Manville sat upright in his chair.

"Alexander Walcott, of course. That man! I had no idea."

"I think perhaps I had better tell you," Adrian said in a defiant voice, "that Candida has been helping me. I have been writing poetry for some time, and I know now that is what I wish to do in life."

"Why not?" Lord Manville asked indifferently, then suddenly added: "So that is what you were always talking about. You used to hide what you were doing when I came into the room. I wondered what it could be."

"I did not wish you to see my poems," Adrian explained.

"I was thinking as I was riding today looking for Candida," Lord Manville said, "that perhaps I have been a trifle high-handed where you are concerned. You can marry your Vicar's daughter, I will give my consent."

"I do not want to marry her now," Adrian answered.

"You are in love with Candida?"

The question seemed to vibrate across the room. Adrian shook his head.

"I love Candida," he replied, "I think she is the most adorable person that I have ever met in my whole life. But I do not want to marry her or anyone else. Besides, she is in love with you."

Lord Manville murmured something inarticulate and Adrian went on:

"I too have been thinking. Something had upset Candida before dinner last night. She looked as though the bottom had fallen out of her world, and she was only half conscious of what was going on around her—a very good thing as it happens. But she was miserable and depressed. It must have been something you had said to her before we went into dinner."

"I did not understand," Lord Manville murmured, almost as though he were talking to himself. "I did not realise—who she was."

"Who she was?" Adrian echoed. "Surely you were aware that she was a lady. I may be a green-horn in your eyes, but I realised that the moment I saw her."

"You do not understand," Lord Manville said. "I bought her, do you hear, bought her with the horse from Hooper and Cheryl Clinton—from the woman who keeps the most notorious "House of Introduction" in the whole of London. How could I imagine that Candida was anything but what she appeared to be?"

Adrian gave a hollow laugh.

"And I have been thinking you are so clever!" he

jeered. "You have always made me feel an ignorant fool, but I was not so thickheaded as to think that Candida was one of those vulgar creatures who were here yesterday."

"But it was Hooper who produced her," Lord Manville said, almost as though he were in the dock facing a prosecution.

"Hooper bought Pegasus for one hundred pounds at the Potters Bar Fair," Adrian said. "When Candida showed him the tricks she could make the horse do he took her to London. But he was shrewd enough to realise that she was not going to be of much value to him unless she was properly bedecked and fur-belowed to attract such fastidious gentlemen as yourself. So he and that woman kept her hidden for three weeks.

She never saw another soul except Foxleigh, who forced his way into the house. Candida was grateful to them, don't you understand, grateful for letting her ride Pegasus and for giving her a roof over her head. When you rose to the bait that was just what those vultures were waiting for."

"My God!" Lord Manville ejaculated, putting his hand over his eyes.

"Candida did not have the slightest idea what was going on," Adrian said. "Her only thought was that she could stay with Pegasus. That was how they persuaded her into coming down here with you to Manville Park."

Lord Manville's hand still covered his face, and Adrian went on:

"She confessed to me—confessed, mind you—that her conscience was worrying her because she could not do what you wished. She could not introduce me to the Argyll Rooms, to Motts and to Kate Hamilton's because she did not know what they were. She had never even heard of such places."

"Then why did she not tell me so?" Lord Manville demanded.

"Because she thought if she did you would send her back as being unsuitable for the position you were offering her," Adrian replied. "Unsuitable!"

His voice should have been heavy with sarcasm, but instead it sounded pitiful, as if he were not far from tears.

"What has happened to her?" he cried. "Where can she have gone? Surely it is impossible for the horse to disappear, let alone Candida?"

"That is what I have been thinking," Lord Manville said. "And she has no money."

"No money?" Adrian exclaimed. "Did you not give her any?"

"I never thought of it," Lord Manville answered. "There seemed no necessity while she was here, and besides, I had the feeling she would not accept it from me."

He remembered Candida's reluctance to take the guineas he had held out for her when they had left Cheryl Clinton's and the manner in which she had contrived that he should throw the money to John. Why had he not realised then, he asked himself, she was not the "Pretty Horse-breaker" he had thought her to be?

"It was her first appearance in Hyde Park that put me on the wrong track," he explained. "In that white habit, Hooper riding by her side, she caused a sensation."

"Candida told me how nervous and embarrassed she was," Adrian said. "But Hooper assured her she was doing it for Pegasus, and she believed him, although she did not realise then he was intending to sell the horse. He promised her he would not."

Lord Manville remembered the fear in Candida's eyes when he had asked the Major what price he was asking. Why had he not understood from the very beginning there was something different about this girl? Why had he been so blind, so incredibly stupid?

"I have been a fool," he confessed, and there was a humility in his tone that Adrian had never heard before. "But I am determined to find her before she comes to any harm. Suppose you tell me what was in the bundle she was carrying."

"Her Father's poems," Adrian replied, "and one or two treasures that were not sold when the whole of her home was broken up. Her Mother died, then her Father broke his neck when he was drunk. It was when he was dead that Candida learnt the full magnitude of the debts they owed to the tradesmen, to everyone in the village.

The only thing she had of any value was Pegasus, and

the money Major Hooper paid for him went to provide a home for their old groom."

"The old groom!" Lord Manville cried. "That is where she will have gone! Do you know where he lives?"

"Yes, she told me," Adrian replied. "It is a village called Little Berkhamstead, not far from Potters Bar."

"I will go there first thing tomorrow," Lord Manville promised, a new light shining in his eyes. "Thank you, Adrian. I have a feeling that tomorrow I shall bring Candida back with me."

"I hope you will," Adrian said in a low voice.

Lord Manville rose and put his hand on his shoulder.

"You are quite sure you do not wish to be married?" he asked. "I was wrong to refuse my consent."

"Candida made me realise I did not love Lucy," Adrian said quietly. "She made me see too that a man should first do something in his life—something worthwhile. When I saw those fops Sir Tresham brought here yesterday, I realised Candida was right. I have never wanted to be a fashionable young man about town, and now I know I have to work. Not to make money—that is unnecessary—but to prove myself, and if possible contribute something to other people's lives."

"Is it Candida who had made you think like that?" Lord Manville asked in a wondering tone.

"She made me understand so many things I had not realised before," Adrian said. "You see, Sir, Candida may have lived in the country, she may be unsophisticated and in your eyes ignorant, but she seemed to me to be exceedingly wise about the things that really matter."

"I am beginning to realise that now," Lord Manville said, and went from the room with his head bent.

In the morning he had already left before Adrian came down to breakfast.

"Do you think His Lordship will find Miss Candida?" Bateman asked anxiously. "We are all worried in the house, a nicer young lady never stayed here. I can say that truthfully, Sir, after being in service here for over thirty-five years."

"I am sure His Lordship will find her," Adrian said consolingly.

"It is obvious," he thought to himself, "that she has returned to Little Berkhamstead," but unable to concentrate on his poem he went down to the stables to talk to Garton.

"Are you quite sure, Garton, that Miss Candida gave no indication of where she was going?" Adrian asked.

Garton shook his head.

"No, Mr. Adrian, His Lordship asks me the same thing. I wasn't here when she first appeared, but I heard something happening in the yard so I comes down, and there they were abringing Pegasus from his stall, and Miss Candida standing waiting for him. She were carrying a white bundle in her hands and she looks so pale that I thought summat were the matter.

" 'It'd be best for a groom to go with you, Miss Candida,' I says to her.

" 'No thank you, Garton,' she answers, 'I want to go by myself. And you have nothing except Thunder that can keep up with Pegasus!'

"It was an old joke between us, and I'd have laughed if I'd not realised how ill she looks, just as though she were agoing to collapse.

" 'You're all right, Miss?' I asks.

" 'I am all right,' she answers. 'Help me into the saddle, Garton, I have hurt one of my arms a little.'

" 'Don't tell me you've got the rheumatics, Miss,' I smiles.

" 'No, it is not that,' she answers. 'I had a fall and my arm is a little stiff, but it will soon wear off.'

"I helps her up into the saddle, light as thistledown she were. But when she looks down at me there was something in her face which seemed to strike at me very heart, and that's the truth, Mr. Adrian.

" 'Good-bye, Garton,' she says, 'and thank you for all your kindness.'

"Then she was gone."

"Did you think then that perhaps she was not coming back?" Adrian asked.

"I was afraid to think such a thing," Garton replied. "I wouldn't have lost Miss Candida, or Pegasus for that matter, for all the money in the Bank of England."

"Nor would I," Adrian agreed.

He went back to the house and waited. He tried to

reckon how long it would take Lord Manville, riding across country, to reach Little Berkhamstead. He was not quite certain of the mileage, but dinner was spoilt once again before Lord Manville came home.

Adrian knew as soon as he heard his Guardian's footsteps cross the Hall that his search had been unsuccessful. Nevertheless he was unable to suppress the obvious question.

"Have you any news of her?"

"The old groom had not seen her or heard from her," Lord Manville replied, "but he told me much about Candida that I should have known the very first moment I met her. I saw her parents' grave in the churchyard and the Manor House where she had lived.

"Adrian, how could I have thought for one moment that she was a 'Pretty Horse-breaker'? I have been asking myself that question over and over again every yard of the journey home."

There was so much pain in his voice that Adrian answered gently:

"I think most people see what they expect to see! That was what misled you. Candida once said to me that we do not use our intuition enough about horses or about people."

"I certainly did not use it about her," Lord Manville said bitterly.

Day after day, with monotonous regularity, Lord Manville left the house in the morning and returned in the evening. Each day it seemed to Adrian he was noticeably kinder and more approachable, but quite obviously more unhappy.

He grew so thin that his clothes seemed to sit loosely on him, but it made him better-looking. He had shed the dissipation and the loose living which, even with his strong constitution, had begun to leave its mark.

After the first week Adrian found it hard to remember that he had ever been the awe-inspiring, frightening Guardian whom he had hated and feared.

Now they talked as man to man; two men who had lost something they both prized, something they both loved. And sometimes it seemed that Adrian was the older and wiser of the two and that Lord Manville looked to him for help and guidance.

190

"What can I do? Where can I go?" he asked not once but a dozen times when he had returned after a day of fruitless searching. "What can she be living on? She had nothing to sell." Then added in a low voice: "Except—Pegasus."

"If she sold him, surely we would find him," Adrian answered. "A horse like that would not go unnoticed."

"I thought of that," Lord Manville said. "I have already sent a groom to London to watch Tattersalls and the other Sale-rooms. And Garton has instructions that either he or one of his more knowledgeable grooms will attend every horse sale within a radius of fifty miles."

"What about Hooper?" Adrian asked.

"My Secretary tells me that neither Hooper nor Cheryl Clinton has heard from Candida since she came here. He is convinced they are speaking the truth."

"She must be somewhere," Adrian said. "Even if she had died there would be a record of it."

"Do not say such things," Lord Manville said sharply.

Adrian, looking at him, realised he was suffering as he had not believed it possible for anyone, let alone His Lordship, to suffer over the loss of a woman.

News was brought them a week later that Sir Tresham Foxleigh had gone abroad and The Towers was up for sale. Lord Manville gave the order to buy the Estate, but there was no elation in his voice or manner. When his agent had gone Adrian said to him:

"That is something you have always wanted, is it not?"

"I would forfeit my chance of owning that Estate and this one as well if I could find Candida," Lord Manville answered, and Adrian knew that incredibly he spoke the truth.

"Why did Sir Tresham hate you?" he enquired. "What was the quarrel between you?"

"It was not important," Lord Manville replied. "I found he had crooked a friend of mine, who was forced to sell his horses to pay his debts. He was young and not very knowledgeable, and Foxleigh beat him down to an absurd figure far below the value of the horses. I persuaded my friend to cancel the sale, and gave him myself what was a right price for the animals.

Foxleigh was furious, especially when one of them

191

won a race at Newmarket. He behaved so badly and insultingly about it that I black-balled him from a Club he wished to join. He swore to get even with me, and indeed he has succeeded."

"He has not got Candida," Adrian said quickly, "that is one thing we can be sure about."

"But I have not got her either," Lord Manville muttered. ·

It was a fortnight later, three weeks after Candida had left, that Adrian came down to breakfast to find Lord Manville finishing his coffee. Adrian had taken to breakfasting early so that he could see his Guardian before he left on his daily search.

"I am sorry I am late," Adrian said, "but I stayed up until three o'clock writing a poem. I want you to hear it when you have time."

"I would like that," Lord Manville replied quite naturally. "I thought the last one you did was one of your best."

"I am not sure about that last line," Adrian said. "If only Candida were here, she would tell me what was wrong with it."

"Perhaps I will find her today," Lord Manville said.

There was little hope in his voice, only a kind of dull misery which made Adrian feel that above all things he wanted to cheer him.

"I dreamt last night that she was back," he said, "and we were all very happy. It was a mad dream because Pegasus was standing in the Drawing Room eating a vaseful of carnations."

Lord Manville tried to smile, but failed.

"I must be getting off," he said, rising to his feet. "I do not know quite where I am going—there is practically nowhere I have not been already."

Bateman came into the room, and there was an expression on his face which made Adrian stare at him.

"Begging your pardon, M'Lord," he said with a note of excitement in his voice, "but young Jim from the stables wishes to speak to Your Lordship."

"He has something to tell me?" Lord Manville asked quickly. "Tell him to come in, Bateman."

A rather under-sized stable-lad came in nervously twisting his cap. Lord Manville sat down again.

"Well, Jim," he said, "you have found something?"

"I thinks so, M'Lord," Jim answered. "Last evenin' I goes over to see me aunt at Cobbleworth. 'Tis about four miles away, as your Lordship knows. I thinks afore I comes back I'd've a mug o' ale at 'The Woodman'. While I was there two grooms comes in. The younger lad starts to chat, and asks if we'd entered anything for the county races next month. I says as how Your Lordship has some fine horses, and he says:

"'We has one in our stables that'll beat any horse-flesh in these parts.'

"'You're boasting,' I says.

"'Nay,' he answers. 'We has a great black stallion. Over seventeen hands he be. And he'll outride and outjump anything as ye could put up."

"I was agoing to ask him more when the groom he was with calls him, he sets down his mug all of a hurry and follows him out of the Inn."

"Who were they? Where did they come from?" Lord Manville demanded, speaking as though he could not contain his curiosity.

"I was just agoing to tell Your Lordship," Jim replied. "I asks the innkeeper—being someone I've known all me life—who them two grooms belongs to. He replies they were the Storr lads, and asks why I didn't recognise the livery."

"The Earl of Storr!"

Lord Manville uttered the words with an expression on his face which made Adrian say quickly:

"It may not be Pegasus, Silvanus! Do not count too much on it. After all, there are many black stallions."

"Yes, yes, of course," Lord Manville said. "Thank you, Jim. If it turns out that the black stallion is Pegasus, you will not go unrewarded. You know what I have promised for the first person to bring me information which will lead me to Miss Candida."

"Yes, M'Lord, I knows, M'Lord. Thank ye very much, M'Lord!"

The stable-boy backed his way out of the door.

Lord Manville turned to Adrian, a light in his eyes which transfigured him.

"That is where she must have gone—to Storr Castle. But why?"

"Do not be too confident," Adrian begged.

He had a feeling that his Guardian would break if this last hope proved to be fruitless.

"I will go and call on Lord Storr immediately," Lord Manville said.

"Not at seven o'clock in the morning!" Adrian protested.

"No, no, I suppose not," Lord Manville admitted, looking at the clock as though its hands must be deceiving him.

"You must at least wait until noon," Adrian said firmly. "You do not wish to cause unecessary comment."

"I will be there half an hour before noon," Lord Manville conceded. "Order my Curricle, Adrian, I will go and change."

He went from the Breakfast Room and Adrian heard him running down the passageway like a schoolboy setting off for the holidays.

"If only this is true," he thought, and to his surprise found himself praying "Oh Lord! Let Candida be there!"

12

Just before 11:30 in the morning The Earl and Countess of Storr were sitting in the Blue Drawing Room at Storr Castle. The Earl, an elderly man, who had once been exceedingly handsome, was resting his foot on a velvet stool, while he read aloud from the *Morning Post*. Finally he put down the newspaper and said:

"You are not listening, Emily."

"Indeed I was, dear," his wife answered, looking up from her tapestry.

"Then what was I reading about?" Lord Storr demanded.

His wife gave a laugh so light and so young that it belied the grey of her hair as she replied:

" 'All right, my dear, you have caught me out', as Elizabeth used to say. I was thinking about Candida."

"Neither of us think of anything else these days," Lord Storr replied gruffly.

"She is not happy, Arthur."

"Not happy!" Lord Storr exclaimed. "Why not? We have given her everything that she wants, have we not? And she has refused a dozen times or more to have a season in London, even though you told her you would present her to the Queen."

"She cries bitterly night after night into her pillow," Lady Storr said, her voice dropping. "Mrs. Danvers told me this; so for several nights I have listened at her door. It is terrible to hear her misery, but I do not like to force her confidence. Perhaps, when she has been with us longer, she will tell us what is wrong."

"What can be wrong?" the Earl growled.

"That is what I keep asking myself," his wife replied. "I cannot believe such unhappiness is entirely caused by her Father's death."

The Earl snorted aggressively and his wife said warningly:

"Now, Arthur?"

"Yes, yes, I know," he said quickly. "I will say nothing about that man to distress Candida. But when I think how he kept Elizabeth apart from us all these years, I could curse him into eternity."

"It was your fault, dear," Lady Storr said gently. "You know that you made little effort to find Elizabeth when they first ran away, and after that, when we made enquiries, we could not find where they had gone. They had simply vanished."

"Very well, it was my fault," the Earl said testily. "But now that Candida has come back to us, we must see she is happy and content. Give her everything she wants, Emily—everything."

"Of course, dear—if it is in my power," Lady Storr answered without conviction. She sighed, and her sweet face bore a worried look.

The opening of the door made them both turn their heads. The butler crossed the room to the Earl's side.

"Lord Manville has called, M'Lord. His Lordship begs that you will see him on an urgent matter."

"Lord Manville!" Lady Storr cried in surprise, and added quickly: "Show His Lordship in—and, Newman, serve the best port, or maybe His Lordship would prefer madeira."

"Manville! I thought he never came to the country," Lord Storr remarked. "A gay blade from all I have heard."

They waited until Newman left the room, and a moment later he announced stentoriously:

"Lord Manville, M'Lady."

Lady Storr rose to her feet as Lord Manville walked towards them. He was dressed with extreme elegance and she would not have been a woman had she not appreciated his good looks and beguiling smile he gave her as he shook first her hand and then the Earl's.

"Nice to see you, Manville," His Lordship said. "Cannot get up because of this damn gout. One of the penalties of old age. Comes to us all in time."

"I am afraid it does," Lord Manville agreed.

"Do sit down, Lord Manville," Lady Storr suggested, indicating a seat beside hers. "It is a great pleasure to see you. Your Mother was a very dear friend of mine, and never a week passed when we did not drive over to each other's houses. I am afraid we were sad gossips, but we enjoyed each other's company enormously."

"My Mother often spoke of you," Lord Manville said. "And my Father too used to tell me how much he enjoyed racing with you, My Lord."

"A fine judge of horseflesh, your Father!" Lord Storr said.

There was a slight pause. Then, as if Lord Manville could waste no more time in trivialities, he said with an urgent note in his voice:

"I called to see you, My Lord, because I feel you may be able to help me."

"Help you?" Lady Storr asked in surprise. "But of course we should be only too delighted, should we not, Arthur?"

"Yes, yes, naturally," Lord Storr said. "What is it you want?"

Before Lord Manville could speak there was a sudden interruption.

"Grandpapa," a voice cried from the open window, "Grandpapa, what do you think?"

A small figure dressed in white came running across the room. She had eyes only for the old man to whom she ran, slipping her hand into his and bending forward to plant a kiss on his forehead.

"You will not believe it, Grandpapa," she said, her voice alight with excitement, "but Pegasus leaped the river, he did really! He saw me on the other bank and he jumped. His hooves never even touched the water, and you know how wide it is. Do you not think that is fantastic?"

"It is indeed," Lord Storr replied, "but then Pegasus is a very remarkable horse. Manville, I do not believe you have met my granddaughter."

Lord Manville had risen to his feet as Candida entered the room. Now she started as though someone

197

had fired a gunshot. Their eyes met, and for a moment it seemed as though they had both been turned to stone.

They stood staring at each other, and there was a tension vibrating between them so that everything else faded away and they were alone facing each other in another world.

Then, with a little inarticulate cry, almost that of an animal who has been frightened, Candida turned and fled. She ran from the room out into the sunshine. After a second, with a muttered murmur of apology, Lord Manville followed her.

"What is happening? What is going on?" Lord Storr demanded irritably. "Where has Candida gone, and why has young Manville gone after her?"

Lady Storr picked up her embroidery.

"I think, Arthur," she said gently, "that we have discovered the reason why Candida has been so unhappy."

"You mean that Manville has upset her?" Lord Storr asked angrily. "Well, I will not have it, do you hear, Emily? And I will not have him taking her away either, if that is what he is after. She has come to us, and if she leaves us now it will seem like losing Elizabeth all over again."

"Manville Park is very near," Lady Storr said quietly, "and I have a feeling, Arthur, that we shall never lose Candida completely, whatever happens."

Candida had stopped at the far end of the terrace. She knew that Lord Manville was following her, and pride would not allow her to run away any further. She rested her hands on the stone balustrade, and as he approached he saw that she was trembling.

Her head was turned from him and he could see the straight line of her tiny aristocratic nose, the soft curve of her parted lips and the way in which she carried her chin proudly on the rounded white column of her neck.

He asked himself again, as he had asked himself by now a thousand times, how he could have been such a fool as not to recognise her for what she was.

He came near to her slowly, and when he saw the little pulse beating in her neck, he knew that she was frightened. After a moment she said in a breathless voice hardly above a whisper:

"You have . . . come for . . . Pegasus?"

"No," he answered, "I have been searching for you."

"It was wrong of me to take him . . . when you had paid for him," she said. "He was your horse, but I could not leave him . . . behind."

"It was not Pegasus that mattered!"

Lord Manville's voice was deep and hoarse. Then, forcing himself with an effort to speak more lightly, he said:

"Can you not realise what a catastrophic muddle you have left us in? Mrs. Hewson has never stopped weeping; Bateman is crippled with rheumatism; Garton has been so bad-tempered that half his stable-boys have threatened to run away; and Alfonse is sending up the most disgustingly inedible meals it is possible to imagine."

Candida gave a little ghost of a smile.

"I am sure that is not . . . true," she managed to say.

"It is indeed," Lord Manville asserted. "And Adrian has written so many poems and torn them up again that the house resembles a paper-chase."

For one fleeting second she glanced at him.

"You know then about Adrian's . . . poems?"

"He told me how much you had helped him," Lord Manville said gently. "Thank you, Candida. You have done so much for Adrian. You realised what he needed, while I was dealing with him in entirely the wrong manner."

"You are not . . . angry about the . . . poems?" Candida asked.

"I am not angry about anything," Lord Manville answered. "I am only glad—and what an inadequate word that is—to have found you again, Candida."

"I thought you were angry with . . . me," Candida whispered. "You said . . ."

"Can we not forget what I said?" Lord Manville interrupted. "I was insane—and I did not understand what had happened."

"But why are you here?" Candida asked. "And why is Alfonse still at Manville Park? I thought you would have gone back to London."

"I have been looking for you," Lord Manville said simply.

"I imagined you were in London," Candida said almost beneath her breath. "I thought of you having a . . . gay and . . . amusing time with your . . . friends."

"I have travelled miles over the countryside. I have ridden every horse in my stables to the point of exhaustion," Lord Manville said. "It would have distressed you, Candida, to see them. But I have bought a horse which I think will please you."

She did not speak and he said:

"It is Firefly."

"Oh I am glad!"

For the first time there was a warmth in her voice.

"I am waiting for you to ride him."

Candida drew a deep breath.

"There is . . . something I want to say . . . to you," she said slowly, and he saw what an effort she was making. "You were angry with . . . me, and though I had not done . . . what you . . . thought I had . . . I had in fact . . . deceived you."

Lord Manville would have spoken but she put up her little hand to prevent him. It was trembling and her whole body seemed to quiver.

"No, no, I have to say this," she said, "I have been thinking of it for a long time. I know now that I was . . . wrong to go to London with Major Hooper when he asked me to do so . . . Mama would not have approved . . . but at the time I could think only of Pegasus and there seemed nothing else I could do not to lose him. Major Hooper was kind to me, but I felt . . . though I would not admit it . . . there was something strange about the other . . . women who rode his horses. It was the same at Mrs. Clinton's. I knew Mama would not have liked her, even though she was so considerate. But I was so . . . foolish that I thought she was giving me those . . . gowns as a . . . present because she wanted to . . . help me. I did not know that . . . you were going to pay . . . for them."

"Candida," Lord Manville said pleadingly, but again her little hand moved to check him, and he knew he must let her say what she wanted to say. He wondered how many times she had rehearsed it in her mind against the day they might meet.

"And when you took me away without a . . .

chaperon," she continued, "and I stayed at Manville Park without another woman being there, I knew . . . yes of course I knew . . . it was wrong. It did not seem wrong, but I was aware all the time that I was behaving in a . . . reprehensible manner, even though I was so h-happy."

She faltered for a moment and her voice broke on the word, and then with an obvious act of courage she went on piteously:

"I did not . . . understand what was . . . happening, I just knew . . . I wanted to be . . . with . . . you. Then when you k-kissed me I knew that . . . I loved . . . you and . . . I thought that . . . you loved . . . me . . . too."

"I did love you," Lord Manville murmured, his eyes on her face as if he could never stop looking at her.

"B-but," Candida stammered, "because I was so . . . ignorant and s-stupid, I thought that it meant we . . . would be m-married and be t-together for ever."

"That was exactly what it should have meant," Lord Manville interrupted.

Candida shook her head.

"I s-saw your . . . face that n-night at the p-party, and I knew you d-did . . . not . . . m-mean that . . . and something was very wr-wrong."

"It was I who was wrong, Candida."

She turned her face away.

"No! It was because I had d-deceived you," she said, and it was agony for him to hear the self-accusation in her tone. "I asked Grandpapa about the Argyll Rooms, Motts and Kate Hamilton's, and he said they were places no l-lady should know about, let alone v-visit. So I knew . . . you see, that . . . you did not think of . . . me as being a l-lady."

"Candida, do not torture me!" Lord Manville begged. "It was all a terrible mistake."

It seemed as though Candida did not hear him, as she continued:

"If I had been honest and told you the truth, perhaps everything would have been all right. But I was a-afraid you would s-send me away and I would be separated from . . . Pegasus. So I p-pretended I was going to do what you wanted, but instead I helped Adrian with his poems! Then . . . those w-women . . . came."

201

"Women you should never have met or even known of their existence!" Lord Manville exclaimed.

"The m-more I thought about . . . it the m-more I realised I . . . was . . . one of . . . them," Candida said, the colour rising in her pale cheeks. "That was why . . . Mrs. Clinton had dressed me up in that vulgar . . . white habit, and why Major Hooper had taken me in the Park, so that I should be l-like them, and y-you, or somebody like . . . you, should pay a high p-price for Pegasus and . . . me . . . too. It is all my f-fault, and . . . I am . . . ashamed."

Her voice broke and the tears overflowed from her eyes and ran down her cheeks.

"Don't, Candida, I beg you not to cry," Lord Manville pleaded.

"There is only one . . . thing more," Candida said, still in that low, lost voice. "I have not told Grandpapa or Grandmama that I have been to London, or indeed that I stayed with . . . you at Manville Park. I had no wish to . . . lie any further, but I thought it would . . . hurt them and they would not understand. And so they think I came straight to them when . . . Papa died, and that I was . . . bruised and . . . scratched because I had a fall on the way. It was a . . . lie, but perhaps it was not a very wrong . . . lie!"

Her eyes sought his for a moment as if seeking confirmation.

"I think it was not wrong but right," Lord Manville said gently, "absolutely right. It is the sort of thing, Candida, that only a lady could have thought of—a great lady."

She turned her face to him and he saw the question in her eyes and the tears standing like dewdrops on her dark lashes.

"Then you do not d-despise . . . me . . . utterly?" she questioned.

He put out his hands and took hers. He felt her fingers tremble beneath his, but she did not draw them away.

"Candida," he said gently, "will you honour me by becoming my wife? I cannot live without you."

For a moment she was very still, and then she said:

"Are you asking me to . . . marry you because . . .

202

you feel you have to . . . because I have found my . . . grandparents?"

"No, that is not true," he said sharply, and his hands tightened so sharply on hers that the blood was almost squeezed from her fingers. "I am asking you because I love you, Candida, because I respect you, honour you, want you, and because I cannot go on without you. Everything that has happened is my fault, not yours—mine because I was blind and criminally stupid. But you must try to forgive me—you must try to understand."

He felt despairingly he had not reached through to her.

"I have done," he went on, "a great many bad and wrong things these last years, Candida. I am not pretending you would not be shocked by my behaviour and perhaps disgusted. I have no excuse save that someone tricked me once and I have never forgotten it. I have been suspicious of women ever since; I thought that they were all the same, all out for what they could get, loving only where their love would be repaid by money or position. That was why, when I found you, my darling, I could not believe you were so different or indeed so—pure."

"It was a woman who . . . hurt you?" Candida stated. "I was sure of . . . that."

"You thought that?" he echoed.

"Yes," Candida answered. "I was convinced that some . . . woman had . . . wounded you, and I was . . . right."

"You have always been right," he answered. "Candida, I say this without meaning to sound dramatic, but if you refuse me now there will be nothing left for me but a life of degradation, a life so useless, so wasteful that I can only hope it will not last long."

She was still looking up into his eyes, and he felt as if she searched his face, seeking for something, so that he cried out in agony.

"Candida, if you will marry me I swear I will not fail you. I love you—I love you with all my heart. They say I have no heart, but I promise you it has hurt me most excruciatingly every moment of these last three weeks while I have been searching for you."

"You really . . . missed me?" Candida asked.

"Missed you?"

He almost smiled at the absurdity of the question, and then she said:

"There is something . . . different about you . . . I do not know what it is . . . Once before you looked like that . . . the day . . . we found . . . our enchanted wood."

"Candida, let us go back to that day," he pleaded. "Let us forget everything that has happened in between. Everything I said and everything I did that terrible night was only because I was crazed with jealousy. I could not bear that any other man should touch you. I thought you belonged to me. I believed you did, and if I had had even a modicum of sense I would have carried you away after those moments of happiness in the wood. We should have gone somewhere where we could have been alone—just you and I."

"If only . . . we . . . had," Candida sighed.

"Can we not go back and start again?" Lord Manville asked humbly. "Oh, Candida, say you will marry me!"

"Are you . . . quite sure that you . . . want me?" Candida asked. "I am so . . . ignorant; I know so . . . little of the life you . . . lead, what you . . . like and what . . . amuses you."

"Oh, my little love," he answered, "I don't know that either. Can you not understand that we are starting again, both of us? I only know that everything I have done in the past seems incredibly dull and not worth remembering. We will both begin again at Manville Park. We will build a new life there—just you and I, with our horses and one day perhaps our children. Will that be enough for you?"

He suddenly realised that through her tears her eyes were shining like stars.

"That is what I have always . . . wanted," she whispered, "a . . . home of my . . . own . . . and . . . y . . ."

She stopped and her eyes fell before his. Then, as though he could control himself no longer, Lord Manville took her in his arms, holding her closer and still closer to him, until lifting her chin he found her lips.

"If you only knew how I have dreamed of this," he murmured and kissed her.

To Candida it brought all the glory, the ecstasy, the beauty, the wonder that she had found with him in the little wood. But now instinctively, though she could not explain it to herself, she knew there was a dedication in his kiss that had not been there before. His lips were at first gentle, then demanding and then passionate, and they awoke a flame within herself.

But there was also something which seemed to her indivisibly linked with her prayers, her belief in God and the glory of the sun.

Impulsively she put her arms round his neck and drew him closer. He would never know, she thought, how lonely and lost she had felt without him. It had seemed as if a part of herself had been left behind when she ran away from Manville Park.

Now with his mouth on hers they were man and woman, yet so close that they were one person, and she knew they would be together for all time.

"Oh, Candida," Lord Manville murmured, looking down at her, "I have found you—found you after I thought I had lost you. You will never leave me, never escape me again, for I know now that you are the only thing that matters to me in life—and I cannot live without you."

"I . . . I-love . . . y-you too," she murmured, stammering from sheer happiness, and there was a flush on her cheeks and a radiance in her eyes which transfigured her. "I love . . . y-you, I love you . . . and nothing else m-matters . . . does it?"

"Nothing, my darling," he answered. "We are together —you and I—and what else is of consequence in the whole world?"

ON SALE WHEREVER PAPERBACKS ARE SOLD
— or use this coupon to order directly from the publisher.

BARBARA CARTLAND

V3587	The Kiss of the Devil $1.25 £	
V2751	Kiss Of Paris $1.25 £ (#38)	
V3474	A Kiss Of Silk $1.25 £ (#30)	
V3450	The Leaping Flame $1.25 £ (#70)	
V3174	Light To The Heart $1.25 £ (#56)	
V2965	Lights Of Love $1.25 £ (#46)	
V2966	The Little Pretender $1.25 £ (#19)	
V3122	Lost Enchantment $1.25 £ (#52)	
V3196	Love Forbidden £ $1.25 (#51)	
V3519	Love Holds The Cards $1.25 £ (#12)	
V2750	Love In Hiding $1.25 £ (#4)	
V3047	Love Is An Eagle $1.25 £ (#49)	
V3429	Love Is Contraband $1.25 £ (#13)	
V2611	Love Is Dangerous $1.25 £ (#31)	
V2824	Love Is The Enemy $1.25 £ (#9)	
V2865	Love Is Mine $1.25 £ (#43)	
V3451	Love Me Forever £ $1.25 (#14)	
V3079	Love On The Run (#50) £ $1.25	
V2864	Love To The Rescue $1.25 £ (#11)	
V2768	Love Under Fire $1.25 £ (#39)	
V2997	Messenger Of Love $1.25 £ (#22)	
V3372	Metternich: The Passionate Diplomat $1.25 £	

Send to: PYRAMID PUBLICATIONS,
Dept. M.O., 9 Garden Street, Moonachie, N.J. 07074

NAME _____

ADDRESS _____

CITY _____

STATE _____ ZIP _____

I enclose $_____, which includes the total price of all books
ordered plus 50¢ per book postage and handling for the first book and
25¢ for each additional. If my total order is $10.00 or more, I understand
that Pyramid will pay all postage and handling.
No COD's or stamps. Please allow three to four weeks for delivery.
Prices subject to change.   P-16

are you missing out on some great Pyramid books?

You can have any title in print at Pyramid delivered right to your door! To receive your Pyramid Paperback Catalog, fill in the label below (use a ball point pen please) and mail to Pyramid...

PYRAMID PUBLICATIONS
Mail Order Department
9 Garden Street
Moonachie, New Jersey 07074

NAME_____

ADDRESS_____

CITY_____STATE_____

P-5   ZIP_____

STRANGER
IN THE
MIRROR

is the story of Toby Temple, super star and super bastard, adored by his vast TV and movie public yet isolated from real, human contact by his own suspicion and distrust.
And the story of Jill Castle, who came to Hollywood to be a star and discovered she had to buy her way with her body.

A lonely man. A disillusioned girl, pursuing dreams of stardom and carrying a terrible secret. In a world of predators, they are bound to each other by a love so ruthless, so strong, it is more than human—and **less**.

Published by
WARNER BOOKS

ATTENTION: SCHOOLS AND CORPORATIONS

WARNER books are available at quantity discounts with bulk purchase for educational, business, or sales promotional use. For information, please write to: SPECIAL SALES DEPARTMENT, WARNER BOOKS, 666 FIFTH AVENUE, NEW YORK, N.Y. 10103.

ARE THERE WARNER BOOKS YOU WANT BUT CANNOT FIND IN YOUR LOCAL STORES?

You can get any WARNER BOOKS title in print. Simply send title and retail price, plus 50¢ per order and 50¢ per copy to cover mailing and handling costs for each book desired. New York State and California residents add applicable sales tax. Enclose check or money order only, no cash please, to: WARNER BOOKS, P.O. BOX 690, NEW YORK, N.Y. 10019.